BROTHER CAN YOU SPARE A DIME?

A Harry Bierce Mystery

JACK MARTIN

Blank Slate Press | St. Louis, MO

Blank Slate Press
Saint Louis, MO 63110
Copyright © 2015 Jack Martin
All rights reserved.

For information, contact:
Blank Slate Press
An imprint of Amphorae Publishing Group
4168 Hartford Street, St. Louis, MO 63116

A Harry Bierce Mystery, Book 1

Manufactured in the United States of America
Set in Adobe Caslon Pro and Desdemona
Interior designed by Elena Makansi
Cover Design by Kristina Blank Makansi

Library of Congress Control Number: 2015948267
ISBN-13: 9781943075089

Dedicated to Anson and Zachary Martin,
tied for the position of my favorite nephew

BROTHER CAN YOU SPARE A DIME?

TABLE OF CONTENTS

PROLOGUE

CHAPTER 1:
"They used to tell me I was building a dream ..."

CHAPTER 2:
"Say, don't you remember, I'm your pal ..."

CHAPTER 3:
"Once I built a tower up to the sun ..."

CHAPTER 4:
"And so I followed the mob ..."

CHAPTER 5:
"With peace and glory ahead ..."

AFTERWORD

PROLOGUE

Giuseppe Zangara was an angry man. First, at God, for having made him less than five feet tall and ugly as a monkey. Then at the capitalists who had started the Great War to line their pockets with money squeezed from the bodies of soldiers. Then at the king and aristocrats of Italy who had drafted him, trained him to be a sniper, and then turned him loose to kill his fellow workers. Then at the Fascists, Mussolini especially, who had persecuted him for his beliefs and driven him to flee to America. But above all, he was angry at America and its promise of freedom and opportunity. America—he could practically spit each time he said the word—was no different from the rest of them. From sea to shining sea, it was ruled by more of the same blood-sucking capitalists. Fascists in all but name. It made him sick.

Three years into the Great Depression and still people bought into the promise. Why couldn't anyone else see it? While the rich lived lives of ease and luxury, millions of people had been thrown out of work, their lives ruined, their families starving on the streets. And now foolish Americans think Roosevelt will be their savior. The bitterness threatened to overwhelm him as he walked along the Miami street. "The millionaire son, of a line of millionaires going back a century," he muttered. He wanted to scream at passers-by, "Can't you see? He is a fraud, a liar, an oppressor of the proletariat!" However, he realized that the man who had given him the money to get to Miami and buy the Colt .32 automatic was right.

His benefactor had said the charming lies and smiling face of Roosevelt had fooled the working class. Something needed to be done to wake up the workers, to free them from the charm of the deceitful, plutocrat. Only then would they realize there could be no hope of better treatment from their capitalist oppressors. Only then would they wake up to the truth that nothing but a glorious revolution would do.

Zangara stopped walking for a moment, and stared at his reflection in a cafeteria window. Even he had to wince. The image that greeted him was of a shabbily dressed, underfed gnome, just one of the millions of "forgotten men" the Depression had bestowed on America. He reached into his coat pocket and fingered the Colt .32. His bitter frown turned into a knowing smile, and he held his five-foot frame a little more erect. Soon, he would not be a forgotten man. Yes, soon the whole world would know who Giuseppe Zangara was.

✦

Franklin Delano Roosevelt laughed as he ran along the warm beach, the incoming waves tickling his feet. He gloried in the exercise of his animal strength, his lean yet powerful six-foot two-inch body easily maintaining a pace few of his acquaintances could have matched. He must have run for at least a mile, yet his breathing was easy, his powerful legs untired. He smiled at the warm morning sun shining on his face as he ran, and ran, and ran....

"Sorry to wake you, Governor, but you need to get up. Folks will be expecting your speech."

Roosevelt opened his eyes to find George, his manservant, looking down at him.

"Got your chair," said George, wheeling the metal contraption to the left side of the bed. "Let me get you in so we can go to the bathroom and take care of the unpleasant duties nature requires."

George drew back the covers and Roosevelt looked down at his legs, two skin-covered sticks, devoid of any strength, devoid of any musculature. Of course the public knew he had suffered from polio ten years earlier and that it had permanently affected his legs. He smiled grimly at the thought that they had no idea just how crippling the damage had been. They'd seen him give public speeches, approaching the podium with the aid of two canes; they knew he wore braces on his legs. Only those closest to him knew he retained no use of his lower limbs whatsoever. The braces simply locked his legs rigid, and he simulated walking by swiveling his hips, enduring pain with each agonizing step. Out of sight of reporters and the public, he always used the wheelchair. Voters would sympathize with his fight against the ravages of the disease, but, if they once saw him in his metal prison, they would regard him as a weakling unfit for public office

George, however, was no weakling. He deftly hooked

his hands under Roosevelt's armpits and lowered him into the chair in a single fluid motion that always reminded Roosevelt of a much-practiced ballet move. As George rolled the President-Elect into the hotel suite's bathroom, Roosevelt once again gave thanks that the polio had, at least, not robbed him of his continence. A small blessing in light of everything else. In light of Eleanor.

He still found her behavior perplexing. She'd made it abundantly clear she wanted no further physical relations and yet had been enraged when she discovered that not every woman was appalled by the ravages of his disease. Perhaps it was just that it was her own social secretary who had welcomed him into her bed. One thing was certain, after all they'd been through together, after all they'd shared, he would never understand his wife.

"There we go, Governor. I'll step outside to give you some privacy. When you be done, just call out. Then I'll come in and shave you."

Settled in on the toilet, Roosevelt couldn't help but laugh. In two weeks he would be the most powerful man in America—possibly the world—yet he was unable to have a bowel movement unaided.

✦

Lillian Cross, a middle-aged unemployed seamstress, had been up since daybreak, waiting to hear the newly elected president speak. Penniless, with two small children to support, she was desperate to hear some words of hope. Anything that would indicate that the remote and uncaring Washington would change under with rapt attention as Roosevelt spoke from the back of some rich man's car. Zangara scowled. The President-Elect spoke into a jerry-rigged loudspeaker system, haranguing the people with lies. The newspapers had said the speech would be short, and Zangara knew he dared not delay else Roosevelt finish, sit down, and roar away.

He slipped through the crowd with ease finding, for once, that his negligible size was an advantage. Closer and closer he drew to the front. Finally, only one woman stood between him and Roosevelt. She would afford him some cover after—and during—the upheaval that would follow, allowing him ample time to flee. Zangara took a deep breath, drew the automatic from his coat pocket, snapped the slide to chamber a round, and took aim.

✦

Except for the fact that the man who had wormed his way up behind her smelled of sausage and sweat, Lillian paid little attention him. She sensed him peering around her and stepped aside politely to give him a better view when out of the corner of her eye she saw the glint of metal and heard the distinctive snap of a gun being cocked. Involuntarily, she turned to see a gnomish man raise an automatic weapon. With an inarticulate cry, she grabbed the man's arm just as he fired. With surprising strength, he tossed her aside and she heard the sharp report of four more shots. She grabbed at him again, but before he could fire another round, several men in the crowd tackled him, disarmed him, and forced him to the ground. She scrambled to her feet and turned to look at

Roosevelt, who was staring directly at her, his face blank with astonishment. At that moment, the driver of the Buick started the massive engine. With a roar, the car shot forward, throwing the President-elect back into his seat with a spine-shuddering thud. Panicked listeners dove in all directions to avoid the car as it lunged through the crowd. Reaching the main street, the driver careened off to the south, back toward the hotel.

✦

Roosevelt was in agony. His braces were still locked in place. He fumbled to release the catches as the Buick sped down the street. Successful after a few moments, he used his arms to drag himself into a marginally more comfortable sitting position.

Hearing a groan from the backseat, the driver screamed over his shoulder, "Mr. Roosevelt, are you hit? Should I take you to the hospital?"

"I'm all right. Just some bruises. Nothing serious."

"Wish I could say the same," came a nearly imperceptible whisper.

Roosevelt jerked his head to his left. Anton Cermak clutched his belly with both hands. Blood oozed through his fingers. In Cermak's pale grey face and glazed-over eyes, Roosevelt saw the unmistakable mark of death.

"My God, Anton, you've taken a bullet meant for me!" Roosevelt leaned forward and screamed at the driver, "The Mayor's been shot! Get us to a hospital!" The driver said nothing, simply shifted the Buick into a higher gear and laid on the horn as he flew through intersection after intersection, avoiding collisions with cross-traffic by mere inches.

Roosevelt pressed his hands over Cermak's and held the dying man's gaze. "This should not have happened to you, my friend. Stay with me, we're almost there."

"I'm glad it was me instead of you," Cermak whispered. "Country needs you. People … need you." Cermak grabbed Roosevelt's arm with his bloody fingers. "You give them hope. Hope no one else can." Anton Cermak shuddered, and his gaze was suddenly dull, fixed. Lifeless. For the first time since his father died, Franklin Delano Roosevelt cried.

✦ MONTHS LATER ✦

Zangara stared moodily at his last meal on Earth, unwilling to partake of the fried chicken, mashed potatoes, and biscuits. In a few hours, he would be marched down the corridor to meet the device the Americans were pleased to call "Old Sparky." To his own surprise, he found he was trembling with fear. He had imagined himself perfectly willing to be a martyr. As a good Marxist, he was an atheist, having no hope of any future life. Yet, the moment the judge had uttered his sentence, it hit him that the state of Florida would extinguish his existence. When death had seemed far away and abstract, this had not worried him, but the knowledge that his life would end at a set time and place, unsettled him more than he had imagined. And, he had not even born the satisfaction of killing Roosevelt, just some unimportant civic official.

In his weakness, Zangara even thought of bargaining for his life, of telling the authorities who had paid him and given him the gun. But, to his amazement, not long after he was moved to death row, that man himself had come to talk to him, the guards having been dismissed.

Nothing drove home the power of the man—and the people for whom he worked—more than him obtaining a private interview with a condemned man, unsupervised. The man had chortled as he casually described Zangara's relatives—down to second cousins—in both America and Italy. He rattled off where they lived, where they worked, and told Zangara what would befall them if he breathed one word of his existence. Zangara looked into the crazy man's eyes and believed him—and remained silent.

Down the corridor, Zangara heard a rattle of keys, then the squealing sound of a metal door being opened, then closed. He listened as brisk footsteps approached his cell. His heart leaped into his mouth. *This is it!* They have come to execute me early. They wish to cheat me of my last few hours of life!

But it was not the guards. A single man appeared in front of the bars to his cell. He was a short, slight, and Zangara noted that he, too, was dressed in an expensive double-breasted suit, a dark fedora perched neatly on his head.

The man, his sky-blue eyes intent, encircled with gold-rimmed spectacles, stared at Zangara.

Still sitting on his bunk, Zangara mumbled, "Who're you?"

"Harry Bierce, Bureau of Investigation," replied the visitor in a soft, cultured voice, with a trace of a Southern accent.

"One of Hoover's thugs," snarled Zangara. "Should have known. Only one of your kind could get onto death row the night of an execution."

"Mr. Zangara, I have an offer. A one time, never to be repeated offer. I know you tried to murder Roosevelt at the behest of others." Zangara started to protest, but Bierce waved him to silence. "Do not waste my time. I know this beyond any doubt. You did not have the money to buy the Colt pistol, much less travel the rails down to Miami. What I do not know is who those people are. I have talked to the Governor in Tallahassee, and he is willing to commute your death sentence to life imprisonment if you provide me the information I need. Well, Mr. Zangara?"

Zangara ached with temptation. His terror of death had been growing with every passing hour. But he thought of his brothers and sisters, his nephews and nieces, and what the earlier visitor had promised would be done to them, if the secrets were spilled. Somewhat to his own surprise, Zangara said, "I have nothing to say to any lick-spittle servant of the capitalist plutocrats." He then rolled over on the bunk and turned his face to the wall. He heard only silence, then the brisk footsteps of Bierce as he walked back to the entrance to death row.

Zangara's mind drew into itself, and he tried to think of the few times in his life he had been happy. He was still searching within when the guards came for him. As if in a dream, observing himself from a distance, he saw himself walking down the short hallway to a small room. There, in the midst of the room, a heavy wooden chair with straps attached to the arms and legs, loomed before him. Wires attached to the back of the chair connected to a junction box on the far wall. A large-handled switch anchored alongside. The guards were efficient in strapping him to the chair, wiping the top of his shaved head with saltwater, and attaching the ominous metal cap. Their experience in this procedure evident.

Zangara then seemed to wake up from his semi-trance state and looked about him. A guard was already stationed by the junction box, his hand firmly gripping the switch, while he stared intently at the clock on the wall, waiting for one minute past midnight. The warden, two more guards, and three reporters stood next to each other, each there as a witness. Standing apart from them, Zangara saw another witness, Harry Bierce, staring at him intently through gold-rimmed spectacles. It occurred to Zangara that it was still not too late, that Bierce could stop the execution, if he agreed to talk. Filled with terror of his impending death, no longer concerned with his family and their possible demise, Zangara opened his mouth to scream to Bierce that he would talk.

And then the whole universe filled with a brilliant, impossible light.

CHAPTER ONE

"They used to tell me I was building a dream ..."

John Edgar Hoover stared at the thin file on the mahogany desk in front of him and frowned. He believed that files were power, the thicker the better. When he had been appointed head of the Bureau of Investigation seven years previously, he had found an organization rife with corrupt and incompetent agents, most of them protected by powerful bureaucrats, congressmen, and senators. Unlike his predecessors, Hoover had decided not to accept the situation. Zealously determined to create an efficient and incorruptible national police force, he had begun assembling files on agents he deemed unacceptable, as well as on their protectors. In less than a decade, he had cleaned up the agency and filled it with the competent, brave and incorruptible. In his more honest moments, he admitted to himself that it was accomplished to a large degree by blackmail. But, he thought, since it was done in the cause of honesty and efficiency, it wasn't truly blackmail. It was patriotism.

He frowned again and rifled through the meagre contents. Harry Doyle Bierce was the one man in his bureaucratic empire who seemed out of his reach. According to Bierce, he was born in Galveston, Texas in

1898. The agent could produce no proof of this because the hurricane of 1900 had utterly destroyed Galveston, killing over 8,000 people and destroying whatever records the local authorities possessed. But that wasn't the only missing piece of information in Bierce's file. There seemed to be absolutely no documentation of any kind on Bierce until May of 1917, when, despite his apparent age of nineteen, he applied for and received a commission of lieutenant in the Army's Military Intelligence. He had been promoted to captain in the astonishingly short interval of fourteen months. The cause for this rapid promotion was officially concealed behind a wall of security, which even Hoover's people could not penetrate. Unofficially, the most astonishing rumors circulated in the army, the most common—and the most unbelievable—was that Bierce had somehow managed to attend General Ludendorff's final staff briefing before the German commander launched his greatest offensive in 1918. An offensive thwarted by Allied knowledge of exactly where the attack would take place. All thanks to Bierce.

Hoover didn't believe such dime-novel melodrama. Nonetheless, Bierce had clearly done something to gain him the patronage of General Pershing, the up-and-coming General MacArthur, and such supposedly incorruptible politicians as that damnable Bolshevik Franklin D. Roosevelt. So, Harry Bierce was protected from the kind of pressure Hoover could normally deliver. Thus he roamed the Agency pretty much as he pleased, taking cases that interested him, declining those that did not. Most fascinating to Hoover was that the cases Bierce did take were often the most baffling, and yet, ended with Bierce solving them nearly single-handedly. That was all well and good, but still, Hoover could not tolerate such a free spirit in his beloved agency, and he intended to rein in his knight errant.

There was a soft knock on the door to Hoover's office. "Come in," barked Hoover.

Harry Bierce entered and closed the door behind him. As he approached Hoover's desk, he said with a hint of the South in his voice, "You wished to see me, Director?"

"Sit down, Agent Bierce," growled Hoover, gesturing to a straight-backed chair in front of his desk. Bierce complied, crossing his legs in a relaxed manner that irritated Hoover, who liked his agents to show healthy fear in his presence.

"Bierce, I got a call this morning from the Governor of Florida. He lodged a very strongly worded complaint against you. He alleges you bullied him into agreeing to offer a commutation of that bastard Zangara's death sentence. He wanted to know if I had authorized you to make this deal. As you very well know, I had not."

Bierce shrugged negligently at his superior, oddly unaffected by Hoover's disapproval. "I suspect Zangara was a tool of other, more powerful players. I felt that commuting the gunman's death sentence would be a small price to pay for exposing the masterminds of this attempt on a President's life. I was able to ... persuade the Governor to cooperate."

Hoover was not surprised by Bierce's admission. He struggled to keep his volcanic temper under control. "Agent Bierce, do you have any idea of what I go through to keep this organization free from the taint of politics?

Do you? I have garnered the power to steer the Bureau clear of the rapids of political influence and corruption, and keep that power only because I do not abuse it—or permit my men to abuse it. And here you are, threatening a powerful ally of Roosevelt, the governor of a state no less, all on your own authority!"

Hoover precipitously stood, and began pacing back and forth in front of his windows, hands clasped behind his back. "Do you know who was sitting in your chair not half an hour ago?" Hoover spun around. "No, how could you? Well, Bierce, it was the Vice President of these United States, John Nance Garner. Yes, Cactus Jack, in the flesh! And do you know what he wanted? He wanted me to call off the investigation by the Houston field office into allegations that some Ku Klux Klansman had abducted a colored preacher who had been urging his congregation to defy the Jim Crow laws." Hoover threw up his hands. "Preacher turned up dead in Arkansas, hanged from a tree, for God's sake. I explained to our beloved Vice President that crossing interstate lines in the commission of a kidnapping was a Federal crime, and in a respectful voice, told him I would not order my people to ignore a violation of Federal law.

"Ever been shouted at by a vice president, Bierce? It's quite an experience. Surpassed only by being shouted at by a president. Garner raved at me for a good ten minutes, reminding me that he had helped deliver the Klan vote to our beloved President, and that Roosevelt would be nowhere without it. I only got him out of here by promising to look into it. Of course, I won't be pulling the Houston office off the case, but it will be some time before he realizes that." Hoover stopped pacing and sat down, his face fire-engine red. Then he slammed his fist on his desk. "And now, after all that, you drag another goddamned political mess into my office!"

Most men in the Bureau quailed before the anger of Hoover. Not Bierce. "With all due respect, I did not feel that the interests of justice permitted any delay in the matter. As I said, I had a strong feeling that Zangara was simply the tool of more powerful men, and, I believed the surest way to get at those men, would be to offer the pathetic little gunman a commutation. My apologies if I neglected to clear the matter with you beforehand. With Zangara's execution pending, time seemed of the essence."

"I'm of a mind to throw you out of the Bureau," Hoover growled.

Bierce's eyes were bland, indifferent to Hoover's rage. "That is your prerogative, sir. I would, however, continue my work, although I would regret losing access to the Bureau's resources. Conversely, you would regret losing my proficiency at solving difficult cases. After all, who produced the evidence that Sacco and Vanzetti were behind that murderous bombing? Who procured the accounting records for Mr. Ness, that allowed the Treasury to put Capone in Alcatraz? Who was responsible for obtaining the evidence that guaranteed the conviction of Secretary of the Interior Albert Fall? At the risk of seeming immodest, I would suggest to you that the Bureau can ill afford the loss of my ... specialized services."

"And dammit, that is why I am not firing you on the spot! But Bierce, don't dare rely on my appreciation for your previous successes. I run this Bureau, and if you persist in defying me, I will be forced to not just fire you, but will certainly deny you any assistance from the Bureau. Besides, Zangara was a lone gunman, a pathetic little wop who sought fame by killing Roosevelt. And failed even at that, only managing to shoot a Chicago party hack. Don't get me wrong, the mayor was a good, honest man, a commodity sadly lacking in Chicago. We should be as concerned about his fate as that of the President."

Hoover struggled mightily to control his temper. The damnable thing, he reflected amid his outburst, was that Bierce was among his very best agents—perhaps the best—and he needed him. He decided to change the subject and get down to business.

"Bierce, I am sure you have been following the news about the wave of robberies, kidnappings, and murders sweeping the Midwest."

Bierce nodded. "Indeed I have, Director. I had hoped the repeal of prohibition would have diminished the lawlessness plaguing the nation. Unfortunately, it would seem that criminals involved in bootlegging haven't turned to law-abiding work, just because alcohol is now legal."

Hoover agreed, but added, "That's only part of it. This damned Depression has left many law-abiding citizens unemployed and bitter. So, they cheer these thugs on, even making heroes of them. The newspapers render accolades, follow their crime sprees with ill-conceived glee, and portray them as modern-day Robin Hoods. Whereas you and I both know they are selfish, murderous lawbreakers, most who would kill a mother and her child for the price of a meal." Again, Hoover pounded his fist on his desk. "This rampage must stop! The country needs to see them for what they are and understand that breaking Federal law is the surest way of gaining admission to one of Uncle Sam's eternal summer camps."

"With respect, what does this have to do with me? You have good men on the ground in all the major cities in the Midwest."

"Not as good as you," replied Hoover in a voice indicating he wished it was not so. "Bierce, I want you to forget this political nonsense and take a new assignment. You're going to be my roving trouble-shooter and rein in these criminals."

"Sir, I don't think—"

"You've heard of Machine Gun Kelly?" Hoover interrupted.

Bierce paused for a moment, his eyes glittering with interest. "His real name is George Barnes. As far as we know, he hasn't killed anyone yet, but the newspapers gave him the nickname because he brandishes a Thompson submachine gun during his crimes. Kelly is just an alias he uses from time to time."

Grudgingly Hoover nodded his approval. "As always, you are well informed. So, you of course know his gang has kidnapped Charles Urshel, an elderly Oklahoma City banker. What you may not know, is that Urshel's family paid a ransom of $200,000, and the banker has been found alive, but emaciated, on a road near the town of Wanette."

"I am glad to hear it. The newspapers reported Urshel has a heart condition, and even if the Kelly gang intended to release him alive, he still might not have survived the ordeal." Bierce turned thoughtful. "Of course, obtaining a ransom of that size will encourage other such kidnapping attempts."

"Exactly. That is why we must catch the gang immediately. Kidnapping has only been a federal crime since the Lindbergh tragedy. We need to show the country, and especially the criminal world, that such kidnappings will not be permitted. I want you on the train to Oklahoma City tonight. Go wherever you must, do whatever needs to be done, but don't come back without the Kelly gang in tow."

Although Hoover had issued an unambiguous order, Bierce seemed to consider it a request. He put his fingers together as if considering a philosophical problem and was silent for a few moments before he favored the Director with a tight smile. "Very well. This assignment is both interesting and clearly in the public interest. I will take it." He stood, bowed slightly to Hoover, and left the room without another word, closing the door carefully behind him.

Hoover needed all his self-control to keep from throwing his desk lamp at the door.

✦

Special Agent-in-Charge William Rorer was not sorry that the road to Charles Urshel's home was in bad repair. He needed all of his concentration to fight the old Model A's steering wheel, barely avoiding axel-breaking potholes and crumbling shoulders, which left him little time to talk to Hoover's hatchet man sitting in the passenger seat—not that Agent Bierce seemed inclined to talk. Rorer and his men had spent weeks working on the Urshel kidnapping case, carefully interviewing witnesses and sifting evidence. He believed they were finally on the verge of tracking down and apprehending Machine Gun Kelly, and now this headquarters agent was moving in to steal all the credit.

"I'm not here to take credit for the collar," Bierce said out of the blue. "You and your men have done sterling work. And as far as the newspapers are concerned, I will not appear in them at all."

Not taking his eyes off the road, Rorer replied, "Then why are you here?"

Bierce shrugged. "Director Hoover decided that he wanted me to, in effect, establish a nation-wide brief on such kidnappings and robberies. What I learn from the way you are handling this case will be useful in future such cases. I understand you have already made an arrest."

"Just a small fry. Jethro Tully, a two-bit gunman Kelly had been using on his smaller robberies. He took leave from Kelly, once he learned of the size of the ransom. He was smarter than Kelly, and he knew the heat would never be off him in a kidnapping of this size. We picked him up almost by accident at the Oklahoma City train depot, buying a ticket to California. He was acting so nervous that the local bulls figured he had to be guilty of something. So, they held him for us. A couple of cracks from the rubber hose, and he broke like a fresh egg. Unfortunately, Tully didn't seem to know too much about Kelly's long-term plans, beyond him repeating that would be his last job." After a moment, Rorer said, "Here we are."

Rorer turned into a graveled drive, much better kept than the county road. Fifty yards away from the road was an immaculately maintained Victorian mansion. The Depression might be continuing, but Urshel had obviously done well in banking. Rorer pulled the Ford up to the front porch, killed the engine, and set the parking brake. Both men exited the car and bound up the steps just as the door opened and a thick-necked, glowering man appeared, hand in his jacket. When he recognized Rorer, he removed his hand from his pocket.

"Hi, boss. Who's this joe?"

"Gus, this is Agent Bierce from Washington. Hoover wants him to, ah, help us out on the Urshel case."

"Don't need no help from Washington," Gus growled. "We'll track down Kelly just fine on our own."

Bierce ignored the sullenness of Rorer's man. "I'm just here to help. I see you've established a bodyguard here. Wise precaution."

"Nobody's getting near him until Kelly is collared," replied Rorer. "That includes newspapermen. Damn vultures don't care that the old geezer's ticker is bad."

"Well, I am no reporter. I would like to talk to him, if he feels up to it."

"As I told you back at the office, that depends on Urshel. Goddamn kidnappers took him without taking along his digitalis, and nearly scared him into heart failure. Then all our questioning put further strain on him."

"Just ask him, Agent Rorer. Tell him Harry Bierce would like a word with him, if he feels up to it."

Rorer shrugged, then walked off into the interior of the house, leaving Bierce and one of Rorer's silent musclemen standing in the entryway. Within a few moments, Rorer was back, a strange look on his face.

"He most definitely wants to see you. In fact, he demands to see you. Gus, take up your regular position, I'll escort Agent Bierce to Urshel." Gus went to a chair by a side window that had an excellent view of the road, sat down, and stared out intently, saying nothing. Rorer led Bierce into the back parlor.

Seated in a padded wingchair with a table at his side cluttered with books, medicine bottles, and a carafe of water, a gray-faced, white-haired man sat with a heavy blanket covering his legs.

"Agent Harry Bierce, Mr. Urshel," announced Rorer.

To Rorer's astonishment, Urshel replied, "I know him. Please close the door behind you." Bemusement written on his features, Rorer opened his mouth to say something, then apparently thinking better of it, he closed it and exited the room, slamming the door behind him a bit more loudly than was necessary.

Gesturing to the room's only other chair, Urshel said, "Be seated, Captain Bierce. It's been a long time."

"Nearly fourteen years, sir," responded Bierce as he sat down.

Urshel looked carefully at Bierce's face. "Hard to believe. You don't look like you've aged a day."

"How are you holding up, Colonel?"

"Better now. There were times I thought my bum ticker was going to give out. Still, it wasn't that bad. Not like some of the things we saw working intelligence under Pershing."

"Let's not think on those things, Colonel. They are long past. I'm here to help Hoover's local people

23

catch the thugs who dared do this to you. With your heart ailment, they might have killed you, even if they intended you no physical harm."

The old man wheezed as he laughed. "Those punks scare me to death? Hell, they couldn't hold a candle to what we saw the Huns do, and what the Hun scientists had in mind for our troops. If I was still the man I was during the War, I would have slapped the Thompson out of that inbred cracker's hands and spanked him with it."

Urshel burst into laughter, but the laughs quickly became breathless coughs. Bierce started to rise to come to the old man's assistance, but Urshel waived him off. Instead, he poured some water into a small glass, then as carefully as his coughing allowed, dropped six drops from one of the medicine bottles into the water. He raised the glass and knocked back the contents like it was whiskey, then leaned back in his chair, exhausted and grey-faced. Bierce was normally an emotionless man, but he felt a pang of pity for his old commander, imprisoned in a failing body.

"Colonel, I shouldn't be troubling you at this time. I know you've told your story to the other agents, but would you please tell it to me one more time? Afterwards, I can leave you to recuperate your strength."

"There isn't much to tell, Bierce. I'd gotten home late from the bank, so it was after dark. Didn't notice anything as I parked the Buick out front. Of course, I had no reason to suspect anything was wrong. No lights were on in the house, but that wasn't strange. My cook and maid live in town, and always leave around sunset. No, wait. Damn it, there was something! The porch light was out. The maid always leaves it on if she goes home before I get back, so I don't have to fumble with the key. Goddamn it! I never would have missed that detail in the War."

"Don't blame yourself, sir. This is rural Oklahoma, not the Marne. I'm sure most people hereabouts don't even lock their doors at night. Go on."

"Well, it took me a few moments to open the door. I step inside to find the switch for the parlor light when I'm grabbed from behind and someone jams a damn sack over my head. I try to get free, but someone hits me with something hard, maybe a gun barrel. I don't think I lost consciousness altogether, but I was sure as hell stunned. By the time my mind was clear, they had tied my hands behind my back and were hustling me out the kitchen door."

"How did you know it was the kitchen door?"

"Kitchen floor's covered with linoleum, makes a distinctive crackling sound when you walk on it. Then they hustle me into a car they'd hidden out back, and took off like a bat out of hell. During all this, they never said a word."

"Pity you couldn't see the car. That could have been a real help."

"Can't tell you the color, but I can tell you for sure it was one of those new Ford V-8s."

Surprised, Bierce asked, "How do you know?"

"Sound was that of a big engine, but it was the rough roar of the new Fords, not the smooth sound of a Packard or Cadillac. Anyway, the Ford is the only cheap car with an eight, and I don't figure kidnappers would draw attention to themselves with a expensive car that would draw stares."

"Do you have any hints as to where they held you?"

"Like I told the other agents, they drove me for what seemed like an hour to an hour and a quarter, then the road turned rough for a couple of minutes, and then we stopped. They hustled me into some abandoned farmhouse."

"How were you certain of that, sir?"

"They kept me there the next few days, and during that time they kept a hood over my head and my hands tied behind my back. Gave me bits of bread and water from time to time, slipping it under the edge of the hood, so I could never get a clear look at them. Still, they couldn't keep me from noticing that there were no sounds coming from the outside, either passing traffic or animal noises. Had to be an abandoned farmhouse."

"So, as I understand it, it took them about four days to arrange for the family to collect $200,000 in cash. Did you overhear any of their calls to your family?"

"Nope. They must have made calls from payphones. Nevertheless, I did hear them talk from time to time. Pretty sure there were only three of them; two men, and a woman. Gave me some bad moments towards the end."

"How was that, sir?"

"It was after they had collected the ransom. Some real arguing broke out. The woman—Kathryn the men called her—said that as they now had the money, they should bump me off, to make sure I could tell the police nothing. Strange, it was the men who wouldn't have it. One man whose name I never got said he hadn't signed on for murder and he wasn't going to fry, not even for his share of $200,000. The other joker—George, the others called him, so I guess he was Machine Gun Kelly himself—agreed with him and started a real cussing contest with the woman. I suppose the other palooka snuck off unnoticed while they were fighting, because the woman screamed that he was gone and they needed to grease me now and scram. Thought my time had well and truly come. But then I heard the sound of someone getting her chops slapped, and Kelly said there would be no cold-blooded murders on his watch. They would take the money and skidoo, leaving me to work myself free as best I could. Then I heard the faint noises of them loading the Ford, gunning the engine, and taking off like a bat out of hell. When I was sure that they were gone, I started squirming along the floor until I worked the hood off, then managed to get to my feet by bracing my back against a wall. Then I was able to find a door-jamb where a missing piece of wood left a sharp edge. After about four hours, I was able to wear through the rope and free myself. Then I started walking. It took me half an hour to reach the county road, and an hour more to come across a working farm. The good people there didn't have a phone, but they treated me right kindly, and drove me into the county seat in their Model T. The rest you know."

"You don't mention that you collapsed at that farmhouse, and they rushed you to the hospital first," said Bierce gently.

"That didn't matter much," replied Urshel gruffly.

"One final thing, sir, before I leave you to rest up from your ordeal. When the man and woman were getting ready to flee, did you hear any words that might give a clue as to their destination?"

"Nothing that seemed important," came the old

man's reply. "Oh, over the days I heard them talking about their plans after they got the ransom. Those plans weren't too solid. Sometimes they talked about getting to Mexico, other times to Cuba or Barbados, that kind of thing. Kelly did seem smart enough to know they would have to lay low for months; the border crossings and ports would be watched for some time. Once he said that they could rest up in the hideout he had rented. Said to that Kathryn bitch that it would be plenty safe to go out to the store and the park after dark, so they wouldn't have to stay cooped up." The old man turned thoughtful for a moment. "Hold on. I think he once said something about Overton being safe at night. Does that mean anything to you, Bierce?"

The agent seemed lost in thought for a moment. He then favored his old commander with a smile and said, "It may very well. I will need to check on a few things."

"Care to tell an old man where your train of thought is headed?"

"With respect, sir, I would like to hold off until I'm certain. I never like to make claims until I am certain of the facts."

Urshel chuckled. "I remember that well and how it used to drive Pershing near insane. He used to damn you to hell one minute, then grumble that if you weren't correct one hundred percent of the time, he'd have court-martialed you. That was a good team we had, Bierce. Damn good men."

Bierce rose. "Sir, I have bothered you long enough. Do take care of yourself. I want you around for many years to come."

"I appreciate the sentiment, Bierce, but that's not up

to me." Urshel extended his hand and Bierce shook it firmly. Then Bierce took two steps back, saluted the old man formally, then turned and left the room.

✦

Every so often Rorer shot a glance at his passenger and frowned at the way Bierce sat placidly, his attention obviously turned inward. Since leaving Urshel's place, they'd been driving in silence for a quarter of an hour, Bierce volunteering nothing about how he and the old banker knew each other. Rorer's fingers gripped the steering wheel until they were white, as if the not-knowing was coiling up inside him in a hot ball of anger.

Suddenly Bierce spoke and Rorer nearly jumped out of his seat, jerking the wheel as if he'd been shot at. "You and your men must accompany me to Memphis. There is a night train we can catch from Oklahoma City."

"Why the hell should we do that?" Rorer yelled, attempting to get the car back under control.

"Because that is where Machine Gun Kelly is. We are going to take him, preferably alive. I promised you and your people credit for the collar, and I live up to my promises. It would be hard to assign credit to you if you are not there."

Rorer started to say something extremely rude, but thought better of it. Something about the way old Urshel had treated Bierce warned him that the young agent was someone with whom he should not trifle. Instead, Rorer asked a simple question.

"Why Memphis?"

"Because of something Colonel Urshel told me. He

said that Kelly and Kathryn had talked of going to places like Mexico, Cuba, Barbados."

"Yeah, so? Makes sense that someone with two-hundred grand would skip the country, and head to a place from which we are unlikely to ever extradite them."

Bierce favored the driver with a tight smile. "Notice that the places mentioned are all easily accessible by water. The best place to take ship to any of those places is New Orleans, but the criminals dare not board a vessel immediately. All the police are on the lookout for them. They will wait a month or so until more recent criminal activity occupies the authorities' attention."

"But why New Orleans for sure? Why not a smaller port, like Mobile or Galveston?"

"Because even after the heat is off, they are most likely to be noticed in a small port with few departures. They are more inconspicuous among the confused bustle of a port such as New Orleans. Furthermore, it will be easier for them to get there with less chance of being recognized along the way. Just a straight shot down the Mississippi on a barge to the Big Easy, a few dollars to a deck hand, and they are home free."

Rorer frowned. "What makes you so certain that they will go down the river, that they won't drive or take the train?"

Once again, Bierce showed his tight, humorless smile. "There are greater chances of being recognized on the road or train then on a single river barge, where they won't have to stop for gas or food. More importantly, they are hiding out virtually on the river. During your talks with Colonel Urshel, you must have heard him say how Kelly mentioned relaxing in Overton."

"Yeah, but that didn't seem to mean anything useful."

"Agent Rorer, I am very familiar with the states of Kentucky and Tennessee, and with their principal cities. For Mr. George Barnes, Overton can only mean one thing. I am certain the gangster was referring to Overton Park, the largest park in Memphis, overlooking the Mississippi."

✦

George Barnes peeked through the curtains of the parlor window of the run-down bungalow and noted that the last traces of sunset were disappearing behind the treetops of Overton Park.

"It's dark, Kathryn. Should be safe to take a stroll across the street. No one will recognize us at night."

The redheaded, hard faced woman lounging on the run-down sofa emitted a most unladylike snort. "Another walk in the park? George, I swear, I'll go bat-shit crazy if I don't get some real night life."

With a sigh, Barnes turned away from the window and studied his wife, briefly wondering how different his life would have been if he had not hooked up with such a greedy, selfish bitch. "I've told you time and again, we can't appear in public during the day. Our mugs are in the papers more than Babe Ruth's."

Kathryn picked up a pack of Camels from an end table, shook out a cigarette, and lit it with a wooden match. Blowing smoke through her nostrils, she said, "Why don't we make the run down to New Orleans, then? Hop on a boat to Havana or Jamaica? With two hundred grand, we'll be on easy street for life."

Barnes counted to ten before speaking. "Don't you remember what that Louisiana shyster said? We wait until he gives us a call at this house to tell us which barge has been squared, then we hop on the barge to the Big Easy, pay him his twenty percent cut, and he'll put us on a boat to Havana with fake passports—simple and easy, with most of the risks taken care of."

Kathryn sighed and ground out her cigarette in the ashtray. "If you say so," she muttered, "but no walks in that goddamn park tonight. I'd rather screw."

As his wife slowly revealed her impressive assets, button by tantalizing button, George remembered why he put up with her.

+

Bierce and Rorer watched as the lights blinked out in the decrepit bungalow. They stood in the shadow of a tree across the street, hidden from view by the gangsters in the house, but watched warily by a dozen men and women—homeless refuse of the Depression—settling down for the night in the park, clutching about them filthy blankets if they were lucky, discarded newspapers if they were not.

"Your men are certain Barnes and his wife are the ones inside the house?" asked Bierce quietly.

"They are certain about George Barnes, less so about the woman. Last night the two went out to the market to buy some food. My men ambled in, and while pretending to make some purchases got a good look. It was Barnes, no question."

"Your men are to be commended for not trying to

make an arrest then. The two of them would have been on the alert and certainly armed. Your men might have been injured or killed. Perhaps even other shoppers."

"Don't like making the collar in the night," muttered Rorer. "Chance of confusion and identifying wrong targets is too great. We should wait for morning."

"Your concerns do you credit," replied Bierce. "On the other hand, they will be least alert in the wee hours of the morning. Also, I have unusually good night vision and will be in the lead. You've told your men who are stationed around the back of the house that you and I will go in at midnight on the dot?"

"Yeah, and that they shouldn't go into the house, just nab anyone coming out."

"Fine. Now all we have to do is wait."

The time passed with agonizing slowness. Impatiently, Rorer checked the luminous dial on his wristwatch every few minutes, grunting from time to time. Bierce did not check his own timepiece—an old-fashioned gold pocket watch—nor did he ever ask Rorer for the time, but just as Rorer was about to tell Bierce that midnight had come, Bierce drew a large Colt .45 from under his coat, working the slide to bring a round into the chamber.

"It is time, Agent Rorer. Follow me." Without a backward glance, Bierce began to run across the street, leaving a surprised Rorer in a rush to keep up, clumsily drawing a revolver from beneath his own coat. Rorer had expected Bierce to at least slow down as he reached the bungalow's front door, but the small agent hurled himself at the door without slowing. To Rorer's amazement, Bierce knocked the door clean off its hinges, and ran with undiminished speed into the black interior of the house.

As Rorer reached the threshold, he heard Bierce shout "Federal Agents! Surrender or be killed!" The voice shocked Rorer, it was much deeper and far louder than Bierce's normal speaking voice, yet was undoubtedly the voice of the small agent. Rorer scrabbled his free hand against the wall to the left of the doorway, found the switch, and flicked on the lights. Although the bulbs were weak, Rorer was blinded for a moment by the contrast with the night's inky blackness. He heard a crash from the direction of the kitchen door, and his two agents, ignoring their orders, stumbled into the living room. Simultaneously, from what must have been the door to the darkened bedroom the sound of a man's voice, high with terror, erupted.

"Don't shoot, G-men! Don't shoot!" Barnes shouted in a squeaky, terrified voice as he stumbled out of the bedroom, bleary eyed, hands high over his head, naked as a newborn babe. From behind him came the voice of a woman muttering curses, followed by the sound of a bolt being drawn back on a machine gun. In his impossibly deep voice, Bierce shouted, "Everyone hit the floor!" He then knocked the terrified gangster to the ground as he literally barreled over him into the dark bedroom. The single, deep boom of a .45 rang out, rapidly followed by a series of most unladylike obscenities. Rorer's two men came up beside him, confusion written on their faces. Bierce called out in a more normal voice that he had everything under control.

Gruffly Rorer said, "Cuff the prisoner." Then he sidled into the bedroom, revolver at the ready, and switched on the bedroom light to reveal Barnes's wife, sprawled on the floor, tightly clutching her stomach, swearing like a sailor. He glanced over to Bierce, who was holding a Thompson submachine gun, carefully examining the weapon's breach, which seemed to be damaged.

"Bierce, we need to get this woman to a hospital, pronto!"

Bierce shifted his attention to the senior agent and favored him with a wintry smile. "Mrs. Barnes' most serious injury is to her pride. When she tried to turn the Thompson on me, I fired. My bullet hit the breach of the weapon, driving it hard into her stomach, and forcing her to drop it. I imagine it felt like being slugged by Joe Louis. Best have your men cuff her and take her down to the Federal building. She will recover from her shock soon enough, and she impresses me as a more dangerous customer than her husband." Bierce carefully uncocked his automatic and restored it to his shoulder holster.

"I have to give it to you, Bierce," said Rorer with grudging admiration. "Hitting the breach of the Tommy gun without putting a scratch on her is quite a feat of marksmanship."

"I fear I do not deserve your praise. I was shooting to kill. Her gun just got in the way."

✦

Still handcuffed, George Barnes sat dejectedly in an interrogation room in the Memphis Federal Building. Across a steel-grey table from him sat an expressionless Harry Bierce, studying the gangster impassively.

After a long silence, Bierce finally spoke. "Well, George, you know you are very likely to get the chair."

The prisoner's head jerked up, eyes wide with panic.

35

"But I didn't kill nobody!"

Bierce shook his head. "It doesn't matter. Congress came down very hard on the issue of kidnapping after the death of the Lindbergh baby. The Lindbergh Act permits the death penalty even if no one died in the commission of the kidnapping. You know, George, it's best for those determined to live a life of crime to keep track of the laws they break."

Barnes ran his handcuffed hands through his hair. "Listen, G-man, what do I got to do to stay out the chair?"

"Well, that would depend on a few things. If the court hears that you have helped the Bureau in its investigations, it might very well give you a life sentence." Bierce took from his breast pocket a silk handkerchief, removed his spectacles, and began to methodically clean the lenses.

"I ain't a fool," Barnes replied desperately. "I kept my group small and independent of the big gangs. I ain't got nothing but chicken feed, and you know it."

"Pity," replied Bierce, carefully inspecting his lenses for any hint of a smear.

"There is one thing I can give you, but you can't ever breathe a word that it was from me."

"So what little morsel of, as you say, chicken feed do you have to give me?" responded Bierce in a bored voice, his fingers drumming heavily on the table.

"There's a shyster down New Orleans way who's got connections," Barnes said. "Word is if you need papers, if you need any sort of favor from the Long crew, even if you need out of the country, he can square it. Name of Abner Rocha. Buddy of mine put me in contact with

Rocha before the Oklahoma job. This was in January. The swells ain't heard of him, but he's well known on the street. Even has an office in a bank building with a regular waiting room. People going in and out all the time, all kinds of people. Just in the short time I was there, a half a dozen people go in and out. Everyone from the Mayor of New Orleans to some little midget wop."

The drumming stopped. Bierce leaned forward, eyes glowing, focused as if he were an animal with prey in his sights. Involuntarily, Barnes leaned back in his chair to distance himself.

In a low voice that was more threatening than anything Barnes had ever heard, Bierce said, "The 'midget wop', describe him to me."

Sensing he was on dangerous ground but not knowing why, sweat broke out on Barnes's forehead and trickled down his back into the waistband of his pants. Bierce could smell the fear and focused his gaze on Barnes until the man practically squirmed in his seat. "Uh, well, I tried not to pay too much attention to Rocha's other visitors. Just like I wouldn't want them paying too much attention to me, you know?"

Bierce said nothing, waiting for Barnes to continue.

"I tried not to look at him, but it was hard not to stare at the ugly bastard. Not more than five feet tall, and an Italian face pockmarked like ten miles of bad road."

"Just how did you know the gentleman was Italian?"

"Gentleman?" Barnes barked out a nervous laugh, then clamped his mouth shut at the withering look Bierce gave him. "Uh, well, the skin color, the face, the way he carried himself. When you've been dealing with Dagos as long as me, you just know."

Slowly, Bierce rose to his feet. His hands flat on the table, back bent, he stared at Barnes—or rather stared through him, as if he wasn't there. Fearing he was about to get the third degree, Barnes cringed pitiably, holding up his cuffed hands to protect his face. But Bierce made no move to strike the prisoner. Instead, he stood stock-still for over a minute. Finally, he spoke.

"I will speak to the United States Attorney and the judge on your behalf. Especially in view of the fact that no one actually died during your crimes, I think that they will agree to not give you the supreme penalty— providing the information you have given me is accurate. It is accurate, is it not? I have recently witnessed an execution by electrocution. There is no good way to die, but that clearly is one of the worst ways."

"I swear, G-man, swear to God, what I've told you is true!"

"One final thing before I go. I presume you wish me to ask for mercy on behalf of your wife."

Barnes considered Bierce's question, and how, because of his wife's vicious greed, he'd been led deeper and deeper into more serious crimes. He shrugged his shoulders. "Doesn't matter much to me, one way or the other."

Bierce peered at Barnes for a long moment, his face still expressionless. Then he walked to the door and exited the life of George Barnes forever.

✦

Abner Rocha pulled a crystal tumbler and a bottle of his favorite bourbon out of his lower left desk drawer. He poured a stiff measure, restored the bottle to its resting place, took a sip, and leaned back in his leather chair, savoring the pleasurable burn as the liquor slid down his throat. The smile taking shape on his self-satisfied face disappeared abruptly when the door to his private office flew open, and his lumbering henchman, Eddie, strode in.

"Hey boss, some bull from the Feds wants to see you. Told him to come back when he has a war—"

Without warning, the big man flew forward, landing flat on his face with a smushed nose bleeding on the imported silk carpet. Rocha choked back his drink and jumped to his feet to see who had dared to knock down his massive bodyguard as Harry Bierce stepped over the stunned man still sprawled on the floor and pulled out his badge.

"Mr. Rocha, I am Special Agent Harry Bierce of the Bureau of Investigation." He restored the badge to an inner coat pocket, not caring whether Rocha had been able to read it. "Please tell your associate to leave quietly. There is business to discuss, just between the two of us."

As Eddie pulled himself to his feet, murder on his face, Rocha waived him off. "That's all right, Eddie. I'll handle this. Please shut the door behind you."

With a surly grumble, the bodyguard did as he was told. Without being invited, Bierce seated himself in the chair before Rocha's desk, crossed his legs, took his hat off and placed it primly on the corner of Rocha's desk. Bierce stared directly at Rocha through the lenses of his spectacles, which, for no reason Rocha could easily pin down, unnerved him. Rocha waited for his visitor to announce his business. But, as the seconds passed without Bierce uttering a word or diverting his eyes, Rocha grew more nervous, until finally, he broke the silence himself.

"You have me at a disadvantage, Mr. Bierce. What business do you have with me?"

"I have business with your business," replied Bierce, his voice soft, barely above a whisper. "Your business is to provide criminals and fugitives with protection in exchange for a percentage of their ill-gotten gains. You provide forged documents. You get the police and state authorities to ignore the activities of your clients and yourself. You get district attorneys to drop charges, judges to solicit rulings in favor of defendants. You are a conduit for corruption. The word on the street is that if one is in legal trouble in Louisiana, or if one needs to leave the country quickly, you are the man to see. Even forged passports and other documents of extremely high quality are procured. All in return for handsome fees. Quite a racket you have, Mr. Rocha."

Rocha, an excellent poker player, allowed no emotion to show on his face, although inwardly, he was seething with anger—and panic. He wondered just how much this G-man actually knew, and how much was guessing and how much was just bluff. The man's face gave nothing away. He decided to play the wounded, outraged, honest attorney.

"Mr. Bierce, I can't imagine who has been telling these detestable lies, or what their motivation might be. I am a respected and valued member of the legal community. No one has ever filed an ethics complaint against me. Please, with my blessings, check with the Louisiana Bar Association. No doubt some local, less-successful attorney has been spreading vile slanders. Besides, if such crimes did occur, they would be in violation of state laws, and hence, of no concern to the Federal government."

"I respectfully beg to differ. The forging of, let us say, United States passports, is a federal crime. And if documents pass through the United States mail, this, is also a crime. Felonies, Mr. Rocha. And if, for instance, one of your clients needed said documents to leave the country after a kidnapping, the Lindbergh Act provides for the death penalty. Even for accomplices."

Rocha allowed himself a smile, rocking his glass of whiskey and watching the amber liquid swirl in the light. "You haven't got anything, G-man. If you had any evidence, I'd be cuffed and on my way to the tank right now. So, now, why don't you just run along and play your little games on someone who wasn't playing them before you were born."

Bierce stood up and settled his hat on his head. "You can cooperate now and turn state's evidence, or you can go to Alcatraz. The choice is yours. Call me at the Federal building should you change your mind. Oh, and as for you playing these 'little games' longer than I've been alive, I sincerely doubt it." With that, Bierce spun on his heel and barged through the door, shouldering Eddie aside and causing the infuriated muscle-man to reach for his gun. Bierce just kept on walking.

✦

Eddie glanced behind him one more time before he entered the seedy, downtown hotel room. Rocha was going down and he had no intention of going down with him. As he closed the door, he spotted the man he had come to see, reclining comfortably in a worn easy-chair. Eddie removed his hat and twirled the rim between his fingers. He tried not to let his voice shake. In a halting manner, he described the visit of the Federal agent to Rocha. The man in the chair grinned broadly, then snickered in a way that made Eddie's fear slither up from his belly and settle at the base of his throat. The man lit a cigarette and blew a ring of smoke at the ceiling.

"So the Feds are suspicious. Rocha appears to have not handled things very well—indeed, not well at all. And, according to you, he all but dared the G-man to prove wrongdoing." The man took a long draw from his cigarette, then shook his head. "Not a smart move. Best to have shown an air of bewildered innocence. Big Brother will not be happy—not happy at all."

"Uh, yes sir."

The man leaned back in his chair and blew several smoke rings before again sitting upright and crushing the cigarette with undue force. "You have done well, Eddie. Your loyalty is appreciated, indeed it surely is appreciated. Now, what to do about Mr. Rocha? No telling how quickly the Feds will be back with warrants, and no telling what he might say to save himself from prison."

Eddie shifted uneasily, but said nothing.

"Still, I imagine Mr. Rocha will meet with an accident before the Feds get back. If that accident occurs in a timely manner, I imagine my brother would be very grateful."

"Uh, how grateful?"

✦

Again, Director Hoover confronted Agent Bierce from behind the expanse of his mahogany desk. Again Hoover fumed at his agent's unerring ability to involve the Bureau in more delicate political issues.

"Congratulations on the conclusion of the Machine Gun Kelly business. The local agents are getting the credit in the newspapers. But I am well aware who was responsible for the operation's success."

Bierce made a deprecating gesture with his right hand. "Agent Rorer and his men did most of the groundwork. I have no problem with them receiving credit for this success. In any event, such things are of little concern to me."

Hoover grimaced. "There is, however, another matter that concerns me. Without permission, you went down to New Orleans to investigate some document forger named Rocha. Already, the Bureau has received a complaint from Baton Rouge."

Bierce frowned in puzzlement. "Why should the State of Louisiana care one way or the other? More importantly, why should the Bureau care that it cares?"

"Are you being deliberately obtuse?" Hoover tried not to shout. "You know as well as I do that Senator Huey Long is dictator in all but name in Louisiana. You also know as well as I that Long is the only possible challenger to Roosevelt for the Democratic nomination in '36. Everything about Long has to be handled with kid gloves, and the White House will not thank you for irritating the senator or his minions back home. So, when Baton Rouge says lay off the Rocha matter, we lay off."

Bierce, his eyes like ice, bore into those of his superior. "Sir, at least let me haul in Rocha for formal questioning. I'm sure that some time under the light would break him."

"I said no, Bierce. Besides, there is no point."

"Pardon?"

"I made some inquiries of my own. This morning the New Orleans office telegraphed me that a grain barge heading for the Gulf picked up a floater. The fish had been at it, but eventually dental records identified the body as your Mr. Rocha."

"So, that is where it ends?" asked Bierce, an edge of fury in his quiet voice.

"That is where it ends." Hoover grimaced as if bile had risen from his stomach. "If the Bureau is to retain its independence from politics, it must sometimes sway with the wind. I like it no more than you, Bierce. But there it is." Hoover swiveled his chair around and stared out the window while he continued to speak.

"Still, we may get lucky. If, for instance, an agent on leave stumbled across some connection between Rocha and Machine Gun Kelly, the Bureau could hardly ignore it. Speaking of which, I understand you have accumulated nearly the maximum amount of leave."

Bierce stared at the back of Hoover's chair, a small smile gracing his features.

"Make no mistake, Bierce, I expect you to spend all your Bureau time helping our field offices clean up the gangster mess in the Midwest and South, but what you do with your vacation time is up to you. Understood?"

"Understood." Bierce stood, nodded curtly at the back of the chair and left without another word.

Hoover continued to stare out his window. "Good day, Agent Bierce," he whispered.

✦

Bierce drove his rented Hudson convertible through the entrance of the large country estate. The Kentucky bluegrass property was enormous, with mature trees and stables obscuring the long distance views. Night had fallen, but Bierce unerringly navigated the roads of the property before he pulled up before a plain Federal brick mansion, the stately home on the century-old estate of Dignitas. He knew the property well.

He exited the car, bound up the steps, then knocked loudly on the door. After a short interval, a somberly-dressed black man opened the door and went to shoo the visitor away.

"Git you! Mrs. Belasco don't see no one at nights...." His voice trailed off when he recognized Bierce. "Beg pardon, Mr. Bierce. Didn't recognize you in the dim light."

"That's all right, Ulysses. Please tell your mistress I will wait for her in the library," Bierce said as he strode past the servant, continued down the hall, and turned left into the mansion's library. An awe-inspiring room, every inch of wall not adorned with a door or windows, was covered floor to ceiling with shelves full of gleaming, leather-bound books. Bierce did a slow circuit of the room, his fingers wistfully caressing the volumes.

"Well, I'm surprised to see you. Here to give me another dressing down on the way I choose to live my life?"

Bierce's heart lurched and he turned and looked for several moments at the tall, lithe woman standing in the doorway. Public records showed that Mrs. Brigid Belasco was over sixty-years-of-age, but her raven black hair was untouched with grey, her face unlined, her voluptuous form showed no signs of sagging. Bierce knew that her image appeared with some regularity in the newspapers, and briefly wondered why none of them commented on her unusually youthful appearance. He supposed that interest in her fabulous fortune, consisting partly of a controlling interest in Standard Oil of Kentucky and partly in her war-profiteering husband's vast holdings, interested readers more than her youthful looks. After all, there is much a woman with a fortune can do to hold back the ravages of time.

Bierce favored Mrs. Belasco with his thin smile. "You need not fear any lectures from me. You have chosen your course, and I must respect it."

Mrs. Belasco responded with a silvery laugh that nearly broke Bierce's stony heart. "Indeed I have. This world is full of endless diversions and pleasures for those with the money to afford them."

"Do you wish to end up like your husband? If he is ever found alive, he will get the chair." Bierce knew he couldn't hide the sadness in his voice, and he didn't try.

Last year, Mr. Belasco had invited twenty-some guests, not including his wife, to a wild, extended party in which to celebrate the completion of his rural Maine mansion. The party had gone on for literally months. The few servants who left Belasco's service in disgust whispered of daylong orgies, drugs, devil worship—even of human sacrifice. The state police were reluctant to interfere with the pleasures of such a rich and powerful man, but as the rumors grew, they were forced to investigate. When they broke down the door, they found the new mansion is utter disarray and twenty corpses littered about the place—Belasco was not among them.

Mrs. Belasco laughed again. "Ah, he certainly knew how to enjoy himself. Too bad he never knew how to keep from going ... too far."

"Be that as it may, you must still be in contact with your brother, who, I believe, is spending far too much time in Germany with those dangerous people in the Thule Society. Can't you persuade him to return to America and perform more, ah, socially useful activities?"

"You poor fool. You still think you can persuade us to share your love for this country and its people? I suppose you will never accept that we don't give a damn for America, or its ridiculous inhabitants."

Bierce found his thoughts turning inward, but he refused to dwell on them. "Well, preaching to you is not the reason I came. I came to ask for $50,000."

Mrs. Belasco threw back her beautiful head and laughed. "Money. I should have known. Washington not paying you enough?"

"My personal needs are few. I am performing an investigation of potentially great importance—one in which Washington can afford no formal involvement. I will require cash of my own for travel expenses, bribes to informers, that sort of thing."

"So, you are off on some quixotic adventure to protect your pathetic country and its even more pathetic citizens. Haven't I already told you that those matters are of less than no interest to me?"

"You have. I do not expect you to give me the money for the sake of 'my pathetic country,' as you put it. I expect you to give it to me for your mother's sake."

A shadow passed over Mrs. Belasco's face as her expression of cynical amusement turned to one of thoughtfulness. She walked over to the large desk, sat down, and drew a checkbook out of the upper drawer. Like her mother, she will always be beautiful, Bierce thought and struggled to push his memories aside as he watched her pick up a gold pen, swiftly fill out a check, sign it, and rip it out of the book. She rose and walked over to him, handing him the check.

"Of course you needn't worry about this being good. Even in these times of bank failures, the Morgan Bank stands solid. Now, if you will excuse me, I have a guest upstairs that I have neglected for far too long." She swept out of the room. Bierce heard light footsteps pattering up the stairs as he stood in silence looking at the door to the library, tears streaming down his cheeks.

CHAPTER TWO

"Say, don't you remember, I'm your pal ..."

The black Ford V-8 coasted to a stop alongside the chain link fence separating the narrow, lonely road from a thriving crop of cotton. Although it was night and the windows were down, the air was muggy and heavy, a typical summer night in Texas. Clyde Barrow lit a Camel, passed it to Bonnie Parker, the woman sitting beside him, and then lit one for himself. He stared with naked hatred past the crops to the buildings looming in the distance. Eastham State Prison.

"Clyde, honey, I wish you would change your mind. Those two troublemakers aren't worth the risk. I'd die if something happened to you. There's only two of us, and that is a goddamn state prison."

"Ain't no good tryin' to talk me otter this. We're getting' my buddies otter there, and givin' the goddamn Texas Department of Corrections the blackest of black eyes. Sides, the guards only watch the fences when the inmates are in the fields. At night, when everyone's locked up, they hardly look."

For a moment Clyde thought back to his incarceration behind this fence nearly ten years ago, when he had been a frightened sixteen year old, convicted of car theft. The indifferent guards threw him into the same cell with a massive old prisoner who proceeded to bugger him almost every night. This continued until one day he found himself behind the prison machine shop, alone with his tormentor. He'd smashed the old pervert's head to jelly with a length of pipe. The guards suspected what he had done, but showed no more interest than they had shown in Clyde's agonized screams in the night. He left Eastham without something he had possessed when he had entered the prison—religiously minded folks would have said it was his soul. In the place of that intangible item, there was now a raging, unshakeable hatred for cops, prison guards, and queers—for society in general.

"Bonnie, we are takin' Hank Methvin and Ray Hamilton otta that hellhole. They's my buddies. Besides, I got a little score to settle with Eastham, and I'm going to settle it tonight."

"Honey, what if we get caught?"

"Hell, we've already kilt seven bulls an' three store-owners. Cain't hang us more than once."

Bonnie sighed. A petite woman, scarcely five foot, she had been a part-time waitress, finding rural Texas excruciatingly dull, until she had met Clyde at a friend's house. She had fallen in love with the dangerous looking gangster the moment she set eyes on him, and swore she would never let him go.

"All right, honey, give me the wire cutters an' I'll get to work making' the hole. You get the BARs out of the back." Clyde handed her the clippers and eased himself out through the driver's side door, while Bonnie slipped out of the passenger door and immediately went to work. Although she and Clyde carried pistols as a matter of course, the Browning automatic was their preferred weapon. A man-portable, fully automatic machinegun firing five rounds per second of the devastating 30-06 ammunition. Not only could it pierce through multiple human beings, it could shoot clean through a car's engine block. The gun intimidated any opponent. To make the massive weapon easier to handle in close combat, Clyde had sawed off half the barrel on each.

By the time Clyde came up to her with the two Browning's, she had already clipped a man-sized hole through the wire. He tossed one of the BARs to Bonnie, along with a spare magazine and then pushed his way through the hole. Bonnie grinned, hefted the heavy weapon in her arms, and followed her lover through the fence.

Picking their way through the rows of cotton by the light of a quarter moon, Clyde led them straight toward the brightly lit buildings that housed the prisoners. The guards, made careless by routine, focused their attention on the prisoner blocks and did not spare so much as a backward glance for the darkened fields.

"Which one?" whispered Bonnie.

Clyde pointed to the nearest building on their right. "There. Ray's letter said they would be there." Jogging as quietly as possible, he headed toward the entryway of the building. Under the illuminated doorway, a lone guard stood idly puffing on a cigarette. His night vision destroyed by the light, the guard noticed nothing until Bonnie and Clyde lunged out of the darkness, both pointing their weapons at his stomach. The cigarette fell instantly from his fingers at the sight of the BARs, and he made no motion toward his holstered revolver. Bonnie relieved him of the gun, while Clyde hissed, "Git that door open, or I'm going to blow your guts all over it!"

Fumbling nervously with the keys, the guard did as he was told. Prodding the guard through the opening, Clyde saw the two night guards for the block engrossed in playing cards at a folding table next to the wall-mounted telephone. They looked up when the guard walked in, hands up. One man froze; the other went for his revolver. Clyde fired a three-round burst, which sent the guard spinning across the hall, dead before he hit the ground. The other guard slowly raised his hands, while Clyde's hostage flattened himself along the wall, wide-eyed with terror. The explosive burst of automatic fire woke all the prisoners in the block. Shouting, cursing, even crying, echoed through the hallways.

"Bonnie, git that bull's gun," said Clyde nodding toward the still-sitting guard. Once she snatched the gun, Clyde prodded his hostage toward the surviving guard with the still-smoking barrel of his BAR.

"Now, you two, you've got ten seconds to take me to the cell where Hank Methvin and Ray Hamilton are—if you want to live." The guards exchanged a single glance, then scurried up to the second story block of cells, Bonnie and Clyde close on their heels. They stopped in front of a cell near the stairwell, and looked apprehensively at the two gangsters.

"Hank, Ray, you in there?" shouted Clyde.

"Hell, that you Clyde?" both prisoners shouted, almost in unison.

"Yep, me an' Bonnie. We're takin' you for a change of

scenery." Clyde then nodded at the one guard with the keys. "Open that door, pronto."

The guard did as he was told. With a metallic screech the door swung open, and out staggered short, bald Hank Methvin and lanky Ray Hamilton.

Hank said, "Goddamn you Barrow, if this don't beat all. Bustin' us out of the state pen."

As Ray came out of the cell, he eyed Bonnie and said, "Miss Parker, aren't you easy on the eyes. Thought I'd never see you agin."

"We'll catch up later," said Clyde, his voice gruff. "Right now, we need to move." With the barrel of his BAR, Clyde motioned for the two guards to enter the cell. They obeyed meekly. Bonnie then locked the door and threw the keychain down the hall.

Ignoring the cries of other prisoners begging to be let out of their cells, Clyde said, "Let's go before the cavalry arrives."

The three men and one woman scurried down the stairs and sprinted past the body of the murdered guard toward the outside door. Before they reached it, the door was jerked open and a guard dashed in, revolver in hand. "What the hell—"

Before the man could finish, Clyde fired a two-round burst. One of the bullets missed. The other struck the officer in his lower right stomach, spinning him clean around. With a piercing scream, the man dropped his gun and crumpled to the floor. Clyde walked up to the inert form, peered at the victim, and smiled.

"Well, well, well. Major Crowson. Bet ya didn't expect to see Clyde Barrow again." He kicked the man in the head, then shouted, "Come on!"

They were almost to the hole in the fence when the wail of a loud siren filled the night. One minute later, the car was out of sight of the prison.

✦

Captain Hamer of the Texas Rangers took his time walking down the corridor of the Eastman Prison's infirmary. Normally, the middle-aged, somewhat overweight Hamer would have strode along purposively, well aware that he had killed forty-nine criminals and survived seventeen bullet wounds inflicted by said criminals and that he need fear no man. But buried deep within the heart of the efficient killing machine that was Frank Hamer lay a sentimental core of love and respect for his fellow lawmen and the people they had sworn to protect.

Two hours earlier, he'd learned that Joe Crowson had been shot and was likely to die. In those two hours, he had covered sixty-seven miles in his rattletrap Chevy, determined to see his old friend one last time. Yet as he approached the hospital room where Crowson's body was losing its fight against Clyde Barrow's bullet, he felt an odd reluctance to enter. He paused for a moment, pinched the bridge of his nose, squared his shoulders, took a deep breath, and strode into the room.

A still form lay on the room's single bed. Over the form stood a doctor and a male nurse. They both straightened up and looked at Hamer, recognizing him from the many times his face had appeared in Texas newspapers. The doctor walked over to Hamer, quickly shook his hand and said, "Captain Hamer, under other circumstances it would be a pleasure to meet you. I understand that Major Crowson is a good friend of yours. I am so sorry."

"Thanks, Doc. Be straight with me. What are Joe's chances?"

The doctor found it hard to look Hamer in the eye. "Captain, they simply don't exist. I'm surprised he's held on this long. It's horrifying what a 30-06 does to a man's guts. We're doing what we can for him, doping him with morphine to keep him comfortable ... but he can go any time now."

The hard-eyed lawman choked back a sob, but then took his emotions in hand. "Is he conscious?"

"In and out. I know it isn't a consolation, but that's probably merciful."

"I'd like to be with him a few minutes. Alone."

The doctor considered for a moment, then nodded his head. Gesturing to the nurse to follow him, he departed and pulled the door shut with a soft click. Hamer took a chair from the corner of the room and placed it so he could sit down and look directly into Crowson's face. Hamer would have sworn the man on the bed was dead. His breathing was so shallow as to be hardly visible; his skin the color of a three-day corpse. Hamer could take it no longer, he buried his face in his hands and silently began to weep.

With great effort, the figure on the bed groaned, and half opened its eyes. Crowson slowly focused his eyes on the crying Hamer. The faintest ghost of a smile crossed his face, and in a barely audible rasp said, "Well, Goddamnit Frank, what's with this blubbering like a little girl?"

Hamer's head jerked up. He swiped his eyes on the arm of his suit jacket and sniffed, a smile erupting over his reddened features. "Hell, Joe, you know how my hay fever acts up this time of year."

"Hay fever, my ass," Crowson said. "Inside, you're soft as my pocket. I remember how you cried for an hour over that little Mex kid that those two white trash bastards had raped."

"Don't remember that. But I do remember that I blew those two bastards' brains all over the wall. By the way, thanks for not telling anyone they had dropped their guns and were trying to give up."

"Hell, Frank, if you hadn't done it, I would have. Besides, I owe you for saving my ass during that riot in Amarillo."

"You don't owe me nothin', not after you saved my sorry ass when I turned my back to that Klan bastard and he tried to drill me that time near Austin." At once, the smile was gone from Hamer's face. "Goddamnit Joe, why did you have to go and leave the Rangers to work for the goddamn Prison Bureau?"

Crowson chuckled. "You remember the reason, my friend. My wife thought it would be safer than being in the Rangers. She kept after me, saying that I owed it to the kids to stay alive." The smile faded. "Frank, I want you to promise me something. When I'm gone, make sure she knows this wasn't her fault. I know her; she'll beat herself up over this, unless someone like you pounds some sense into her."

"Hey, you tell her yourself, when you get out of here."

Crowson, still smiling, said. "Frank, you never were good at bullshitting. You know I'm on my way out, and that's all right with me. Both of us know the risks that go with the badge. I just want you to let her know I love her and that I don't blame her."

Hamer hated himself for the small sob that escaped his lips. "Sure, Joe."

"Two other things, Frank."

"Anything, Joe."

"One, make sure Austin doesn't try to cheat my family on the pension."

"I'll kill any paper-pushing bastard who tries. What's the other?"

The smile was now gone from the dying man's lips. "I want you to kill Barrow and Parker for me. I want you to do it yourself—no one else."

"Joe, I promise you that—" Hamer paused, noting that Crowson's eyes were locked, staring, and his jaw had fallen open. Slowly, Hamer rose from his chair, and without a backward glance, walked out of the infirmary room. The doctor had been waiting, smoking a cigarette. He started to ask the lawman a question, but stopped, the stunned expression on Hamer's face revealing all the doctor needed to know. Throwing the cigarette to the floor and crushing it underfoot, he hurried into the room, while Hamer, walked woodenly down the corridor to the door leading outside.

Once the door closed behind him, Hamer stopped and stared for nearly a minute at the volcanic red sunset. Then, in a quiet, clipped tone, he said, "Barrow and Parker, I'm coming for you." He paused again, then bellowed, his voice echoing throughout the prison yard, "BARROW AND PARKER, I'M COMING FOR YOU!"

✦

Harry Bierce sat in an easy chair in the living room of the late Mr. Rocha's French Quarter apartment, calmly reading a leather-bound notebook. Around him was a wild clutter—contents of drawers scattered about, the stuffing of furniture ripped out and tossed onto the floor, and the pages of books, their bindings slit, lay in heaps. The flash of his badge to the doorman of the building had been enough to gain Bierce access. Fortunately, the squat, surly man did not ask him if he had a warrant. Finally, after hours of methodical searching, Bierce had struck gold.

The notebook in his hands contained surprisingly explicit records of Rocha's transactions—exact amounts received from criminals and lowlifes, and exact amounts paid to certain corrupt government officials in New Orleans and Baton Rouge. Apparently, Rocha had kept such records as insurance, should his protectors in the Louisiana government ever decide he had outlived his usefulness. It would appear that Rocha's insurance was not nearly as comprehensive as he had supposed. Although no Federal crimes were indicated in the records, in most states the notebook would have resulted in various state charges and scores of prosecutions.

Bierce was well aware, however, that Louisiana was not most states. Former Governor, and now United States Senator Huey Long, ran the state from top to bottom with an iron fist. Even the current governor was well known to be a slavish puppet to Long, a current joke holding that he didn't dare sneeze unless Long said so. The state judiciary was equally indebted to Long.

When one judge had dared to defy his wishes, Long ordered the state legislature to eliminate the judge's position. It was not merely corruption that gave Long an iron hold on the state, Louisiana's black population also adored him because he had built hospitals and schools that admitted blacks. The rural poor of both races worshiped him because of the roads, schools, and free textbooks he provided for them. They did not care that Long's construction companies provided most of the concrete for the schools and roads, or that he got a cut on every textbook the state bought. His control of the state was cemented by the fact that there was no civil service in state government, and that literally every state employee was appointed by the Long organization, and each served at his pleasure. With unemployment over twenty percent, this guaranteed the loyalty and support of every state employee, despite the fact that Long demanded each donate ten percent of their salary to his organization, "voluntarily," of course.

A sigh escaped Bierce as he tucked the slim notebook into his inner coat pocket. The book was proof of the massive corruption of the Long machine, but he was well aware that there seemed to be no federal charge on which Long and his cronies could be prosecuted, and that no Louisiana court would dare convict them. He also knew that information uncovered in the future might, in combination with Rocha's records, lead to Federal charges. A long shot to be sure, but Bierce had seen long shots come in before. In fact, he had often helped those long shots come in. So, he was determined to keep the book.

There was a brisk knock at the door to the apartment.

In a loud, Southern drawl, the intruder called, "Agent Bierce, please open the door." In one fluid motion, Bierce came to his feet while drawing and cocking his Colt .45. He gained the door in three long steps, threw it open, and stuck his gun into the face of one very surprised young man.

"How do you know my name?" Bierce commanded softly.

To his credit, the stranger did not seem unduly panicked or afraid. "Why, the doorman told me your name, Mr. Bierce."

Bierce's gun was rock steady as he continued to point the .45 at the man. "You have me at a disadvantage, sir. You know my name, but I don't know yours."

The young, dark-haired man smiled, a smile Bierce did not like. There was something abnormal, something demented behind it.

"Why, I'm Earl Long, sir. My big brother is Senator Long." Unperturbed by the gun in his face, Earl brushed by Bierce and continued, "You are a hard man to track down, Mr. Bierce. Very hard indeed. But what Big Brother Huey wants, I do my damnedest to do." Earl turned around to face Bierce. "Huey likes having me do this and that for him. And just now, Huey wanted me to track you down and invite you for a little meeting. Nothing formal, mind you, Mr. Bierce. Just a little talk, private-like, between two gentlemen having mutual interests."

Bierce contemplated Earl Long for a long moment before lowering his gun, slowly uncocking it, and restoring it to his shoulder holster. "Very well. I have long suspected I would need to meet with your brother.

Might as well be now, as later. When do we leave for Baton Rouge?"

Earl Long gave vent to a not quite sane giggle. "Oh, no need to go that far, Mr. Bierce. Brother Huey is here. At The Roosevelt Hotel, 'meetin and greetin', as he calls it. I'll take you there right now, if you don't mind. After you," he said, gesturing to the open door.

"I think not, Mr. Long. After you." Bierce waved his hand toward the door.

Earl Long sniggered again. "As you wish."

Senator Long's entourage seemed to have taken over the entire seventh floor of New Orleans' best hotel. The moment Bierce and the senator's brother stepped out of the elevator, two hulking men in ill-fitting suits confronted them. One said, "Afternoon, Earl. Who's your little friend here?"

"Why, this is Mr. Harry Bierce, come clean from Washington City. Huey sent me to invite him over for a little talk."

The other guard looked suspiciously at Bierce's left armpit. "Seems the G-man is packing a heater. He'll have to hand it over before he sees the Senator."

"I will do no such thing," responded Bierce mildly.

"Then I'll have to take it from you."

Bierce locked eyes with the guard. "You are entitled to try," replied Bierce

"Now, now, boys, let's not exercise ourselves over a small formality," interrupted Earl. "I'm sure brother Huey don't mind if we let one of Mr. Hoover's boys keep his gun. After all, we're all friends with Washington City, now that Huey is a United States Senator."

Both of the guards stared stonily from Bierce to Earl, and back to Bierce again, then simultaneously both shrugged and moved aside. Cheerfully, Earl said, "Now, Mr. Bierce, follow me, if you will." The Senator's brother ambled down the hallway, followed by a somewhat amused Bierce.

The door to the largest suite on the floor was wide open. Bierce's gaze swept the room as he entered. Two elderly men, dressed in the planter style white suit so common among southern politicians, stood in front of the room's large bed. One man was tall and portly, the other short and thin. Both sported white moustaches and goatees. And although chairs were available, they both stood, their faces reddened by suppressed rage.

Sitting on the bed, back supported by several pillows pushed up against the headboard, was United States Senator Huey Long, coat and tie discarded, sleeves rolled up, eating with his fingers from a heaping plate of fried chicken while his eyes constantly roved about the room. As a man with formal habits and an austere lifestyle, Bierce frowned at the sight of the absurd figure on the bed—short, greasy-fingered, pot-bellied, with a wild tousle of black hair. Slovenly was the word that came instantly to Bierce's mind.

The taller of the gentlemen spoke through gritted teeth. "Senator, you know that the proposed Army air base in Caddo Parrish is vital to my constituents. The Depression has hit the whole country hard, but especially hard in places like Caddo. The hundreds of jobs and millions of dollars Washington would spend means everything to my constituents."

"I expect that it would," replied Long as he selected a chicken leg and tore a chunk of meat off it with his teeth.

"Don't play games with us, sir!" said the shorter man, the high pitch of his voice indicating his anger. "You know very well that the Army will only give us the base if we can get that additional land from the neighboring parish. And for that, we need permission of the state government to exercise eminent domain in another county."

"So, go to Baton Rouge and get the legislature and governor to give you permission," replied Long around a mouthful of masticated poultry. "What does this have to do with me, a humble United States Senator?"

"Don't treat us like children," said the taller man, voice trembling with rage. "The whole state knows your organization controls Baton Rouge. If the boys in the statehouse have held up permission, it's because you told them to!"

Long swallowed his mouthful of chicken, threw the half-eaten leg on the plate, and wiped his greasy fingers on his trousers. "I suppose it's true I have a little influence in Baton Rouge. Now you gentlemen, the two most powerful people in Caddo Parrish, come asking me to use that little influence. I have to ask myself why should I do such a thing? I have no trouble helping my friends, but the good folks of Caddo have not exactly been friendly to me. The two times I ran for governor, they voted by a wide majority for my respected opponent. Same thing happened when I ran for the Senate. Now that was hardly friendly."

The two elderly politicians looked at each other,

then the taller began to speak. "All right, Senator, we understand. You want something from us. Tell us what you want. The folks of Caddo Parrish are in dire straits, some are actually starving. Tell us what we need to do, and we will do it."

"Oh no, gentlemen. Not me. I don't have much influence with Baton Rouge. Go up there and talk to the governor. Tell him that I really hope he can reach an agreement ... an accommodation with you both. Perhaps something to do with the deduct box." The two elderly politicians glared at Long for a moment, then slightly nodded their heads. Without a word, they turned and trudged out of the room.

"Earl, close the door," the senator told his brother. "Don't want the boys hearing what Agent Bierce and I've got to discuss."

"Want I should go, too?" asked Earl as he walked over to close the door.

"Nope, little brother. You're family, and I trust family. Most family, anyway."

Earl Long closed the door and leaned against it, eyes fixed adoringly on his big brother.

"Now, Mr. Bierce," Huey Long began, "you seem to be nosing around some of my ... ah ... interests here in Louisiana. What happens here is of no interest to Washington City or to Mr. J. Edgar Hoover. When I first heard of you sniffing around New Orleans, I had myself a nice little talk with Mr. Hoover. Nice little talk. He understood that it was best for everyone concerned if you stopped making such hurtful inquiries about state matters in Louisiana. Imagine my surprise, my hurt, when I learned you were carrying on just like before. I understood Mr. Hoover to be a gentleman of his word. My hurt is so great that I may feel it necessary to use my position as United States Senator to demonstrate the degree of my hurt in the budget of Mr. Hoover's organization."

"Senator Long, I am not here at the behest of the Bureau. In fact I am on vacation, as you can easily verify by making a simple call to Washington. How I spend my vacation time is not your business, nor, with respect, is it the business of Mr. Hoover."

Huey Long's flabby features usually gave him the appearance of a buffoonish rube. At this moment, however, Long's features transformed. The mask of the genial, rural politician had dropped to reveal features that conveyed implacable hatred and fury. Bierce had seen such features before, most recently on German shock troops storming the trenches in France.

"So, that's how it'll be," replied Long. "Well, Mr. Bierce, I hope you enjoy your vacation here in Louisiana. However, a word of caution: outsiders who aren't used to our humid, insect-choked climate can find it mighty unhealthy. The longer they stay, the more unhealthy it becomes for them." With a wave of his hand in dismissal, Long said, "Be that as it may, enjoy your time in my state. Brother Earl, open the door for our visitor."

Earl Long did as he was told. Bierce gave the governor a shallow bow, turned on his heel and strode out the door, which Earl Long closed behind him. The young man turned to his older brother and spoke.

"Huey, that feller impresses me as right stubborn, and unlikely to take the hint. Want that I take some cash from the deduct box and have our Texas friends go visit that feller up north who does those special little jobs for us?"

Senator Long had resumed eating his chicken. He chewed for a while, swallowed, then said, "Not yet, little brother, not yet. Bierce is after all a Fed. Let's see if Mr. Hoover can rein in his little doggie before we do anything, ah, irreversible."

✦

"I would like to see Agent Pierre Lanier," said Bierce to the pinch-faced receptionist at the Bureau's New Orleans office.

The middle-aged woman stared sourly at him, replying, "I'll see if he's available. Who may I say is asking?"

"Harry Bierce. He knows me."

The receptionist spoke into an intercom. To her surprise, no response came over the device. Instead, a fiftyish, somewhat overweight man virtually exploded out of an inner office and grabbed Bierce's hand, shaking if effusively.

"Goddamnit Harry, this is a surprise! Haven't seen you since the business with the missing lunatic up in Providence, and before that, the professor with a crazy story of beasties up in Vermont. Hear you're doing great work in Washington. Come in, come in." He led Bierce into his office and closed the door, leaving the puzzled secretary to speculate in her own mind how her boss and this slight visitor were connected.

Lanier steered Bierce into an old but comfortable leather armchair alongside his desk, then planted himself in the swivel chair behind the desk. "I'd offer you a drink and a cigar, except I remember you don't indulge in either of my favorite vices. So, what brings you to the Crescent City? Vacation?"

"Technically I am on vacation, but it is a bit more complicated than that. May I speak off the record?"

Lanier's cheerful expression slumped into a worried frown. "Of course. You're here about the Long organization, aren't you?"

Bierce nodded. "At first I thought it would be a straightforward investigation into the forgery of federal passports and other documents. But when I came down here to follow a lead, I found myself running headfirst into Senator Long's people. Officially, Hoover ordered me off the case and advised me to go on vacation." Bierce smiled. "Turns out I have quite a few accumulated vacation days."

"Not surprised," Lanier said. "And unofficially?"

"Unofficially, the director would not be displeased if I could dig up proof of corruption on the state's beloved senator."

Lanier pulled a sour face. "Just like that two-faced bastard Hoover. He will hang you out to dry if you fail, and take all the credit if you succeed."

"True enough. Still, he has done a good job of keeping political influence on the Bureau to a minimum so he deserves credit to that extent. In any event, I need a favor. I would like you to give me a briefing on Long and his organization—a briefing based on your knowledge and suspicions, not just documented material."

Lanier chuckled ruefully. "How long do you have? I'll give you the short version first. Believe everything you've heard and double it. Huey Long isn't just a powerful political boss, he flat out owns this state. Politically, he is an absolute dictator. Reminds me of that Jew-baiter who just took over Germany. Here in Louisiana, Long controls over two-thirds of each house of the state legislature, the state supreme court, and all the state boards and agencies. And without exception, every single state employee holds office at the pleasure of Long. Do you know about the deduct box?"

"I have heard it referred to. Just what exactly is it?"

"Rumor has it that it is a four-foot high tin box, filled to the brim with cash money. Each and every state employee must 'voluntarily' pay ten percent of his salary, in cash, to the Long organization. The story going round is that Long never deposits this money in banks, as that would leave a paper trail, which might be inconvenient. You of all people would appreciate that, considering your involvement in the Capone case. Rumor has it that at any given time, Long has over $2,000,000 in cash in that box."

"So, Long has the ready resources to bribe anyone who opposes him, including any district attorney or grand jury who looks into his actions. He can outspend by a wide margin any political opponent running against his machine in a state as dirt-poor as Louisiana. Without leaving a paper trail."

"It's not just the money, Harry. The people of Louisiana, especially the poor people, love the bastard unreservedly. Partly, it's his cornpone up-from-poverty act in his speeches. In fact, he is from a wealthy family in the northern part of the state. But he is also the first politician in the history of this benighted state to ever give a damn about the poor. Poor whites couldn't afford schoolbooks for their children or hospitals when they were sick. The poor blacks were essentially excluded from both schools and hospitals. Long built scores of new hospitals, hundreds of new public schools—providing free textbooks—for both whites and blacks, and built thousands of miles of all-weather paved roads so the poor could have access to them. The poor know that Long is raking off enormous amounts from all this construction, but they simply don't give a damn. 'A dollar for Huey and a dollar for the people' is a popular saying hereabouts. Before Huey, there was no dollar for the people. There was barely a single red cent. And the old, entrenched money liked it that way just fine. Make no mistake, the rich and the large landowners hate Long like poison, but it seems there is nothing they can do about him."

Bierce frowned. "I would have thought the business community would have been in active opposition. If nothing else, businessmen know that corruption is bad for commerce."

Lanier laughed bitterly. "Long has actually brought them into his system, making sure that those who contribute to him get favors, tax breaks, special permits, while those who don't ... well, a story is told about that. I don't know if it is literally true, but it illustrates how things work here. Supposedly, back when Long was governor, he called some of the wealthiest and most influential businessmen in the state for a meeting in his office. Very bluntly, he demanded 'campaign contributions' from them. When they balked, he supposedly said, 'Those who give a lot will get a lot of the pie; those who give a little will get a little of the pie; those who give nothing will get … good government."

The corner of Bierce's mouth turned up slightly. "An intriguing man. I would like to hear more about what you have learned. I suggest we do this over dinner. It is close to five, so why don't you pick the best restaurant in town. I'm buying."

✦

"Agent Bierce, can you hear me?" J. Edgar Hoover yelled into the mouthpiece of the telephone, the difficulty of his being understood exacerbating his already foul mood.

"Yes, Director," responded Bierce, his voice soft as ever, and yet, somehow going through clear as a bell over the crackling line between New Orleans and Washington.

"What the hell have you been doing?"

"Doing? I have been vacationing, as you recommended, sir."

"I know damn well what I recommended! Well, you certainly hit pay dirt! The President called me over to the White House and raked me over the coals pretty damn good. Mentioned you by name. Told me to get you out of Louisiana, or he would fire my ass and replace me with someone who would fire yours!"

"Mr. Director, I don't want you to risk your position on my behalf," Bierce said, a note of genuine concern in his voice.

Bierce could not see the predatory smile spread across Hoover's face. The Director was thinking of the file he had already started to assemble on Roosevelt. A file being filled with transcripts of sprightly conversations the President had with his mistress, and even more disgusting photographs taken by hidden cameras of his trysts with the charming woman. He had to hand it to the crippled Bolshevik. Who would have imagined he could be as energetic in bed as he evidently was? Hoover decided that it was about time Roosevelt learned of the existence of the file.

"Bierce, don't worry about that. Neither you nor I are going to be fired. For now, none of this can be on the record, but I want you to dig deep enough to get what we need to send Long to Alcatraz for life. But I also want you to dig into the Barrow-Parker business. They've been crossing state lines to commit their crimes, so it's a Federal case. And they've been active in Louisiana, so that's why, officially, you're down there investigating. You can juggle both cases at the same time, can't you?"

Bierce hesitated for a moment. "Yes, I believe I can."

"Good. As of now, your vacation is officially over. If the politicians press me, I can truthfully tell them I have you working on Bonnie and Clyde. I want you to do real work to bring in those two, but discretely, and without creating waves, continue to dig into Long's doings. No jumped-up cracker politician is going to put the squeeze on the Bureau of Investigation!" Hoover slammed his phone into its cradle.

As he hung up, Bierce's face bore a puzzled look. He had fully expected Hoover to cave to political pressure at some point. Well, the pressure had been applied, but all it had done was turn Hoover into a raging bull. He shrugged, deciding he had underestimated the Director.

What bothered him more, though, was his near-certainty that he had heard a third-party breathing on the line. The breathing had been extremely quiet, and most people would have missed it, but Bierce's hearing was extraordinarily sharp. He could not be certain, but he had a hunch who the silent listener had been. He stood up quickly, buttoning his double-breasted suit as he headed for the door of his hotel room. He decided to play the hunch and see where it led.

In a room one story below Bierce's, Earl Long gently removed the headphones to the telephone-tapping machine and shook his head wistfully. Earl was essentially a man of peace, and liked everything around him agreeable. Still, it looked like there was no way around it. He was going to have to tell brother Huey about this. He had no doubt Huey would order him to take a big sum in cash to their friends who specialized in taking care of Huey's particular problems. Earl sincerely hoped Agent Bierce had no loved ones.

Earl left the hotel room, locking it behind him. Whistling a jazz tune, he strolled down to the elevator and rang for the car. When the operator opened the cage door, he strolled in without a backward glance. If he had looked around before entering the car, he might just possibly have spotted Agent Bierce waiting in the shadows at the end of the corridor.

⟡

Texas Highway Patrolmen Hughes and Bryant had parked their motorcycles on the shoulder of the state highway and were munching their lunchtime sandwiches in the noonday sun.

"Pretty damn boring," said Hughes after a long silence.

"What, you want to get in a shootout with some of those gangsters up North?" replied Byrant. "That's not for me. I get all the excitement I want chasing speeders and drunks. When you get down to it, that's saving lives, and it gives me a good feeling."

Hughes swallowed, then chuckled. He was older and more cynical than his partner, but he liked the younger man, and hoped he lost his idealism before some punk put a bullet through him. "Hell, you're not even that strong on speeders. I've seen you let folks going ten, even fifteen over the limit go with just a warning."

"Hey, it's rough times on most folks. Even a small fine can make some of them go hungry for a week." The young trooper nodded toward an approaching Ford. "Like that feller there. I suppose he's doing about five over the limit, but what's the point of spoiling his day over such a small crime."

✦

At the wheel of the Ford, Bonnie Parker frowned. "Clyde, lookit. Two state troopers. How we going to handle this?"

"How do we always handle Texas bulls?" snarled Clyde Barrow from the passenger seat. He twisted toward Methvin and Hamilton in the back and shouted, "Gimme the BAR!"

Methvin frowned. "Clyde, they aren't showin' no sign of trying to stop us. Maybe we should just roll by and see what—"

"Gimme the goddamn BAR!" screamed Barrow in a voice that seemed scarcely human. Methvin shrank back into the seat, while Hamilton scrabbled the heavy weapon off the floor and thrust it at Clyde. Clyde took it and worked the bolt to bring a round into the chamber. Yelling, he said, "Bonnie, slow down!"

Bonnie silently agreed with Methvin, but had long ago learned not to argue with Clyde when he was in one of his moods. She dropped the Ford into first gear just before she drew abreast of the two officers. Clyde thrust the stubby, sawed-off barrel of the BAR out the passenger window, and held down the trigger of the weapon for four seconds, sending twenty 30-06 rounds at the Texas lawmen. The tremendous detonations of the powerful rounds in the enclosed cabin of the Ford temporarily deafened all the car's occupants, so Bonnie did not hear Clyde scream to hit the gas. Bonnie needed no urging, and quickly shifted into second, then third, and the roaring V-8 sent the car careening down the road.

As the sound of the Ford died away, absolute silence reigned over two motionless, torn bodies. A single crow circled the scene, then landed and began to peck at a half-eaten sandwich.

✦

Director Hoover scowled as he was led into the Oval Office by a thin male secretary who offered him a chair in front of the enormous desk and then slipped out, closing the door behind him. Hoover sat and placed his briefcase on his knees, staring across the desk at the man he so despised. For no reason he could easily pinpoint, even the jaunty angle with which the President held his cigarette-holder irritated Hoover. Roosevelt tapped the ash of his cigarette into a massive marble ashtray and frowned back at Hoover. Most definitely not the famous smile that cameras and newsreels loved and endeared him to his fellow countrymen.

"Director Hoover, I have asked you here to discuss your inability to control your agents. I believe I made it clear in our previous meeting that your man Bierce, the one supposed to have a sterling reputation, is off the reservation. The fact that he once did a service for me some years ago does not buy him immunity from discipline. Bierce was to cry off looking into Senator Long's affairs. Those were my explicit orders. Yet, I have received further complaints from the Senator. Are you unable to control your men?"

Hoover surprised himself by immediately leaping to Harry Bierce's defense. "Sir, Agent Bierce has evidence of massive corruption on the part of the Senator, some of it pertaining to Federal violations. I have told him to pursue this wherever it may lead." Hoover often found Bierce's arrogance infuriating, but if he needed reprimanding—which he didn't since he was acting on Hoover's direct orders—Hoover would do it himself. He would be damned if he would let this crippled Bolshevik discipline a man of Bierce's record.

The President's face reddened. "Goddamnit Hoover, there is more at stake than some petty violations of Federal law. Despite all that I try, the economy remains in the toilet! The public won't be patient much longer. I need time, time to work us out of this mess. The Republicans can't do anything to stop me for the foreseeable future, but Huey Long can! He is the only one in the Democratic Party who could take the nomination away from me in two years' time. You're a smart man, you know what that would mean. Long acts an awful lot like that strutting fool in Italy and the Jew-baiter in Germany. With mobs of hungry, desperate people behind him, he could sweep into this office in two years and create a dictatorship. I cannot allow that to happen."

"Your political concerns are no affair of mine," replied Hoover, opening the thin briefcase on his lap.

"Then Director Hoover, you leave me no choice but to ask for your—"

Several large photographs plopped on the desk before the president. He froze for a moment then snatched them up and began to examine them, eyes widening as if he could not believe what he saw. Hoover casually threw several pages of transcripts onto Roosevelt's desk. The President glanced at the papers, then looked up to Hoover, ashen-faced.

"Mr. President, my agency and my agents are not to be interfered with while we pursue this or any other investigation involving violations of the laws of the United States of America. If it is any consolation, I believe Agent Bierce may be able to take care of your Long problem." Without further ado, Hoover snapped his briefcase shut, then rose and walked toward the door.

"What about … these?" Roosevelt asked, gesturing feebly at the pictures and transcripts.

"You may do with them as you wish. After all, they are only copies. Good afternoon, Mr. President." Hoover let himself out of the Oval Office, softly closing the door behind him.

For several moments, Roosevelt stared at the documents that could destroy his career. Then, hands shaking, he crumpled them into tight balls and put them in his large ashtray. He took the gold-plated lighter from his desk and ignited the paper. He continued to stare at the ashtray long after its contents had been reduced to fluffy ash.

✦

Constable William Campbell, the only lawman in the small Oklahoma community of Commerce, edged himself out of his Model T and slowly stretched his aging body. An unforgiving sun beat down on his sixty-year-old frame as he wiped the sweat off his lined face with a dirty bandana. He felt older than his age. In truth, he had felt that way ever since his wife passed away in '22. Shouldn't have married her, he thought morosely. Too many years between us. Besides, the child planted inside her is what killed her. Still, for a few years we were happy; not much money, but we were happy.

He shook his head and tried to concentrate on the positive. The job of constable didn't pay much, but he was paid more than many who lived in the Depression-sacked Midwest, enough for him to support his daughter. His little girl was the one true joy of his life, and he was grateful for her. Intelligent, attractive, hard working around their motherless house, he viewed her as God's blessing on his declining years. All he wanted now was to live another ten years and see her safely married to a good man. Then he would gladly join his wife.

Campbell started at the sound of a single shot coming from the town's lone bank. Without conscious thought, he began running toward the bank building. As he fumbled to draw his heavy revolver, he saw three men and a small woman erupt from the bank. To his amazement, he saw that the small woman was holding an ungainly BAR, a weapon he had not seen since his service in the Great War. Before he could think of what to do, the woman swiveled toward him and fired three rounds in one second. Constable Campbell felt himself fly backward as several hammer blows drilled into his torso, felt the impact of the dusty street on his back as he landed, his head bouncing on an old paving stone, then he felt nothing more.

As the dusty Ford V-8 roared out of town, screams of passers-by on the streets and customers as they burst from the bank filled the air. From the ramshackle schoolhouse only half a block away, teachers and students of various ages alike poured onto the street, afraid, yet desperate to see what had happened. A gangly twelve-year-old girl detached herself from the crowd and ran to the body that lay in the street. She looked down, expressionless for a long moment, then she sat and moved the bloody head into her lap. Silently, she began to cry. It would be several hours before she could be persuaded to let the body be taken from her.

✦

Frank Hamer and his three fellow lawmen arrived in Commerce in two dusty Plymouths just as the young girl, numb from grief, was being led away from her father's body by a sympathetic teacher. The cars stopped short of the small crowd, and Hamer eased his bulk out of the driver's seat of the first car. He quickly took in the gathering—mostly dirt farmers and their worn-out-looking wives, with a few obvious merchants, all of them visibly beaten down by the Depression, as well as the Dust Bowl conditions that had ravaged Oklahoma, sending not only their best topsoil whirling away in vast choking clouds, but their livelihood, too. Hamer took in the body lying on its back, along with the several gaping holes and a large puddle of coagulating blood. The crowd turned to look at Hamer as he approached, flashing his Texas Ranger badge.

"Bonnie and Clyde," Hamer said in his drawling yet authoritative voice. It was a statement, not a question.

A thin, stooped man in a threadbare suit stepped forward. "It looked like them to me, sir. Who are you? Your badge says you're Texas Rangers, but this here's Oklahoma."

"Name's Hamer," the Ranger responded, ignoring the question as to his legal jurisdiction. "Been chasing Bonnie and Clyde for weeks now. Found they had been spotted up near Wanette, heading in this direction. Who are you?"

"Dallas Burton. I'm the mayor. I also run the bank over there, for what it's worth. That gang cleaned us out. About $220 total."

"That's not much."

"Folks hereabout don't have much. Lot of them owe on their mortgages, but what would be the point of foreclosing on them? They'd have to pack up a Ford and go to California looking for work, and the bank would just have a bunch of worthless farms." Burton looked down on the body. "Besides, that bitch thought $220 was worth a good man's life."

"Who is he?" asked Hamer, gesturing at the body.

"William Campbell, our Constable. Good man. Widower with a twelve-year-old daughter. God knows what will happen to her."

Hamer thought of the fatherless children of his friend Joe Crowson, and his face hardened. "Which way did Parker and Barrow go?"

The mayor gestured vaguely at the road leading south. "That way. It leads to Southern Arkansas, but there is a paved connecting road that could take them into Northwest Louisiana."

"Thanks. I'd like to use your telephone to alert police departments in those directions. Single officers, or even pairs of them, must not try to take the gang by themselves. They'll just get killed trying. After my phone call, we'll be hitting the road ourselves."

"Sure. Use the phone in my bank. In the meantime, if you've no objections, we need to take Campbell's body to the county seat. We haven't a coroner, or even an undertaker."

Hamer nodded and abruptly turned and marched toward the bank, his fellow Texans hurrying to catch up. Ted Hinton came up alongside his boss, and speaking in a low voice, said, "I know I've brought it up before, but as this mayor mentioned himself, I've got to say that we shouldn't be following Bonnie and Clyde outside of Texas. We don't have the legal authority to arrest them outside of our state."

"That's not a problem, Ted."

"And why's that, Frank?"

Hamer, grim, focused forward. "Because we won't be making any arrests."

✦

It was nearing sunset the following day. Earl Long looked out the window of Huey's enormous office in downtown Baton Rouge and sighed heavily. He turned to the thickset thug, a state policeman, who had escorted him into the office and said, "I do thank you kindly, officer, but you can go now. Brother Huey has some business he wants me to conduct private-like."

The scowling guard normally would never have left a person alone in the Senator's office, but this was Huey's half-crazed little brother, who, for some reason, Long trusted above all others. Without a word, the thug turned and exited the room, closing the heavy oaken door behind him.

Earl again sighed, then cackled incongruously. Part of him was worried, even frightened, about how his brother had not only given him instructions on the Bierce matter, but had added directions on another, even more sensitive matter. Another part of him, the strangely twisted part, was vastly amused that he, poor little old Earl Long, the one called simple by his own family, was trusted with such important duties by the next President of the United States.

He strode over to the tall bookcase behind the Senator's desk chair, felt around the top right edge, and heard a small snick. Then tugging, the bookcase slid open. He now saw the familiar space hollowed out of the wall, and the familiar object it contained: the rumored deduct box. It was a simple tin box, three foot high by three foot long by two foot deep. He grunted as he picked it up and carried it over to the desk where it landed with a thud. From his pocket, he produced the simple key his brother had given him, unlocked the box, and opened the lid wide.

Packed inside was the largest amount of cash money any mortal was ever likely to see in one place, outside of the Treasury. After all, ten percent of all state salaries came to quite a sum, even in these hard times. Most of it was gathered into neat blocks of $100, $50, and $20s, but there was still an amazing amount of loose cash that had not yet been counted or sorted.

Earl feasted his eyes on all that wealth for more than a minute. Then he opened a battered briefcase that was propped up on the credenza, and carefully counted out bundles of $100 bills, until he reached $60,000. He then shoveled the money into the briefcase and snapped it shut. He locked the deduct box and restored it to its hiding place. Whistling a jaunty tune, he opened the door to the office and waved good-bye to the scowling guard. With a light step, he exited the building and climbed into his Chevrolet, throwing the briefcase casually onto the passenger seat. He started the car with a roar and pulled out into the street, nearly hitting a trolley. Earl Long had a lengthy drive ahead of him, and wanted to get to his destination as soon as possible.

Half a block behind him, Harry Bierce sat behind the wheel of a powerful Hudson Convertible Coupe. Smiling to himself, he started the engine and pulled carefully out into the light traffic, taking care to get neither too close, nor too far from Earl Long's Chevy.

✦

It was nearly two in the morning when, after the long, hard drive Earl Long got to the little run-down motel on the Louisiana-Texas border. He turned off the rattling engine of his Chevrolet and yawned long and loud. He would give anything to check into this fleabag motel and sleep for twelve hours, but he knew sleep would have to wait. The previous day he had placed a call from a payphone to a cousin of Clyde Barrow's. A few hours later, the cousin had placed a return call indicating a time and a place for a meeting in a terse, clipped voice. The early morning hours were the time; this decrepit motel was the place.

He rubbed his eyes and exited the car, taking the briefcase with him. He went to the room with the number he had been given and knocked softly. The door was thrust open, and Clyde Barrow, holding a heavy Colt automatic in his right hand, greeted him. In the room, Bonnie, Methvin, and Hamilton lounged on the bed, holding pistols just in case.

"'Bout time," growled Barrow in a low, menacing voice. "Git in, and keep your voice low. There's nobody in the rooms to either side of us, but you can never tell how far a voice carries at night."

With no outward sign of any fear of the gangsters, Earl entered the room. Clyde closed the door behind them.

A quarter mile down the road Harry Bierce stood

beside his Hudson. Even with his keen eyesight, he could not make out who had opened the motel door to Earl Long. He took in the situation: there was no real cover between him and the motel, but the night was moonless and there was little illumination provided by the motel's dim neon sign. Deciding swiftly, he began to approach the motel as silently as a cat stalking its prey.

Inside the room, Earl and Clyde stood, facing one another, while the others lounged with feigned indifference on the beds. Clyde was the first to speak.

"This better be important, Long. Told you the last time to only call my cousin on the most important things. If the bulls pick him up because of this, I'll kill you, Senator's brother or no."

"Relax, Clyde, there's no way your kin will get in trouble because of this," replied Earl, ignoring the others. "Besides, you're not going to kill me. You're relatively safe in Louisiana. You see, my brother has told the state police on the sly that he regards you as a very low priority. You can't say that in Texas, Arkansas, or Oklahoma. People there are riled up about your latest string of killings. Big brother will make this state hotter for you than all the others combined if you kill me." Earl stopped, as if contemplating his next question. "I understand the two Texas troopers, but was it really necessary to machine-gun that old constable? He was a widower with a kid." Earl shook his head sadly.

"He pulled a gun on us," snarled Bonnie, making her voice deliberately harsh to hide the regret she harbored over that particular killing.

Clyde glared at Earl for several moments before replying. "Never mind. We don't have much to show for all our jobs. Banks and stores are as poor as the people in the Midwest. We need cash to keep moving. Say your piece, Earl."

Outside, Harry Bierce held himself flat against the motel wall next to the single open window to the room.

Earl continued. "You know where all this is leading. Brother Huey can only protect you to a certain extent. You keep up this string of robberies and killings, and it's only a matter of time until you are all dead, either from a policeman's bullet or the electric chair."

Methvin and Hamilton exchanged glances—they had already come to that conclusion. Bonnie grimaced. Only Clyde showed no concern.

"If it happens, it happens," he replied offhand.

"What if there was a way out?"

"I'm listening."

"Two more jobs, and you can be on easy street," Earl said.

"What jobs?" interrupted Bonnie. She had never liked Long, and feared they were being set up.

"They should be simple, considering your … experience," replied Earl with a conspiratorial grin. "There's this federal agent, name of Harry Bierce, who is operating out of New Orleans. His health should be taking a turn for the worse very soon. The sooner, the better."

"That's one job," replied Clyde. "What's the other?"

"We need you to visit our acquaintance up in Chicago like you done before. You are to give him $30,000 and a message. Tell him that he is to try again, only this time he's to do it himself instead of getting some Dago. And, tell him when it's done, he'll get another $30,000. For your part, you'll get $30,000 now. When the jobs are finished, you will get another $30,000, along with new passport documents and visas allowing you to get into Mexico under new names. Especially in Mexico, that amount of money should allow you to set yourselves up on a beach for life." Earl smiled.

Clyde thought the proposition over for nearly a minute, then said, "Got the money with you?"

"Sure do." Earl unclasped the briefcase, turned it upside down, and shook out bundles of money onto the bed where Bonnie, Methvin, and Hamilton sat. Clyde bent over and riffled through one of the stacks of banknotes, then he turned to face Earl Long.

"What's to keep us from killing you right now and keeping all of this dough?" Clyde stopped the smirk finding its way across his lips.

Far from being frightened, Earl merely smiled, his eyes dancing with amusement. "You could do that. You could indeed. Though the way I see it, you still might have trouble getting out of the country and settin' yourselves up on easy street without the documents you need. 'Sides, brother Huey would be mighty displeased. You've never seen him displeased. It's truly a sight to behold, it is. You wouldn't be safe anywhere in the U.S. of A. And if somehow you did manage to get out of the country, you wouldn't be safe then, either. The people in Washington City probably couldn't touch you, as they have this naïve belief in this here 'due process'." Earl snickered. "I don't believe brother Huey believes in that due process. No, not at all." Earl's face turned somber. "There's no place on Earth, no, none at all, where his people wouldn't run you to ground." Long's face again took on his characteristic grin. "So the way I see it, your best bet is to do as Huey wants."

Watching the senator's brother, Clyde thought that the rumors that Earl Long was as crazy as a bedbug might well be true.

Clyde ground his teeth for a few moments, then in a surly voice said, "All right. It's a deal. Where do I find this Bierce?"

"Don't know where he hangs his hat, but I imagine he goes in and out of the Federal building from time to time. Oh, before I forget, here's what he looks like." Earl took a photo from his inner jacket pocket and handed it to Clyde.

The gangster looked at the picture intently. It had obviously been taken from across a street, as Bierce was leaving a large office building. After a moment, he chuckled. The man in the photo was small and thin, wearing wire-rimmed spectacles, dressed in an expensive-looking double-breasted suit, a dark fedora perched evenly on his head. The man looked like a bookkeeper, or a high-school teacher. Clyde smiled as he placed the photo in his pocket. Such a pipsqueak would give him no trouble at all.

Earl walked over to the window and stared at the first faint glimmerings of light in the east, unaware that Harry Bierce was only two feet away, just out of his line of sight. Earl stretched as he again yawned.

"Well, I better hit the road. Sunrise ain't far off, and I want to be far away from here before it's light enough for someone to recognize the Senator's brother. Good luck to you all." He strolled over to the door, opened it, and walked out into the night. The light in the room having temporarily destroyed his night vision, Earl Long could not have seen Bierce, even if he had been looking for him.

Clyde turned to Bonnie and said, "Honey, soon as it's daylight, I need you to call that special Chicago number for me. Tell our friend we'll meet him at that motel in Kentucky where we last met."

"Clyde sweetheart, that's a two-day drive, even if we don't take the side roads. There's a good chance we'll be spotted."

"Not if we keep going and don't stop for anything but gas. We'll spell each other driving."

Methvin and Hamilton glanced at each other. They didn't say anything, but they didn't need to. Years sharing a jail cell had given them the intuitive ability to read one another. They didn't understand everything Earl and Clyde referred to, but there was no need. They knew Clyde, and Clyde had committed them to something even more dangerous than what they had done to date—and to leaving the country forever once it was done. Both men had families they were fond of and neither had any intention of never seeing them again. With no words spoken between them, the two men agreed to abandon Bonnie and Clyde at the first opportunity.

In the whole of his unusual life, few things had shocked Harry Bierce. Finding that the brother of Senator Long was meeting with Bonnie and Clyde was one of those few occasions. Still flattened against the building, he evaluated his options in a flash. He knew it could be suicidal to tackle the four, armed murderers by himself. Harry Bierce had not a particle of cowardice, but he did not believe in futile gestures. He briefly considered slipping away to notify the local police, but after a moment dismissed that notion. It would take time to persuade them to mount a raid on this motel. Plus, Earl Long's chatter convinced Bierce that the local police might not be inclined to help capture the gang. Besides, by all accounts, Barrow and Parker had BARs and were skilled in their use. The parish police might easily be massacred trying to capture the gang. No, he decided, the best course would be to follow the gang when they left the motel and wait for an opportunity to call the Bureau. Without a sound, he crept back to his Hudson, quietly opened the door, and slipped in behind the wheel. He settled down for a long wait, eyes never leaving the motel.

✦

It was almost noon when the dusty V-8 Ford passed the Shreveport city limits. Bonnie was at the wheel with Clyde chain-smoking in the shotgun seat. Methvin and Hamilton were in the backseat, even quieter than usual.

Bonnie frowned as she glanced at the grimy streets. Many storefronts were boarded up, and shabbily dressed men and women shuffled aimlessly along the sidewalks. Most pedestrians kept haunted eyes straight ahead, their shoulders slumped with despair. The Depression had taken its toll in Shreveport, as it had in cities across America, and it wasn't near done yet, especially in the South and Midwest.

Bonnie looked down at the gas gauge. "Clyde, honey, we need gas. Food and things to drink as well."

"All right." Clyde lit another cigarette, then turned to face Methvin and Hamilton in the back seat. "We'll drop you two at the grocery store up ahead on the right, then go up to the next gas station. You buy us whatever we need to keep going for a couple of days. It's bad enough stopping for gas, I don't want to stop in restaurants. Too much time for someone to recognize us." He threw a wad of bills into Methvin's lap as Bonnie pulled over to the curb. Methvin and Hamilton exited the Ford. Without backward look, Bonnie put the car in gear and roared off.

As they watched the Ford recede down the street, Hamilton said, "You thinkin' what I'm thinkin'?"

"Yep. Now's the time to ditch 'em. We owe them for getting us out of the joint. But the way they're goin', it's goin' to end in a bloodbath, and I don't want no part of that." Methvin looked at the wad of money Clyde had given him, and saw that it was about $120. "How much you got on you?"

"Thirty, forty dollars."

"Me, too." Methvin gave roughly half of the wad to Hamilton. "We'll split up now. That way, if one of us is caught, he can't rat out the other, even if he wanted. A hundred and twenty ain't much, but if we hotwire a couple of cars it's enough to get us a fair distance. Good luck."

The two friends briefly shook hands, and then went off on separate side streets, looking for cars to steal that would be out of site of the returning Barrow and Parker, knowing that their soon-to-be former partners would not respond well to being abandoned.

A block away, Harry Bierce sat parked in his dusty Hudson convertible. For one of the very few times in his eventful life, he faced an agony of indecision. He recognized the two men who had alighted as Methvin and Hamilton. That left Barrow and Parker in the car. He was confident that he could take down two of the criminals at a time. He desperately wanted to seize the opportunity to bring in Bonnie and Clyde and considered waiting for them to return. Then again, he needed at least one of them alive, to explain fully just what it was that Earl Long had asked them to do. He calculated he could take them by surprise and kill them easily enough, but if he tried to take them alive, one or both might open up with their BARs. The street was full of cars, the sidewalks full of pedestrians. There was too great a chance innocent civilians would die. He decided instead to take Methvin, who had already gone down a side street with little traffic. He could take him alive without too much trouble, and even if he didn't know what Earl and Clyde had been talking about, he could help lure Clyde and Bonnie into a trap where there would be less risk to the innocent.

Harry Bierce vaulted out of his car and dashed after Methvin. The criminal was busy casing the occasional parked car on the side street, and didn't realize he was being pursued until Bierce was less than twenty feet away. He turned at the sound of Bierce's footfalls, saw the small man drawing an enormous Colt .45, and instinctively went for his revolver. Moving almost too fast for the eye to track, Bierce brought down the heavy barrel of his gun on Methvin's hand with bone-breaking force. Reflexively, Methvin pulled the trigger as his wrist broke, sending a bullet through Bierce's jacket but only grazing his ribs. Quick as lightening, Bierce tossed his gun into the air, grabbed it by the barrel, and brought the weapon's butt down on Methvin's skull with stunning force.

As Methvin's shot rang out, two dusty Plymouths were approaching the intersection of the main road and the side street. In the lead car, Frank Hamer rode in the passenger seat, his arm dangling out the open window. His response to the shot was spontaneous.

"Turn right!" he shouted at Ted Hinton, who responded instantly. Tires screeching, Hinton took the corner virtually on two wheels, the second Plymouth following automatically. Hamer and Hinton instantly took in the scene before them, two men struggling, a pistol lying on the sidewalk. Hinton hit the brakes. Hamer was out of car the instant it stopped, a large Colt revolver in his hand. He didn't think that this had anything to do with Bonnie and Clyde. Hell, this wasn't even his state. Regardless, when Texas Rangers were confronted with crime, they never paused to think things through. "Show me your hands, you two!" Hamer shouted in a gravelly voice.

Bierce, who had just finished cuffing Methvin's hands behind his back, shoved the stunned criminal across the hood of a car. Still holding his automatic by the barrel, Bierce turned slowly and said, "I am a Federal Agent in the act of arresting a criminal."

As Hamer's three companions rushed up, Hamer said, "Drop that gun and put up your hands, or you're a dead Federal agent."

A knowing smile crossed Bierce's face as he placed his gun on the roof of the car. "If you permit, I have identification in my coat pocket proving that I am a Federal agent,"

"Just stay there with your hands up, or I'll make your birth certificate a worthless document!" Hamer approached Bierce carefully, patted him down for additional weapons, and then removed Bierce's wallet containing his identification. Scowling, Hamer read it, then with a certain reluctance handed it back to Bierce.

"Guess you are one of Hoover's boys. Take your piece."

As Bierce holstered his automatic, he asked, "May I have the honor of knowing your name?"

Hamer laughed at Bierce's formal diction. "Who are you Bierce, some kind of Limey?"

"I've simply had an excellent education," replied Bierce mildly.

"Well, I'm Frank Hamer of the Texas Rangers. My boys here are Ted Hinton, Manny Gault, and Bob Alcorn."

Bierce nodded once. "I've heard of you, Mr. Hamer. What are you and your ... ah ... companions doing in Louisiana? A bit outside your jurisdiction, isn't it?"

"Don't give a goddamn about state lines or what the courts say about it. Barrow, Parker, and their gang killed my best friend, leaving his wife to raise her little ones on her own. They can run to Mexico, India, Russia, it don't matter. There ain't no place on Earth they can run to where I won't find them."

Bierce, grimfaced, managed a smile. "Well, if you're after Barrow and Parker, you're in luck. I believe this gentleman can lead us to them." He jerked Methvin off the hood of the car, and showed him to the Ranger. The reaction was not what Bierce expected.

Hamer howled like an animal, and with a surprisingly

powerful left hand jerked the dazed criminal away from Bierce, slammed him against the side of the car, and thrust his revolver into the man's mouth, breaking off several teeth.

"Hank Methvin, you cow-raping bastard! You have two choices. One: die right here, right now. Two: tell me where to find Barrow, Parker, and Hamilton, and I'll let you live long enough to meet the hangman in Texas."

Calmly, Harry Bierce said, "Mr. Hamer, I think our goals coincide. I also want to take Barrow and Parker. However, Mr. Methvin can hardly tell us how to go about that with the barrel of your gun in his mouth."

While everyone's attention was on Hamer and Bierce, Bonnie and Clyde's Ford rolled into view at the intersection of the main drag and the side street. The gangsters were on the lookout for Methvin and Hamilton. Sharp-eyed Bonnie spotted the small crowd down the side street, and recognized Methvin by his clothes. He was obviously a prisoner, and Bonnie had no desire to go up against what looked like half a dozen undercover cops. With exaggerated casualness, she shifted the car into second gear, and as the Ford gathered speed she began to explain to Clyde why it was necessary to leave without their two henchmen.

Back on the side street, Hamer reluctantly removed the barrel of his revolver from Methvin's mouth. Methvin spat some blood and pieces of teeth, then looked fearfully at Hamer and Bierce, who said, "Mr. Methvin, it is of the greatest importance that I bring in Mr. Barrow and Miss Parker. You are going to help me do so."

Still visibly frightened, Methvin nonetheless said, "Don't gotta say nothing. Want to see a lawyer."

"You'll next be seeing an undertaker if you don't co-operate," growled Hamer.

"I'm afraid a public defender isn't going to do you much good," added Bierce in a reasonable voice. "They are not of very high quality, and I doubt you have the money to afford a skilled advocate."

"Ah can get a good lawyer," replied Methvin. "My pa lives not far from here, in Bienville Parrish. Got a small farm, he'll mortgage it to get me a good shyster."

Bierce turned to face the Ranger. "Mr. Hamer, I believe I have an idea as to how we can bring in Bonnie and Clyde."

✦

The following morning a dazed Hank Methvin was hustled out the rear entrance of the Shreveport Courthouse. Three cars were parked in the dingy alley: Bierce's Hudson convertible, and the two Plymouths behind it. Alcorn and Gault were at the wheels of the Plymouths. Hamer shoved the handcuffed Methvin into the backseat of the middle car, then turned to Ted Hinton and said, "You ride in this one. I'll be in the lead car with Bierce. If the bastard gives you any trouble, shoot him."

"No problem, boss," Hinton replied laconically.

Bierce had already installed himself behind the wheel of the Hudson. As soon as Hamer had eased his bulk into the passenger seat of Bierce's car, Bierce pressed the starter, slammed the car into gear, and roared down the alley at a speed the Plymouths struggled to match. The cars shot out of the alley, made a reckless right turn after two blocks, and were soon on the main road leading north out of Shreveport.

For some minutes, Hamer was silent as the poverty-stricken city slowly disappeared to the south of them. Finally he addressed Bierce, raising his voice to be heard over the wind that whistled around the open car.

"All right, Bierce. Tell me how in hell you knew the judge was going to release Methvin. The bastard's helped kill five lawmen, whether he pulled the trigger or not. That business about me not having jurisdiction to make an arrest is crap. The judge knew that you are a G-man, and if I didn't have the jurisdiction, you did."

Bierce was silent for a minute, eyes never leaving the road. Then he responded. "Although Texas is famous for its sense of rough justice, you know as well as I that corruption is not unknown in the Lone Star State. Still, nothing could prepare you for the depravity of Louisiana under the rule of Huey Long. Although I cannot present proof that would stand up in a court of law—even an honest court of law—I have reason to believe that the Barrow/Parker gang enjoys the protection of Senator Long and is safe from Louisiana's legal system. I knew, too, that the judge would receive orders to release Methvin from Baton Rouge, and, would be unable to resist those orders."

So, the plan now is to go hellbent for leather to the Texas border?"

"Not quite yet, Mr. Hamer. We are taking Methvin to meet his father, at his farm in Bienville Parish."

Hamer turned his head to fully face Bierce. He favored the small blond man with his thousand-yard stare, the stare that over forty criminals had last seen.

"You aren't letting that bastard go. One way or another, he's dying. Get in my way, and you'll die, too."

Bierce still didn't look directly at Hamer., but he smiled in an odd way. "Oh," said the agent, "he will be yours eventually. I simply assumed you would want Mr. Barrow and Miss Parker as well."

"Just what are you getting at?"

"I've contacted several reporters, and have engaged in a financial transaction. This transaction will guarantee, that at most, in a few days, Bonnie and Clyde will be at the home of Mr. Methvin's father. He lives in the country. No innocent bystanders to be caught in a cross fire, plenty of time to prepare a trap from which they cannot escape. I believe they will see that, and surrender without a struggle. I very much want to take them alive, at least for a while."

Hamer grunted. "What about Hamilton?"

Bierce took his right hand off the wheel and waived dismissively. "He is a true small fry. Without Barrow and Parker, he will eventually fall into our hands. The real danger is from Barrow and Parker. It will be tricky taking them alive."

Frank Hamer said nothing.

✦

There was a knock at the door of the run-down motel room Bonnie and Clyde occupied. Clyde cocked his Colt .45 and went to the door. "Yeah?"

"It's me, Barrow. Let me in." Clyde recognized the voice of the man from Chicago. Uncocking his automatic, he unlocked the door. A thin, handsome man with a pencil moustache slid through the door, which Clyde swiftly closed and locked.

"You're pretty nervous, Clyde," said the visitor. "No need. The people in this part of southwestern Kentucky have no use for the state bulls, much less the G-men." He turned his attention to Bonnie. "Miss Parker, good to see you again. Now, just what do you have that is worth my coming all the way from Chicago?"

Clyde went over to a valise on the crumpled bed, opened it and poured out its contents. Thirty thousand dollars. The visitor's eyes were riveted to the money. Ever so slowly, a smile crept across his lips.

"Thirty thousand dollars now, another thirty thousand when the job is done."

The visitor laughed out loud. Then he did the most outrageous thing. He bent down, placed the palms of his hands flat on the floor, and then in one smooth motion kicked his feet into the air. Walking on his hands, laughing the whole while, he made his way to the bed, pushed up with his deceptively slim arms, and launched himself into the air, landing on his back on the bed. He then grabbed bundles of the cash and hugged them like a lover. Bonnie giggled with delight. Even the grim Clyde smiled.

"Where'd you learn to do that?" asked Bonnie, laughing.

"A trick I picked up doing a spell in prison, had to keep occupied somehow." The visitor continued to erotically fondle the money.

"This is heaven sent, I don't mind telling you. I've got troubles in Chicago, but you can buy yourself out of any trouble there with enough cash." He sat up on the bed, and turned more serious. "So what's the job? I imagine your boys in Louisiana aren't letting go of this kind of dough for knocking over some bank."

"It's a big one," replied Clyde. "Remember that dago of yours who fouled up the Florida job back in '33? Well, it needs to be done, and done right this time. You need to do it yourself. Personally."

"Jesus!" the visitor exclaimed. "That's going to be a tough nut to crack. Good chance I'll end up meeting Old Sparky."

"That's why there's another $30,000 waiting for you when the job is done."

"It's not enough."

"Remember, I'm just a messenger in this. You don't want to get on the wrong side of these Louisiana people. On the other hand, they can give you a lot of protection afterwards. We're proof of that."

"Sixty-thousand dollars more when the job's done, or no deal." The man from Chicago was not a coward, whatever his other moral failings.

Clyde sighed. "I can't make a promise, but I'll tell you this. Do the job so it doesn't come back on Louisiana, and I reckon they will accept your deal." Sure as hell hope so, he thought.

The visitor sprang to his feet, and began cheerfully stuffing the money into the valise. "Then we've got an arrangement. Tell your people I will need a month, maybe two, in order to arrange things." He snapped shut the valise, shook Clyde's hand, winked at Bonnie, and sauntered cheerfully out of the dingy motel room.

After a moment Bonnie said, "Well, it's done. Clyde honey, let's get some sleep."

"Wanna eat first," he responded grumpily.

"Got some bread, cheese, and meat at the store where we filled up the Ford. Got a newspaper, too. Here, read it while I fix us some sandwiches." Bonnie casually tossed the newspaper to Clyde, who caught it easily. While Bonnie laid out the ingredients of their meal on room's drab dresser, Clyde kicked off his shoes, sat on the bed, and unfolded the paper. In only a few seconds, his attention was riveted to a small column on the front page:

MEMBER OF BARROW-PARKER GANG
RELEASED FROM SHREVEPORT JAIL

Hank Methvin, suspected member of the Bonnie and Clyde gang, was released from the jail in Shreveport yesterday. Methvin had been apprehended by Texas lawmen led by the famous Texas Ranger Frank Hamer. Hamer, who has killed forty-two men while wearing the badge, is notorious for his lack of consideration for due process and the rule of law. He had no legal authority to perform arrests in the state of Louisiana. Local police could have re-arrested Methvin when he was released, but rumor in the Shreveport Police Department and the State Police holds that he has been given immunity from all charges in return for helping apprehend Clyde Barrow and Bonnie Parker, and for testifying for the state at their subsequent trial. It is reported that Methvin is staying out of the public eye for the time being at his father's home in Bienville Parish....

Clyde read no further. A vein pulsed on his forehead

and his hands began to shake with rage. "Bastard! Ungrateful, backstabbing bastard! After I broke him out of the state prison."

Bonnie looked up from making the sandwiches.

"Clyde, honey, what's wrong?" she asked in a careful voice.

Struggling to keep his voice from becoming an animal scream, Clyde said, "Do you remember how to get to Hank's dad's farm?

✦

Hamer smiled as he read the newspaper article, then threw it onto the table where the handcuffed Methvin could see it. He then tuned to Harry Bierce and said grudgingly, "Damn smart of you. Still, don't you think Barrow and Parker could smell a rat and stay away?"

Bierce turned to face the seated Methvin. "Well, Hank, what do you think? Is Clyde Barrow smart enough to smell a rat, or will he let the rage inside him govern his actions?"

Methvin just glared up at him, and Bierce turned his attention to the elderly man who stood behind the handcuffed criminal, one hand slightly trembling, not with fear, but from the onset of Parkinson's disease.

"Mr. Methvin, I understand that your son has brought Barrow and Parker to your farm more than once. Do you think they will smell a trap? Or will their sense of betrayal require them to seek vengeance?"

The thin old man first looked at Hamer, then at Bierce. "They'd be animals, Mr. G-man. Animals. Know'd that afore they started this string of killings.

Tol' my boy to have nothin' to do with them, but Hank was always pig-headed. They'd be comin' here to kill my boy, will probably kill you all too. They'd both be crack shots with them Army BARs, and they can kill twice you's number."

Hamer emitted a barking, ugly laugh.

Bierce replied, "We will be taking them alive, if possible."

The old man ignored Hamer and focused his tired brown eyes on the small, bespectacled Bierce for nearly a minute, then said, "Well, maybe you can. I want a promise, want to hear it from you."

"If I can honor what you request, I will."

Old man Methvin glanced over at Hamer, jerked his thumb at him, then looked back at Bierce. "That Ranger feller's meanin' to kill my boy. Seen a lot of bad people in my life, and I knows the killin' look. If'n he has his way, Hank will never make it to prison in Texas." Hamer scowled, but the old man ignored him. "Hank aren't much, but he's all the family I got. You read the newspapers, an' you know my boy aren't a mad dog killer like them two. You know he didn't drop the hammer on those prison guards, or those three policemen. You want me to help you ketch Clyde an' Bonnie? I'll do it, but only if I have your word my boy will live to get to the Texas prison an' serve his time."

Bierce studied the old man, beaten down by a half century of poverty, backbreaking toil, and grief. Then he gave a single nod, not for Hank Methvin, who Bierce regarded as a worthless animal, but for the old man who still loved his criminal progeny.

Seeing Bierce nod, Hamer surged out his chair. "Now

just a goddamn minute, you little bastard—"

Bierce raised his right hand, like a traffic cop ordering the cars to stop. A small gesture, yes, but something in it, some indefinable menace, stopped Hamer short.

"Mr. Hamer, I have given my word. I am a representative of the Federal government, superior to any state authority, even that of the Lone Star state. I believe that issue was settled in 1865." At this point, Bierce chuckled, as if at a private joke. "Providing young Mr. Methvin behaves himself, he will be delivered to your courts alive and … relatively … unharmed."

All of a sudden, Hinton burst into the decrepit cabin, breathless from running. "Frank, I think it's them! Saw them about a mile away with my binoculars. It's a Ford V-8; not many of them out here in the sticks. Got to hurry to get into place."

"Come on, old man," growled Hamer, grabbing the elder Methvin's arm. "Down to your truck."

Hamer dragged the elderly farmer into a swift jog down the dirt path, which after two hundred feet turned into the county road. Bierce and Hinton stayed close behind. At the junction, the old man's decrepit Model T pickup was parked, the hood already up, as if it had broken down.

"Now lean in there and act like you're tinkering with it, just like we discussed. They'll recognize you and slow down. That's all we need." Hamer and Hinton then ran over to where Manny Gault and Bob Alcorn had mostly concealed the Plymouths and the Hudson with branches and brush.

"Very well," announced Bierce. "Once they slow down, I will step into the middle of the road, drawing my pistol. You four—" Bierce's voice trailed off. Without speaking, Hamer and Hinton had opened up the trunks of the Plymouths, and were handing out weapons. Each of the four Texans was given a BAR and a Winchester pump-action shotgun. Bierce heard four metal clacks as the bolts of the powerful army weapons were drawn back, bringing deadly 30-06 rounds into the chambers.

"Where did you get those weapons?" asked Bierce, his normally soft voice eerily deep.

"Texas National Guard Armory," replied Hamer, emotionless, as he and his three companions rushed to where half a dozen trees grew at the side of the road, giving cover. Behind him, Bierce heard the distinctive clunk as the Ford downshifted, reducing its speed.

Sensing what the Texan's were going to do, Bierce ran up to Hamer and said, "No! I must have at least one of them alive! Show them the BARs so they know resistance is futile, but don't…."

There was an audible thump as the butt of the heavy machine gun impacted the side of Bierce's head. He fell to the ground, only dazed by the blow, which should have reduced him to unconsciousness, if not death.

Hamer looked briefly at the Federal man, and, without emotion, said, "This is for Joe Crowson." He then turned his eyes toward the Ford, less than seventy feet away. The old man, sensing what was going to happen, took off running back to his shack. The driver of the Ford, also sensing something was wrong, shifted down into second gear.

His voice curiously quiet, Frank Hamer said, "Open fire, boys."

A deafening roar erupted. In four seconds, eighty

30-06 rounds hit the still moving Ford, causing it to judder uncontrollably. The four men threw down the empty BARs and grabbed the fully loaded 12-gauge shotguns, and began to blast round after round of buckshot into the Ford.

Bierce staggered to his feet. In an unnaturally low, penetrating voice he screamed, *"NO-O-O-!"* and ran straight for the car as it gradually slowed to a stop at the side of the road. As Bierce barreled across the line of fire, Hamer threw up his arms and waved frantically, shouting for his men to stop shooting.

Bierce staggered up to the Ford V-8, which was leaking fluids and hissing steam like a dying beast. Drawing his Colt, he jerked open the driver's door. Clyde Barrow slumped out of the car and onto the asphalt, deader than Caesar. His torso and head a score of bloody holes, a baffled look of surprised rage frozen on his face. The normally unemotional Bierce stifled a howl of anger and disappointment as he leaned in to check the body of Bonnie Parker.

To his amazement, despite a dozen prominent wounds, she was alive and barely conscious. Her eyes began to close. Viciously, Bierce pinched her cheeks. "The name, Miss Parker! The name of the man from Chicago!"

She did not seem to hear him, but began murmuring unconnected thoughts. "Oh Clyde, honey, told you to forget 'bout Methvin ... Chicago feller sure was funny, walking on his hands ... oh, Clyde—" She closed her eyes, exhaled a long breath, and died.

Bierce lowered his head to hide the exasperation, the outrage, the disappointment that gathered and filled him. Then, out of the corner of his vision, he saw Hamer and his men come up, still clutching their shotguns. Hamer nudged Barrow's corpse with the toe of his boot, then addressed Bierce.

"The Parker bitch dead?"

Bierce nodded his head jerkily. Then in a fluid motion he rose and faced Hamer, his light blue eyes behind his gold-rimmed glasses blazing with fire. "Do you know what you have done?" His voice quiet, but nonetheless distressed at his nearness to the unspeakable violence that had occurred.

Hamer did not flinch from Bierce's stare. "I've put down some vicious murderers, and avenged my best friend. What do you think I did?"

Bierce almost told the Texas Ranger that his desire for vengeance had stopped the prevention of a greater crime. Instead, he decided that Hamer simply would not believe him or if he did, this relentless lawman would suffer from guilt for the rest of his life. Besides, alongside the raging demons Bierce kept barely under control, was a strict code of fairness. He had known what it was to want vengeance, and to avenge the loss of someone he loved. He remembered a long-ago day of flame and blood, and a round of horror sailing through the air. He could not judge Hamer harsher than he had judged himself so many years ago.

Bierce's unusually acute hearing picked up the faint sound of a distant siren. Some nearby farmer with a telephone must have heard the gun battle and called the police. Bierce quickly went to his Hudson convertible, pulled off the concealing brush and branches, and leaped into the driver's seat.

"Where the hell are you going?" asked Hamer.

"Away from here. You and your men can have complete credit for this bloodbath. Do not mention me, or the Bureau, to any officials or reporters—especially reporters. And, if Hank Methvin does not reach prison alive, I will be coming for you." Bierce started the Hudson's powerful motor, smoothly executed a bootlegger's turn, and roared off down the road. The last thing the astonished Texans heard was the car slipping into third gear and accelerating into the distance.

CHAPTER THREE

"...Once I built a tower up to the sun,
brick and rivet and lime..."

"I'm not happy with you, Bierce," said J. Edgar Hoover in a voice that barely carried across his large desk. "Not happy at all." His subordinates at the Bureau were well aware that his angry, loud blustering was reserved for small offenses, and when he was truly enraged, his voice sank to nearly a whisper.

On the other side of the desk sat Harry Bierce, his double-breasted suit neatly pressed, legs crossed in a relaxed manner.

"Director, I do not understand the cause of your concern. In addition to the Long matter, you sent me to investigate the wave of murderous crime sweeping the Midwest. Bonnie and Clyde are dead, Methvin and Hamilton back in prison. What more could you ask?"

"Cut the crap, Bierce. The newspapers are giving all the credit to those Texas crackers Hamer and Hinton, when you and I both know that you were the one who lured Bonnie and Clyde in. You're not stupid, so don't pretend to be. You know that I need a record, a public record of Bureau successes to assure our budget on the Hill, and to keep the politicians off our backs."

"There would be precious little glory for the Bureau

in what happened in Louisiana. As I have said, it was a lynch mob, nothing more, nothing less. I do not care that Parker and Barrow are dead; they well deserve to be. I believe some effort should have been made to bring them to trial, prove their guilt before a jury, and then send them to the chair. You follow what Hitler did in Germany just recently? They are now calling it 'The Night of Long Knives'. Officially, only a few score died over what was supposedly a thwarted coup, but I have it on good authority the real total was over a thousand. Not just brown-shirted street thugs, but politicians, generals, university professors, journalists. Director, I was under the impression you did not want to see the United States become a country of force and violence, of lawlessness and injustice."

"Damn it, Bierce, you know I don't want that! The Nazis are as big a threat to civilization as the Bolsheviks, perhaps bigger. It's just that I'm under a lot a pressure from the Hill to show results for the Bureau."

"Not from the President?" asked Bierce perceptively.

Hoover looked for a long moment at his subordinate, then said, "No" in a tone of voice that indicated further questions on the subject would be extremely unwelcome. He then made an obvious change of subject.

"That Chicago bastard you overheard talking to Barrow and Parker. He didn't say it out loud, but you must have drawn the same conclusion I did about the job they wanted him to do."

Bierce smiled thinly. "You mean aside from my murder?"

Hoover laughed. "I'm not worried about that. Somehow, I'm sure you can take care of a Chicago torpedo who's fool enough to try to take you on personally. No, I mean the other job."

The expression on Bierce's face became unreadable. "The President must be the target."

"Yes, the President. Of course we would have a hell of a time proving it in a court of law, as names were not used, but you and I both know who was meant. I want you to drop everything else. Forget Long. Forget the Midwest bank robbers. I want this bastard in Alcatraz or dead. Don't care which."

"Of course, Director." Bierce hesitated and then added, "Would not it be better to flood Chicago with a team, twenty or even thirty agents?"

"Think about it, Agent Bierce. Baton Rouge may be the most corrupt town in America, but Chicago runs a close second. We may have put Capone away, but his subordinate, Frank Nitti is still running a pretty effective vice ring, and has half the local officials on his payroll. We stomp in there with a score of agents flashing badges, and the town will close up tighter than a clam. Find out who this guy is and where he is, and you'll have all the agents you want for the takedown."

Bierce nodded, then stood up. "I will be on the night train to Chicago. By the way, I'd like to review the evidence from the Zangara case. There might be something of use in running down this assassin."

The Director shrugged. "Everything's in the basement. Ask the archivist to help you locate what you need. "Thank you, Director." Bierce stood, bowed slightly to Hoover, and left the office.

What a strange man, thought Hoover. That curious old fashioned bow. It's like he's from the last century.

Could be the devil himself for all I care, so long as he gets the job done.

✦

"You're in luck, Agent Bierce," wheezed the archivist, plopping a box down in front of the agent. "It was covered up by some of those damnable red X files the Director keeps sending down here. Nothing but lies and tall tales of strange happenings and beasties in the night. Been fixated on some town up in Massachusetts, folks doing who knows what. Should burn the lot of them, but he's obsessed with keeping every quotidian bit of information just in case. In case of what, I couldn't tell you. But I'd welcome not having to go up and down the stacks all day long."

Bierce noted the aging man had a prosthetic left leg, and thought it likely the man had lost the original serving his country in the Great War. Only this kept him from being short with the grudgingly helpful clerk.

"I can't let you take anything out of the basement, but you can use the desk over there for as long as we're open."

"Thank you," replied Bierce, who took the box to the indicated desk, sat himself at the lone chair, and began to go through its contents. They were sparse, and for the most part uninteresting. A cheap edition of *Das Kapital* by Karl Marx, who Bierce considered a poorly educated neurotic whose whimsical political theories had already caused the world more grief than Kaiser Wilhelm. Some letters from family members. A few stubs of pencils. Then, the only truly interesting thing in the box: a Colt .32 automatic. He held it in his hands, and actually shivered. This small weapon, firing an underpowered bullet, came close to having changed the course of American history. He closed his eyes for a few moments, remembering a long-ago time when he rushed up a flight of stairs and heard a muffled gunshot. Too late, forever too late.

He opened his eyes and glanced into the window set in the door to the archives. He saw reflected in that window that the crippled clerk was busy with something on the worktable behind him. With no noise whatsoever, he swiftly pocketed the easily concealed Colt, then added an identical pistol he had purchased the previous day. With an audible sigh, Bierce rose from the chair, took the box over to the clerk's window, and said, "I'm done."

The crippled veteran turned around clumsily and took the box. "Find anything useful?'"

"Not really," replied Bierce, who tipped his hat to the man and left the archive.

As Bierce left the Justice Building and entered the brutal sunlight of summertime Washington, he shook his head ruefully. He was not by nature, a thief. Far from it. But some deep-seeded instinct told him that this gun might be crucial at some time in the future. He fully intended to return it to the archive when the case was over. A thoughtful look on his face, he began walking toward his apartment building on DuPont Circle. He needed to pack quickly if he was to make the night train to Chicago.

✦

Francesco Raffaele Nitti—"Frank" to those outside the

Organization, "Mr. Nitti" to those inside it—sprawled on his office sofa, rubbing his stomach through his vest, silently cursing the reappearance of his goddamn ulcer. He looked at the enormous, solid-looking capo who stood before him, and did not answer the question that had just been asked. The man asked the question again.

"Mr. Nitti, I want permission to take out one or two of those bastard Micks. They know the south side is our territory, but they have been moving in, block by block. Dominic tried to explain the matter to them, and one of the bogtrotters put a bullet in him. We need to send a message."

"Like Al sent the north side boys on St. Valentine's Day?" growled Nitti. "We both know that's when Al's slide began, the slide that put him in Alcatraz. Up to then, we were sitting pretty. Local government bought off, beat cops on the payroll, the public that wanted its booze, not caring who provided it, or how. And then Al greased seven of Moran's boys at the garage. Yeah, that scared the Mick off our territory, but it made Al too hot to handle. City Hall wouldn't cover us, the Feds stormed in like Pershing in France, judges, too afraid to take our bribes, backed off. And when the dust settles, Al is sitting in the middle of San Francisco Bay, leaving me to pick up the pieces!"

"Mr. Nitti, we can't do nothing about Dominic."

Nitti absently massaged the spot over his ulcer. "Dominic going to pull through?"

"The docs say so, but they also say he'll never be completely well again."

Nitti chewed his lip. "All right. You go to the hospital and tell Dominic we're taking care of all costs and his family. Then you go see his wife, and tell her when she needs money come to me. Then I want you to gather the boys and organize them into teams. We're going to hit all the Mick whorehouses, number joints, and nightclubs on the south side. Make sure that there's a guy with a chopper at each place to keep the Mick torpedoes from getting frisky, while the rest of them bust up the place—and a few heads with baseball bats. No shooting unless shot at! We'll send a message to the Irish bastards all right, but with no killings if it can be helped. No headlines, no pictures of corpses lined up on the sidewalks. Quiet as can be. You understand?"

The expression on the huge man's face was unhappy, but he had been trained to absolute obedience by Capone himself. "I understand, Mr. Nitti."

"Now get on it! I need to get some fresh air in the park. This goddamn ulcer is killing me."

"Want me to get one of the boys to go with you?"

"I'm not a coward," snarled Nitti. "I can spend an hour in the park without a gunsel at my side."

✦

Frank Nitti ate the last bit of his hot dog, drank the last of his Coke, and threw both wrapper and bottle into the wastebasket at the end of the park bench on which he lounged. He began to rub his stomach again, and knew he would pay for not sticking to a mild diet. To hell with it, he thought, if I can't enjoy an occasional red hot and soft drink, I might as well be dead.

A small man nattily dressed in a trim suit and neat Panama hat, eased himself down at the other end of

Nitti's bench. "Good afternoon," the man said. "Thank you for agreeing to meet with me at such short notice, and alone."

"Yeah, well, didn't have much choice, did I, Bierce?" replied Nitti, scowling. "I know you can order the Bureau down on my operation, and pretty much shut me down."

"I certainly could, Mr. Nitti. But afterwards, people would still be demanding prostitutes, gambling, alcohol. Someone else would inevitably replace you to meet those needs, someone who would not show your … restraint in business practices. Chicago could not stand another Alphonse Capone, the streets literally running with blood.

Nitti grunted and nodded in agreement.

"Oh, make no mistake, Mr. Nitti, I regard you as an amoral criminal. Nevertheless, as things stand now, you are the lesser of a number of evils. Besides, I saw for myself fifteen years ago that there is more to you than a two-bit hoodlum."

Nitti hesitated, then spoke. "Captain Bierce, I run several flower shops, and no one can prove otherwise. I pay my taxes in full, unlike Al. So, let's play a pretend game, if you like. Let's pretend that what you accuse me of is true; that I picked up the pieces of Al's organization. Does Washington really have a bone to pick with me? No more machine-gunning like the one on St. Valentine's Day. No more protection schemes on respectable businessmen. Certain services desired by the good old American public are provided to them, and no one gets hurt. The little operators are even allowed their cut, so long as they don't get greedy. My imaginary organization stays out of the cocaine and heroin shit—what's sold in

Chicago is sold by low-life punks who have nothing to do with my organization. Now, continuing to talk pretend, what do you think would happen to Chicago if me and my organization was busted up by the G-men?"

"I would hope that honesty and good government would return to this fair city." Bierce sighed. "But we both know that won't happen. Anton Cermak was the last chance this city would have for decades."

"Didn't cry no tears when he caught that bullet meant for FDR," snarled Nitti.

Bierce's mild features took on a strange, almost enraged look. Nitti involuntarily leaned backward, immediately afraid. As quick as the threatening expression had come to Bierce's face, it was gone.

"Yes, Mr. Nitti, you have no respect for Chicago officials. To be fair, why should you, when you regularly buy and sell them like cabbages in the marketplace? Nonetheless, I think you have some concern for the people of Chicago, despite your illicit activities."

"You mean that business in the winter of 1919?"

"People want to forget about the Spanish influenza. Only fifteen years ago, it killed over half a million Americans. Bodies literally lined the streets—this very town had mass burials because of the lack of coffins. Yet today, no one talks of it. No one wants to think of it. That's understandable. Who wants to think on the overflowing hospitals, the stink of rotting flesh, the brave doctors and nurses who worked selflessly until they caught the disease themselves and died?"

"Never had much use for the Government men. But I gotta admit that the Army doctors, nurses, and officers came in and did what they could." Nitti looked appraisingly at Bierce. "I remember you coming in with that field hospital group, walking up and down among the sick, giving them antitoxins and experimental drugs, even cleaning the soiled bedclothes when there was a shortage of nurses. Rumor was you were a hero in France, but I had never seen anything braver than how you acted in those months."

"You give me too much credit, Mr. Nitti. I appear to be immune to the influenza. Although, I do remember seeing you when we worked Little Italy. Of course, you were not the important man you are now. A skinny young punk working numbers for the Capone organization—already a professional criminal—and yet there you were, going into tenements to bring out the sick, stacking the dead for disposal, running the risk of death every day, for no monetary gain I could see."

"They were my family, my people," replied Nitti, almost grudgingly, looking into the distance as he remembered. "I couldn't leave them alone in dirty tenements to slowly die as their lungs filled with blood and snot. Couldn't help them all, but I had to help some. Then I caught it; guess I always knew I would. I was burning up, beginning to choke to death. I remember my fingertips were even turning blue." His eyes snapped back and focused intently on Bierce. "And then some goddamn Army captain began injecting me with the most God-awful burning shit, and from that point I began to get better."

"There was never enough. Columbia University couldn't produce it fast enough, and besides it was still an experimental antitoxin and usually made no difference. You were one of the lucky ones."

"Why me?" asked Nitti softly. "There were all kinds of people in that field hospital. Kids, grandmas, priests, doctors themselves. I never got a chance to ask you, why me? Why a nobody street punk?"

"It's hard to explain, Mr. Nitti," replied Bierce reflectively. "Perhaps it was because you were there when you didn't have to be. Doctors, nurses, Army officers—we were all there because it was our duty. There were very few professional volunteers, and the few that did volunteer were doctors, priests, and teachers—the sort of people everyone expects to have high civic values. But there you were, as you say, a worthless street punk, already a career criminal, risking your life for complete strangers. In any event, I wasn't sure the antitoxin would work; it didn't for most."

Bierce sighed and looked at Nitti. "Anyway, that small particle of humanity in you, so rare in a someone in your line of business, is why I have come to you for help today. I need the name of a Chicago criminal, and I need it soon. You know as well as I do, that the Chicago police will be useless."

Nitti scowled. "I don't snitch on my boys. They're loyal to me, and me to them."

"The morality of the Dago gangster," murmured Bierce. Nitti glared at Bierce for the slur, but Bierce ignored him and continued speaking. "In any event, I seriously doubt that one of your people is the man I want. The crime he intends to commit is not exactly in your organization's line."

"I told you, and it's true, I don't deal drugs."

"No, nothing as mundane as that. He intends to murder the President."

Nitti stopped massaging his ulcer. "Jesus Christ! You're shitting me!"

"I truly wish I were. Fortunately, I was able to overhear the plot being hatched. Unfortunately, I was unable to see the assassin, or even learn his name. All I know is that he is a desperate criminal who operates out of Chicago."

"That's it? Mary Mother of God! Do you know how many torpedoes that could cover in this burg?"

"And I know that you are probably the only man in Illinois who has even a remote chance of giving me a lead. He's well-funded, and you know what that means."

Nitti nodded his head. "He can buy off the local bulls. Now, you G-men aren't for sale, I'll give you that. But there's not that many of you, and you don't really know this city."

"And that is why I have come to you."

Nitti scowled. "Just what is in this for me? Why should I care if Roosevelt is ventilated?"

"Just ask yourself, Mr. Nitti, what would happen if the President of the United States is assassinated, and it's traced back to a Chicago gangster? Rightly or wrongly, Americans look upon Roosevelt as their last hope. They would scream for the blood of Chicago criminals, any criminals. The Bureau of Investigation, the Department of Treasury, and for all I know, the United States Coast Guard would descend on this city like the wrath of Jehovah. All known criminals, especially those working for you, would be thrown into Alcatraz on any charges—or no charges—Bill of Rights be damned. Your whorehouses, gambling dens, Speakeasies would be rolled up like a cheap carpet. Your tame Chicago police would not be able to help you, and probably would not want to help you. And the icing on the cake would be you. Everyone knows you're the top gangster in this city, and the public will never believe you were not somehow involved—damn the lack of evidence. You will spend the rest of your life as a cellmate to your old boss Capone. What you would gain for helping me is that none of these unfortunate things would happen to you should I locate the assassin before he could strike."

Nitti began rubbing the spot over his ulcer again. "You make a strong case, Captain Bierce. You should've been a lawyer."

"I was, but that was a very long time ago. So, what is your response to my offer?"

"Here's what I'll do. I'll have my boys hit the streets, asking whether anyone has heard of a freelance hit man taking big jobs."

"Why just freelance?"

"Because my boys all know how I feel about killing that isn't strictly in defense of our interests. Hell, even those crazy Mick gangs wouldn't take on a job like that. Oh, they've got some skilled button men they use in their turf wars, but they are only used against competitors for territory. Even the dumb bogtrotters aren't stupid enough to try and bump off the President. No, if this guy is a Chicago thug, he's one of the independent operators— like those ham-handed crackers Bonnie and Clyde and the Barker gang. I can't promise nothing, but I'll have my boys shake the trees to see what falls. I suppose I owe you for saving my life in '19, and for not digging too deep into my business interests." Nitti paused for a moment, his face reddening slightly, almost as if he were embarrassed. "Besides, it ain't right to mow down the President. That's the way the Fascists do in Italy. It ain't right that their way of business becomes ours."

"Thank you, Mr. Nitti," responded Bierce politely. "I will meet you in three days at this bench, same time, to hear what you've been able to learn." Bierce rose from the bench smoothly and walked off without a backward glance. Frank Nitti continued to rub the spot over his ulcer, his thoughts turning to Milk of Magnesia.

✦

The Hudson Essex was a light car with a powerful engine. It barreled along the road from South Bend to Chicago, passing everything in sight. At the wheel sat John Herbert Dillinger, America's most famous bank robber. A tall, darkly handsome man of about thirty he was usually in a good mood, except when someone failed to give the "g" in his last name a hard, Germanic pronunciation. He was not in a good mood now, pushing the Hudson six-cylinder engine for all that it was worth, putting as much distance as possible between the car and the Merchants' National Bank of South Bend.

"Slow down, John," grunted the small man who sat beside Dillinger, clutching a Thompson submachine gun. "We've left the local bulls far behind. All you're doing now is attracting the attention of motorcycle cops." The speaker was Lester Gillis, known as Baby Face Nelson because of his youthful features and small stature. Despite his humorous alias, he was a sociopath who loved killing, especially policemen. In this, he differed from Dillinger, who viewed a killing during a robbery as a sign of bad planning.

"You stupid little bastard!" snarled Dillinger, not even deigning to glance at Nelson. "The cop walked in expecting nothing, didn't even try to pull his piece. You could have held him at bay with the Tommy gun. Now every cop between Philly and Denver will be after us."

"Don't get all pious on me, John. You got no trouble with killing. I've seen you do it."

"Only when money is at stake, you stupid Mick. Greasing that bull won't bring us a penny."

"I hate cops and G-men," snarled Nelson. "I'll gun down every last one of the bastards I can. I'll never forget what they did to me in the Chicago lockup!"

"Yeah, right. That cop you left bleeding on the floor of the bank is the one that raped you," muttered Dillinger sarcastically over the roar of the engine. He was an intelligent man who bitterly resented that his father's poverty had placed college out of reach, and that the Depression had taken away any prospect of a good job. He reflected on how he had dreamed as a teenager of being an engineer or architect. Dillinger frowned slightly as he realized he could not seem to recall how his petty crime thefts as a kid had led him to this time and place. He shook his head as if to clear it, then made his decision.

Dillinger saw that he was on a long, straight stretch of road, with no sign of cars in either direction. He pulled off the pavement onto a grassy shoulder, stopping the car, but keeping the engine running.

"Hey, what the...." said Nelson, who realized that somehow, Dillinger had produced a .380 Colt automatic and was holding it to his head.

"No sudden moves," Dillinger said quietly. With his left hand, Dillinger deftly plucked Nelson's pistol from under his coat, and tossed it out the open driver's side window. Then he took the heavy Tommy gun from Nelson's grasp. Nelson did not resist, although his face had turned nearly purple with rage. Clumsily, Dillinger shoved the chopper out of the window, where it clattered metallically on the edge of the pavement.

"Now, this is where you get out, Nelson. The witnesses at the bank will surely have recognized a mean little shrimp like you. All the bulls in two states will be looking for you, and I'm not going to be there when they find you."

Nelson finally spoke. "So you're going to stiff me of my share and leave me defenseless when the cops come! You Goddamn, lousy—"

"GET OUT OF THE CAR!" Nelson had never heard the soft-voiced Dillinger shout before. He scrambled for the handle, found it, and half fell out of the Essex. Never taking his eyes off Nelson, Dillinger reached into the back seat and brought a bulging valise into the front. Unlatching it, he began throwing bundles of currency at the feet of an astonished Nelson. Finally, he stopped.

"That's about fifteen grand. I'm leaving that with you, along with the guns I threw out the other side. That should give you a chance." Dillinger reached over and slammed the passenger door shut. Slipping his automatic into his shoulder holster, he gunned the engine and put the car back on the pavement. As Dillinger rapidly sent the car through second and into third gear, Nelson ran to the Thompson, picked it up, worked the bolt, and took aim at the rapidly disappearing vehicle. With a snarl of disappointment, he lowered the weapon. Dillinger was already over a hundred yards away, well beyond the range of the Thompson's .45 caliber round.

✦

Ana Cumpanas sat at the desk in the small bedroom that served as her office, frowning over her ledger. She sighed and leaned back in her chair. America was supposed to be the richest country on Earth. Men always wanted women, and would pay as much as they could afford for them. In America, that would be more than anywhere else, at least if she provided a quality product. And she did provide a quality product. Her girls were attractive, healthy, and free of obvious signs of disease. Furthermore, she made sure that her girls were at least superficially educated and fluent. As an experienced madam, she understood that the best paying customers often wanted company as much as sex, and she did her best to provide both.

No, this small, somewhat shabby apartment building on Chicago's busy Halsted Street should have been a gold mine. It was not. Times were hard, and the number of men who could afford Cumpanas' prices had declined steeply. Then there were the leeches, Nitti's Italian bastards who demanded "protection money," and even worse, the so-called law—policemen and aldermen—who demanded "consideration" for her violation of the anti-prostitution laws. Many of them were more than willing to tolerate, even enjoy, her establishment most of the time. But on the first day of each month, they would show up, shocked to find vice in their pure city of Chicago and demand money to salve their shattered nerves. Since she paid her whores better than most brothel owners, this left surprisingly little for her at the end of the month.

She shook out her long black hair then stood up from the desk and stretched, revealing a tall, lithe figure. She then took a pack of Camels from the desk, shook out one to place in her mouth, and lit it with a gold-plated lighter. Breathing deeply, she expelled the smoke through her nostrils and strolled over to the window and looked through the curtain. Hearing a commotion directly below her, she looked down at the sidewalk outside the front entrance to her apartment building. She was stunned to see Gino, her massive, if dim-witted bouncer, arguing with a beefy man in an ill-fitting suit and a straw boater. The stranger pulled a revolver with his right hand, and with his left, he produced some sort of badge. It took Gino a moment to process the situation before he nodded and led the stranger through the door.

Cumpanas felt her heart lurch with panic. She strode quickly over to her desk and crushed the cigarette out in an ashtray. She then grabbed her ledger full of incriminating information and, after a moment's thought, ran to the window, opened it, and slid the ledger onto the eight-inch brick ledge that circled the building. She believed—no, hoped—that even a bull doing a thorough search of the room would not think to open the window and examine the ledge. Just as she quietly closed the window, she heard a knock at the door. Working to control her breath, she strode to the middle of the room, smoothing her hair and bright orange dress before calling out, "Yes?"

The door was violently kicked open, and the stranger lumbered in, revolver now holstered but clearly visible, a smile creasing his flabby face. Behind him, the bovine Gino was stuttering, "Mrs. Cumpanas, I tried to tell him you don't see no people this time of morning."

"That's all right, Gino," she replied in a throaty voice redolent of Eastern Europe. "Go downstairs and watch the front door."

The bouncer half-saluted, turned, and walked out of sight, his heavy tread fading away.

In a cold voice she said to the newcomer, "Who are you, and what is your business with me?"

"Top of the morning to you, Miss Ana Sage," replied the big man in a voice shaded with an Irish lilt. "Or rather, should I say, Mrs. Ana Cumpanas, the name under which you entered this fine country of ours? I'm Patrick Burke of the immigration service."

The cold organ that was her heart seemed to skip a beat. "Immigration?"

"Oh, bless me yes, Mrs. Cumpanas."

"I don't know what you could want with me. I received my naturalization papers four years ago."

"You did indeed, lass, you did indeed," replied Burke in a friendly voice. "Ah, you see, you identified yourself as Ana Sage, a person who I fear does not exist. Instead, a little bird has told us that you really are Ana Cumpanas." He whipped a dog-eared notebook out of a side pocket and consulted a page towards the middle. "Ana Cumpanas. Born in eastern part of the late Austro-Hungarian Empire in 1889." He glanced up at her and smiled. "May I say you carry your forty-four years well?"

He turned his attention back to his notebook. "You have a police record with the Kingdom of Roumania. Arrested in 1923 for prostitution, procuring, and—bless my soul—theft and moral turpitude. Escaped custody by seducing a guard—what a bad girl we've been." The man continued. "Then obtained a falsified passport and immigration visa to enter our fine, upstanding country. Tsk. Tsk."

"But I am now an American citizen."

"Well, that's the pity of the thing, Mrs. Cumpanas. No one of low moral character may be admitted to this country. You concealed your low moral character, and as a result, your citizenship was obtained by fraud. It can be revoked for that reason, and your sweet self can be returned to the welcoming arms of Roumania."

Cumpanas was genuinely shocked. "But … but … I have been in this country now for over ten years! Why do you raise all this now?"

The smile left Burke's face. "Now that be the pity of the matter. You could say that there are many more deserving of deportation that yourself, and Patrick Burke wouldn't call you a liar. But when an alderman in this fine and honest city of Chicago levies an accusation with my superiors, and they give me my orders, now I ask you, what am I to do?" His face turned dark, angry. "I have heard, Mrs. Cumpanas, that you refused to increase your bribes to the said alderman, who then decided to peach on you to Uncle Sam. If things ran as Patrick Burke would have them, he'd be the one thrown out of the country, not your lovely self. Sad to say, things never have been run as Patrick Burke would have it, and probably never will."

Cumpanas was proud and seldom begged. This was one of those few times she would beg.

"Please … I would have paid him if I had the money, but I do not. Don't send me back to Roumania. You have no idea what it's like. The Iron Guard under that bastard Antonescu takes what they want from whoever they want, kills at random—Jews, Gypsies, or anyone who doesn't worship Antonescu or that bastard in Germany. Please."

Burke looked genuinely sorrowful. "Far be it for an Irishman to deny that the world is a hard place. The sad fact is that me, and my superiors, have no choice against the kind of political pressure being brought." He reached into his inner coat pocket, removed a paper, and threw it down on her desk. "This is a summons to appear in our offices in ten days' time for your hearing. Please be sure to show up. And don't be thinking of leaving town. You won't get far, and I'll be very unhappy if you put me to the trouble of tracking you down."

Burke nodded and tipped his hat to Cumpanas. Then he left the room, closing the door behind him. Ana Cumpanas stared at the document on her desk as if it were a poisonous snake.

✦

It was 2:00 in the morning, and Cumpanas was still tossing in her bed, unable to sleep. But it was not the occasional noises from the rooms of her whores that kept her wide awake. After all, she had trained them to be relatively decorous in their behavior with the customers. No, it was the thought—and fear—of being sent back to Roumania—the Roumania that Antonescu and the Iron Guard were busily turning into an approximation of Hell on Earth. Her body was telling her to run. Her mind was telling her that she didn't have the money to run, or for that matter, get very far if she did. Filled with terror of deportation to Roumania, she gazed wide-eyed at the ceiling, even in the total darkness of the room.

Sighing, she decided to give up on sleep. Turning on the lamp on the table beside her bed, she sat up, swung her legs around, and slipped on her slippers. She grabbed a pack of Camels she kept next to the lamp, shook out a cigarette, ignited it, and took several deep drags in rapid succession. Suddenly, there was a slight rapping on her window, which startled her and she dropped her cigarette. Quickly, she ground it out with her heel. Then she grabbed a snub-nosed revolver from the nightstand and carefully approached the window. She lightly slid the edge of the curtain aside and peered through the glass. She nearly cried with relief. Throwing her gun onto the bed, she unlatched the window and carefully drew it up. A soft-sided valise was thrown into the room and was immediately followed by an athletic man who crouched, his feet on the sill and then fell forward, catching himself on his hands, balancing his body upright. The acrobatic visitor walked on his hands about the room, then with a smooth spring, landed upright on his feet. Cumpanas giggled.

"John, you stupid bastard! I could've shot you!"

A grinning John Dillinger folded her into his arms and planted a deep, lingering kiss on her lips. Then he said, "Ana, you're such a bad shot, I figured the risk was worth it."

Cumpanas stood back and looked at him seriously. "It's not that I'm not glad to see you, but what brings you hear now, at this time? And why through the window?"

Dillinger himself turned serious. "I'm hot, Ana. That bloodthirsty bastard Nelson machine-gunned a bull when it wasn't necessary. Can't count on buying protection from our boys in blue. No matter how much they're on the take, you know how they feel about cop-killers."

"Where's Nelson now?" Cumpanas said, uneasiness in her voice. She did not know the word "psychopath," but she knew one when she saw one, and she had seen the diminutive Nelson.

"Dumped him on the road, with guns and half the swag. If he were smart, that would allow him to lay low, maybe get out the country. But I don't expect him to be smart. He may even try to track me down. That's why I need someone I can trust to stay with."

"Honey, I hate to tell you this, but you aren't safe here. The Feds are on me, said they'd deport me."

The normally cheerful Dillinger frowned. "The hell you say! You've got your citizenship papers and everything."

"They say they have proof I lied on my citizenship application."

"How'd they get that, after all these years?"

"I'm not sure, but I can make a guess. The others running fancy houses in this burg know I get more than my share of the best paying customers. They'd like me out of competition, so they did a little digging. Wouldn't have been hard. Whores, even my whores, don't keep secrets very well. Anyway, they've given me an order to

Purvis walked over to the body and, to everyone's surprise, kicked it viciously in the head. "Bates," he snarled at one of his men, "find the nearest telephone and get on the line to the Chicago office. Nelson's bitch-of-a-wife won't be able to get far. Take her alive, and find out the places Dillinger might hide out."

"Then we set a trap to catch him?" asked Bates.

"No. Then we kill him." He lit another cigarette and started walking back to his Plymouth. He did not notice a burly man with dark features watching him intently from behind the small group of early morning onlookers.

❖

Frank Nitti and his two bodyguards occupied a table far back from the restaurant's front window, the bodyguards facing the door. Nitti poked disconsolately at his food, then put down his fork, took the cold glass of milk and sipped at it as if it were medicine. His attention was taken from his ulcer by his bodyguards' quick movements, jamming their right hands under their coats, more slowly removing them. Nitti looked up to see one of his capos walking through the door. The man approached Nitti's table, removed his hat, and waited respectfully to be addressed.

"I assume it is important for you to interrupt my meal," grumbled Nitti. "Take the last chair."

"Thank you, Mr. Nitti," the bulky man replied as he sat down. "I would not disturb you, except you said it was important to give you news of killers not part of the familia. Lester Gilles, the one they call Baby Face Nelson, has been found dead. He killed two Feds, but not before they filled him with lead."

"I wonder if this is the gunman who so interests the Bureau of Investigation," muttered Nitti to himself. In a louder voice, he asked, "Have the Feds called off the manhunt they've had going on for the last few days?"

"Doesn't seem so, Mr. Nitti. Word downtown is that they're looking for Nelson's wife, and for Dillinger."

A thought occurred to Nitti. He could dismiss Mrs. Gillis. She often strung along with her husband, but never seemed to be involved with the shooting. But Dillinger ... Dillinger ... was a killer as well, but not a rabid, mad-dog killer like Nelson. Dillinger tried to avoid killing as much as possible, unless there was gain in it. So, he knew no one in their right mind would try to hire Nelson to do a high profile assassination. But Dillinger ... that was another matter. Nitti addressed his capo.

"I remember hearing that when he's in Chicago, Dillinger stays in one or two preferred whorehouses. Find out which ones. Bring him to me, or if he's gone, bring the madam running the cathouse. In either case, alive and uninjured."

The capo nodded solemnly. "Yes, Mr. Nitti. Without another word, he stood up and strode out of the restaurant.

A stab of pain shot through Nitti's stomach, which he rubbed gingerly.

✦

Harry Bierce sat alone at a table in a rather dreary restaurant, not far from the Loop, reading the *Chicago*

Tribune. His meal was only half-finished, but he had eaten as much as he could tolerate of the rather greasy viands. And the meat, which he preferred rare, so rare that blood would spurt out as he chewed, was so overdone, he couldn't stomach another bite. He sipped at his glass of strong tea as he read, having never acquired a taste for coffee. When his eye caught something on the page—the glass hovered motionlessly for nearly a minute. Then with exaggerated care, he placed the glass on the table and slowly stood up.

No one was watching him, but if someone had, they would have been shocked to see what little color Bierce's face held. At that moment, he resembled a living statue of marble. He threw a dollar bill on the table, then walked over to the empty telephone booth by the checker's counter. Closing the door firmly behind him, he inserted some change into the slot. After much delay and argument with trunk operators, a connection was made.

"Bierce, what the hell are you doing calling me at this time of night," said the tinny, far-away voice of John Edgar Hoover.

"Don't try to tell me you didn't know about what I just read in the newspaper," replied Bierce in a voice filled with sorely concealed rage.

"You mean the president coming to Chicago in eight days to make a speech to the labor convention," stated Hoover. Although it may have been the static over the long distance line, Bierce thought Hoover's voice sounded dejected, almost defeated.

"Yes sir, that is what I mean. Why didn't you stop him? Didn't you tell him of the risk to his life?"

"I most certainly did. Talked to him for over an hour. It did no good. No good at all."

"Despite what happened in Florida eighteen months ago?"

"Especially because of what happened. He says he trusts the Secret Service to protect him. Has some idea of proving his courage." The Director did not add his suspicion that FDR's buckling in to Hoover's blackmail over his mistress had filled the President with a desire to prove he was not a physical coward.

Hoover literally ground his teeth in frustration. He despised the President, not only for his politics, but for his weaknesses. And yet, to his own surprise, he found himself deeply concerned about the man's safety. He turned his attention back to the waiting Bierce.

"The president is coming to Chicago. Flat out, that's a given. Bierce, you have to stop that torpedo. You've got eight days."

Unable to keep the sarcasm out of his voice, Bierce replied, "Didn't you think to alert me to this before I read about it in the newspaper?"

"Bierce, I know you. You have only one speed. Full throttle. I know you are doing everything you can. There was no point in giving you some distracting news. Anyway, I've instructed the Chicago office to give you any help that you request. Now, if you don't mind, it's been a long day, and I need some rest. Goodnight, Agent Bierce."

Bierce heard a click, followed by a dial tone. Still gripping the receiver in his hand, he fought the temptation to rip it out by the cord and destroy the booth.

✦

Dillinger was a very light sleeper. Cumpanas' building was after all a brothel, and there were comings and goings at all times of the day and night. Those sounds he managed to ignore. However, the creaking of floorboards made by big men quietly moving in, did disturb him.

Instantly, Dillinger was fully awake. Dumping the still sleeping Cumpanas onto the floor, he threw on his clothes with lighting speed, grabbed his gun and valise, and vaulted out the fire escape just as the door to the room crashed open. Nitti's capo moved into the room warily, large automatic held out in front of him, followed by one of his men. *BANG!* A shot boomed from outside the window. Swearing in Italian, the capo rushed over to the window, screaming "Luigi! I told you the boss wants him alive!"

The man was halfway out the window when he froze, catching site of the man he had stationed on the fire escape to catch anyone fleeing. It was clear Luigi had not fired the shot, unless, that is, he had shot himself through the forehead. The capo frantically scanned the alley in both directions, but saw no one. He re-entered the room, where his man was holding onto the naked, dazed Cumpanas.

"Puta!" he snarled as he slapped her across the face with his meaty open hand. "Your boyfriend has killed my sister's boy! What shall I be telling my sister, about how Luigi is never coming home again? Now, where did that bastard go? Speak!"

Cumpanas was confused, and in truth did not know where Dillinger had gone. After a few moments of her silence, the capo struck her again, this time with a closed fist. As Cumpanas gasped for breath through a bloody mouth, the huge gangster pointed the Colt .45 between her eyes. Before he could pull the trigger, his minion hurriedly said, "Remember how the boss feels about killing kids and dames. We should talk this over with him before doing anything that can't be undone."

The capo thought for a moment, then slowly, he lowered the hammer of his automatic, his face contorted with hate. "Get dressed, bitch. We're going for a little ride. Oh, and just give me a reason. Any reason. Please."

✦

Some fourteen hours later, Harry Bierce trudged into his dingy hotel, frustrated and tired from a wasted day of trying to track down leads from the corrupt and inefficient Chicago police.

Before he could ask the desk clerk for the key, the untidy young man with bulging eyes said, "Telephone message for you, Mr. Bierce," and threw a folded piece of paper across the counter.

Bierce picked it up, rapidly scanned the contents, and sighed. It had taken him a quarter of an hour to find a parking spot for his hired Hudson convertible, and now it appeared he would have to be taking to the streets again. Without saying a word to the clerk, Bierce turned on his heel and hurried out of the hotel, taking the two blocks to his car with surprising speed for someone so tired.

A short drive brought him to the downtown hotel. Surprisingly, very few cars were parked along the street, and he was able to find a place for his Hudson virtually at the front entrance. A small, thin man with crazy eyes, hands buried in the deep pockets of his overcoat, walked up to Bierce as he locked the car. Not removing his hands from his coat pockets, the small man said, "You the G-man?"

Calmly Bierce replied, "I am indeed."

"Come with me. Boss said to bring you right up. Room 2322."

The two entered the lobby side-by-side. The clerk at the reception desk glanced up from the copy of the *Chicago Tribune* he was reading, frowned, and hurriedly returned his attention to his newspaper. They rode the elevator up to the twenty-third floor in silence, then proceeded along the corridor. The crazy-eyed man opened the door to a suite and gestured for Bierce to go in. Bierce entered, but instead of following Bierce into the room, the small man remained in the hallway, pulling the door closed.

To the right of the entry, Bierce saw three people sitting in the suite's living room. Bierce walked into the room to find Frank Nitti lounging on a sofa, left hand massaging his stomach through his vest, while in his right hand, he held a drink that looked surprisingly like milk. A woman sat huddled in a padded chair, and from behind a bruised face stared at the newcomer with fear-filled eyes. The enormous capo stood to the right of his master's sofa, huge hands clenching and unclenching as he glared at Bierce.

"Good evening, Mr. Nitti," said Bierce, making a slight bow to the man on the sofa.

"Evening, Captain Bierce," responded Nitti brusquely, draining his glass in several large gulps, then setting it on a small table beside his sofa.

"Mr. Nitti, I don't see the good of this," uttered the capo in a strained voice. "Word gets out you're talking to a G-man, some of the boys will get strange ideas."

"The boys don't need to know nothing. Only us in this room, and Carlo outside guarding the door, know this meeting's taking place. I'd be very unhappy were that to change, understand?"

The large man visibly paled, but nodded once. Nitti turned his attention back to Bierce.

"Captain, as a personal favor to you, I've had my boys out looking to find a freelance torpedo who might undertake a … high-profile killing. Ain't certain, but I think my boys have come up trumps. That bitch in the chair is Ana Cumpanas, runs a high-end whorehouse. Word on the street is she sometimes shacks up with John Dillinger. Normally, I don't care about those hayseeds who spray bullets, whether needed or not. Chicago bulls ain't smart, but they're smart enough to round up hicks like them. But I thought it over a bit, and it seemed Dillinger was a cut above, and just might take the kind of job you were talking about. So, I send three of my boys over to Cumpanas' place to invite Dillinger over for a little talk. Bastard was as quick as a lizard, and deadly as a rattlesnake. Made a clean break after blowing the brains out of one of my men."

"It was my sister's boy," interrupted the capo, still clenching and unclenching his enormous fists.

Nitti grimaced. "As I told you before, I like things quiet on the streets. This is different—blood requires blood. Normally, we'd handle this within the family, but I made you a promise. Now can you promise me this bastard is going to die? No deals, no plea bargains?"

"I can make that promise. I might need to keep him alive to testify at the trial of another, but after that he will pay for all he has done."

Eyes blazing with rage, the capo started toward Bierce. Nitti held up his hand, and despite his anger, the gangster stopped. He had worked for Al Capone.

"You're the only G-man whose word I'd take."

"So, do you know where I can find Dillinger?"

"Not exactly. But I know how he can be found." Nitti gestured at Cumpanas. "This bitch knows more about his hideouts than anyone else. She wasn't inclined to share her information at first, but we persuaded her in the end. Hey, whore," he turned to Cumpanas, "tell the nice G-man where Dillinger hangs out."

Cumpanas did not look at Bierce. Gingerly touching the large bruise under her eye, she began speaking in a low monotone. "Johnnie likes to go to Cub games. Doesn't matter if the heat's on, he won't miss one. There's also a whorehouse a few blocks from Wrigley Field, he goes to ground there when he has to. Used to have a thing with the madam. That's all over, but they're still pals. And movies, he likes to go to the movies at night when it's hot, like it is now."

"How did you come to be involved with such a mad-dog killer?" Bierce asked Cumpanas softly.

The beaten woman managed a smile. "Johnnie's good company. Always has good stories, can make you laugh no matter what. Like the way he can walk on his hands all over the room. Funniest thing you ever saw…."

Cumpanas didn't notice Bierce go absolutely rigid for a few moments, adjusting to the idea that Dillinger, without a doubt, was the man about whom the dying Bonnie Parker had raved.

"I've paid my debt to you, Captain Bierce. Now we're square," said Nitti.

"What will you do with her?" asked Bierce, gesturing toward the battered woman.

"Not your concern, Captain," replied Nitti, glancing over to his capo.

"I disagree. I may need her to lure Dillinger out of hiding. I will take her with me."

The woman and the capo looked at Bierce—one with faint hope, the other with barely suppressed rage. Nitti was silent, and the issue hung in the balance. Then Nitti rubbed his ulcer, sighed, and said, "All right, you can have the whore." He then looked up at his furious capo. "She didn't plug your sister's boy. Dillinger dropped the hammer on him. The important thing is to get him." He then shifted his attention to Bierce. "Captain, I think it's in both of our interests if we don't meet again. Close the door on your way out."

Bierce nodded slightly to Nitti, then walked over to the chair and took the woman's arm, pulling her into a standing position. He guided her to the door, opened it, nodded to the crazy-eyed gunman who had been standing sentry, and guided her down the hallway to the elevator. Only when the elevator had started its descent did she begin to speak.

"Why did you take me out of there? They were going to kill me. I am nothing to you."

Bierce looked at her, and his set features softened somewhat. "I rather disapprove of the murder of women, even those in your line of work. Besides, you remind me of someone I knew many years ago."

"Where are we going?"

"To my hotel room. Tomorrow, I'll get you some respectable clothes, then you will help me catch your boyfriend, the man who left you to the tender mercies of the Nitti gang."

"And what happens to me after that?" she asked in a small voice.

Bierce made no reply.

✦

At 11:00 the following morning, Bierce maneuvered his Hudson into the nearest parking spot, a mere three blocks away, to Wrigley Field. He vaulted easily out of the driver's seat, went around to the passenger side and held the door open for Cumpanas. Gingerly, she stepped out of the low-slung convertible, smoothed the wrinkles out of her brand-new orange dress, and adjusted her cloche hat to a rakish angle. Bierce cast an appreciative eye over her.

"Mrs. Cumpanas, you are to be congratulated. I feared the dress would not fit you well, but the last-minute alterations you made are splendid. It now fits you like a glove."

As they began walking toward the stadium, she replied, "I once supported myself as seamstress, back in Roumania. I liked it, but it paid pennies. As soon as I could, I got away from it and started catering to the lusts of men. It paid much better."

Bierce looked as if he were going to reply, but in the end said nothing. They covered the remaining distance to Wrigley Field in silence.

When they arrived, a large crowd was already jostling through the gates, even though it was nearly two hours to the start of the game. Many in the crowd were obviously among the unemployed, their ragged, shabby clothing testifying to that fact. However, unlike their usual appearance, there was a cheerful, festive air about them. For a few hours they could forget their problems, thanks to America's pastime.

To the left of the main entrance, Bierce spotted four men standing around in neat but inexpensive suits, the uniform of a Federal agent. Bierce led Cumpanas over to the men, and shook the hand of the smallest of them.

"Mrs. Cumpanas, allow me to introduce Special Agent Melvin Purvis, one of the Bureau's best." He did not bother to introduce the other three, nor did they bother to introduce themselves.

"Well, Bierce, when I got your call late last night, I have to admit it seemed a screwball idea. Dillinger, the man being sought in three states, going to a daytime baseball game? Still, I'm running out of ideas, and I'll grasp at any old straw. This the woman you talked about?"

"Yes. Mrs. Cumpanas knows Dillinger very well. I know we've all seen pictures of him, but photos are never as good as an eyewitness."

"Don't need a woman to finger him for me," muttered the gloomy Purvis. "I see that bastard's face in my dreams."

"I agree," replied Bierce. "Still, it's better to be doubly sure."

"So, Bierce, should we split up?"

Bierce shook his head, and gestured to the thickening

stream of baseball fans before him. "That's the only way in, a true bottleneck. Besides, I must have him alive."

"He murdered two of my best men," replied Purvis in a low, hatred-charged voice. "He must die for that."

Bierce jabbed a forefinger at Purvis. "He must be taken alive, if at all possible. Once he has testified about … about another case, he will be bent sent to the electric chair."

Cumpanas had not yet decided whether she would help finger her lover. As the two G-men conversed, she looked at the sea of faces passing her into Wrigley Field. Like a flash, there he was, bold as brass, jacketless in the Chicago heat, straw boater perched jauntily on his handsome head, a loose white untucked shirt. Almost in a hypnotic state, she quietly walked away from the agents, feeling her way through the packed crowds. She touched his arm, and he whirled around in surprise.

"Johnnie, the Feds are here. You gotta run."

At the same moment, Bierce became aware Cumpanas was no longer at his side. He scanned the crowd franticly. His pale blue eyes locked on Dillinger.

Dillinger did not speak, did not hesitate. Grabbing Cumpanas roughly by the arm, he dragged her through the crowd, using blows and kicks to clear a path to the turnstiles, elbowing his way past the astonished ticket-takers. Bierce drew and cocked his .45 Colt automatic, and began fighting his way forward, shouting in a surprisingly loud and deep voice for so slight a person, "Out of the way! Federal Officer!" He was closely followed by Purvis, who in turn, was trailed by his three agents.

Running at full tilt, the crowds on the other side of the turnstiles cleared the way for him. Dillinger, hampered by the high-heeled Cumpanas he dragged along behind him, swerved left onto the first aisle, forcibly shoving past the relatively few fans who had not yet found their seats. Still, he could not go as fast as the unencumbered Bierce, who ran with the shocking fluidity of a mongoose. When a space cleared between them, Bierce's now deep voice boomed, "Halt or I'll shoot!" Bierce paused for a second to decide how best to inflict a nonlethal wound on Dillinger. It was a second too long.

Moving with the speed of a striking cobra, Dillinger released Cumpanas and grabbed a pregnant young woman who had been trying to settle into a seat in the front row of the section. He swung the shrieking woman in front of him, and as Bierce hesitated, the gangster produced an automatic from under his shirt and fired a single shot at Bierce. He then released the young woman, grabbed Cumpanas, and darted down a connected aisle leading into the bowels of the stadium.

Bierce was standing stock still as Purvis and his agents reached him. "Where did he go?" screamed the frustrated, red-faced Purvis as he swiveled his pistol around in all directions, much to the terror of nearby baseball fans. Bierce did not answer. Instead, his automatic slipped slowly from his hand to clatter onto the concrete of the aisle. He brought his hand up to the section of his expensive double-breasted coat that was right over his silk handkerchief, and brought away fingers dabbled in blood. As the horrified Purvis looked on, Bierce smiled weirdly and murmured, "It has been a long time, but I am finally coming, my love." Then his eyes closed and he collapsed to the concrete. like a puppet whose strings had been cut.

"Go get that bastard and his bitch and kill them both!" screamed an enraged Purvis to his men. He then grabbed a terrified hot dog vendor, shoved his pistol in the young man's face, and yelled. "Go find whoever's in charge! Close the gates! Then call the Bureau Office and have them send an ambulance and every man they have! Now move, or so help me God I'll make it a bad day for your mother!" Purvis then dropped to his knees and setting his gun aside, commenced doing everything he could to stop the bleeding.

✦

Dillinger and Cumpanas were sharing a dingy room in a no-questions-asked downtown hotel. Dillinger was busy cleaning a Springfield rifle with a telescopic sight that he had stored in the room some days before.

Cumpanas was chain-smoking while sitting on the bed, her hands trembling with delayed shock. Finally, she broke the silence. "Johnnie, there was no need to shoot that G-man. You had a hostage. You could've demanded that he throw his gun away, and then we could have made our escape."

"No time for that," Dillinger responded sourly. He then placed the cleaned rifle across the room's desk and turned in his chair to face Cumpanas. "I'm more interested in what you were doing with the Feds. Thinking of selling me out?"

"It wasn't like that, honey," she replied, a tremble of fear in her voice. "After you took off from my place, shooting the young punk on your way out, the goddamn dagos took me to Nitti."

Dillinger gave a low whistle. "Frank Nitti himself. That's quite an honor."

"They wanted me to give you up. They beat me pretty good. I think they had decided to take me for a ride, when Agent Bierce—the G-man you shot—showed up. It was strange. He took me away from them, just wanted me to identify you. I went along with it, but only to warn you when they caught up to you. That's what I did."

Dillinger gave her a long, hard look, then his features softened. "Okay baby, I believe you. This will be our new plan. You stay here. Only go out for food and such. I got things to do, people to see. I'll be dropping in from time to time. When I finish my job, we're out of here and off to Canada. Got the picture?"

"Sure, Johnnie, sure."

"All right then, come here. I'm in serious need of some loving."

⚜

The room in the west wing of the seventh floor of Chicago Memorial that Melvin Purvis was approaching resembled an anthill that some kid had disrupted with a stick. Purvis stood still for a minute, watching white-clad doctors and nurses scurry in and out, strange looking expressions on their faces. He had left here just four hours before, desperate for some sleep in one of the bunks reserved for the night interns, leaving strict orders to be awakened when it looked like Bierce was about to die. He had awakened on his own, looked at the clock on the wall and decided the staff had ignored his request, and had allowed Agent Bierce to leave this world with no fellow agent to witness his leaving. Now, staring at the commotion in Bierce's room, he realized Bierce had not yet died, although he suspected the end was imminent. He jogged the rest of the way to the room, and grabbed one of the doctors at the entrance. Shaking the man by the shoulder, Purvis asked, "When will Agent Bierce … pass on?"

The young doctor stared at Purvis, then bit his lip before saying, "I think you should talk to Dr. Stein. He's in the room." Then he pulled free of Purvis and ran down the hall as if he were in fear of his life.

Purvis paused for a moment, then entered the room. The pale, still form of Harry Bierce lay motionless on the bed, an intravenous line snaking into each arm. Two doctors and two nurses hovered over Bierce. "Which one of you is Stein?" asked Purvis with more harshness than he had intended.

They all turned to look at Purvis. The elder of the two doctors said, "I am Stein."

"What is happening to Agent Bierce? I was told four hours ago that he had only a couple of hours to live."

The balding Stein turned to his colleagues, and in a voice tinged with a German accent said, "Please leave for a few minutes." They glanced at each other, but filed out of the room wordlessly. Stein closed the door behind them and turned to face Purvis.

"Frankly, this case baffles me, Agent Purvis. When I initially examined Agent Bierce, I was amazed he had lived to reach the hospital. X-rays confirmed that the bullet had transited the left lung, exiting under his shoulder blade. It had nicked his pulmonary artery; internal bleeding was extensive. Frankly, all I did was stop the external bleeding and administer morphine, so that he would be comfortable while he died—yet, he has not died. In fact…."

Dr. Stein closed his eyes for a moment and reeled. Purvis reached forward to catch him, but the doctor's eyes flew open and he steadied himself. "Pardon, but what I have witnessed has shaken my belief in medical science." The doctor hesitated, as if deciding how to say what he'd seen. "When I changed his bandages, the entry and exit holes were almost completely … healed. And it seems unlikely that any substantial scar tissue will form." He shook his head, still in disbelief, and spoke as if trying to convince himself. "His internal bleeding appears to have stopped. Even less believable, his collapsed left lung has spontaneously re-inflated. Of course, I ordered additional X-rays." Then looking directly at the agent, he said, "You know, Agent Purvis, if I were not a man of science, I would say that this man isn't—"

"Isn't what, doctor?" asked a thin but firm voice from the bed.

Dr. Stein jerked his attention over to the bed. Harry Bierce's sky-blue eyes stared at him calmly. Visibly swallowing, Stein replied, "It's not important, Agent Bierce. What is important is that you are making an astonishing recovery."

"Harry, this is amazing!" exclaimed Purvis, moving closer to the bed. "Dr. Stein and his staff have performed a miracle!"

"We cannot take the all the credit," said Stein. "Much of this recovery seems due to a remarkable immune system. When you are better, I would like to run a number of tests on you."

Bierce's attention had drifted from the doctor. Seemingly to himself, he murmured, "Still here … still here … still not done." He looked back at Stein and said, "Doctor, I would be very grateful for a glass of water."

"Of course." Stein opened the door to the room and barked some orders.

"Harry, I'm damned glad to see you conscious," said Purvis. "I've had to bury too many Bureau men. Didn't want you to be another."

"Did you capture Dillinger?"

Purvis contorted his face as if he'd bitten into a lemon. "No, and I blame myself. Should have had more men waiting outside the park. We had the place locked up tighter than a Scotsman's wallet, but it was five minutes too late. Looks like his love of baseball paid off. He seems to have known every nook and cranny at Wrigley Field."

Bierce nodded slightly. "The woman get away as well?"

"Yeah, the bitch as well. Don't worry, Harry. They're dead—they just don't know it yet."

"I need them alive!" snapped Bierce with surprising emphasis for someone who'd just been so close to death's door. "Take them alive, and bring them to me. I need your word, Purvis."

With visible reluctance Purvis said, "If I can do it with no risk to my men, I promise. But I'm not letting Dillinger kill any of my men. I'm not going to bury another comrade!"

"Fair enough."

Stein re-entered the room with a carafe and a glass. "Here is your water, Agent Bierce."

"Excellent, Doctor. Also, could you have some food brought to me? I'm famished. Preferably steak, as rare as possible."

✦

Ana Cumpanas was lingering on one of Chicago's busiest thoroughfares, window shopping the various dresses on display in various shops, painfully aware that she could afford none of them. Dillinger had barely given her enough cash to pay for a meal before he had taken off early in the morning. Her clothes that she had worn the day before were decent enough in appearance, but they were the only clothes she had. She had just decided she was going to have to beg Dillinger for enough cash for a couple of decent dresses when a rough hand nearly jerked her left arm out of its socket. Simultaneously, she felt the barrel of a gun jabbed into her lower back.

"Take it easy sister," said a man in a low, gravelly voice. "Federal agent. Damned if Purvis wasn't right, that you would still be wearing that orange number. Stands out like a socialite in a strip joint."

✦

Harry Bierce was sitting up in bed, to the utter amazement of Melvin Purvis, Doctor Stein, and various nurses. They all knew the wound he had sustained was fatal, and that if Bierce had pulled through at all, he should have been crippled for life. Yet the latest set of X-rays confirmed what the doctor had suspected—the internal bleeding was not only stopped, all the blood enmassed in his gut had been completely reabsorbed into the agent's body. Although it was harder to interpret the soft tissue of the lung, it seemed, too, that the damage was healing itself with inhuman speed. All those around him, save Stein, felt an increasing uneasiness in the presence of Bierce. As to Dr. Stein, he occasionally muttered in his native German tongue which often contained the words "Nobel Prize."

Bierce handed the seated Purvis his food tray. Purvis grimaced as he placed it on the table to his right, the bloody residue on the plate disgusting him almost as much as had the sight of Bierce devouring the near-raw steak. Sated for the moment, Bierce leaned back into his pillows with a sigh. He then turned his attention to Purvis.

"Not the slightest clue as to Dillinger's whereabouts?"

Purvis shook his head dejectedly. "None. And we're fairly sure that he hasn't left Chicago. We're watching the airport, the train stations, and the major roads out of town. With his face in all the newspapers, we should trace him down soon. It's only a matter of time."

Bierce removed the gold-rimmed glasses from his face and rubbed the bridge of his nose. "We do not have time, Purvis, three days at the most. If he is not apprehended within that time, there could be the most horrific consequences."

"I keep hearing refer to such 'consequences'. What the hell are those consequences?"

"I have told you before, I am not at liberty to reveal—"

There was a commotion at the room's door. A thickly built agent entered, roughly shoving Ana Cumpanas before him.

"Here she is, Mr. Purvis. We should be able to shake something about Dillinger out of the bitch."

Frowning, Purvis asked, "Why did you bring her here? Why didn't you throw her in the can?"

The agent shrugged. "Well, Mr. Purvis, you know that the Bureau don't have its own jail in Chicago. Chicago police run the jails here, and I don't trust them as far as I can throw them. Thought you might have a quiet place where we could put the questions to her, with no one to interfere or complain if the questioning gets a little … loud."

At that, all the medical staff exited the room quickly, not wanting to know the rest.

Cumpanas paled at the last comment. Purvis thought it over, and then nodded. "Right. The Bureau has a safe-house over in Cicero. We'll take her there and get to work on her."

Surprisingly, Bierce said, "I would prefer if you leave her with me. I have errands I need to send someone on, and she will do as well as another."

Purvis' eyes narrowed to slits. "Have you lost your mind, Bierce? This is the whore who ruined our bust on Dillinger, not to mention got you shot!"

Bierce turned his attention to Cumpanas. "You love John Dillinger, don't you?"

Cumpanas lifted her face and for the first time looked Bierce in the eyes. "I did. I still do, I think. People outside my profession think we are not capable of love, but we are … sometimes. But Johnnie does not love me. I see that now. I gave him warning so he could get away, but he dragged me along so he could use me as a shield. Then he used that pregnant woman as a shield, then he fires into crowd, where if he missed you, he maybe would kill some good man or woman or child who were there only to see game. I knew him to be bad man, but didn't care. But he is worse than a bad man—and he does not love me."

Bierce replied to her in what was for him a surprisingly gentle voice. "Mrs. Cumpanas, if John Dillinger is not stopped, at least one other man will die. A good man, on which many other good people rely. Can I count on you to help us catch him?"

She waited for a long moment, then said, "You promise not to kill Johnnie?"

"Yes. I need him alive."

"Then I'll help, but with one condition: you let me stay in this country. I do not want to go back to Roumania."

Bierce gave a short, barking laugh. "Yes, I imagine not. You have my word."

Through gritted teeth Melvin Purvis swore creatively and at length. Then he stood and growled, "All right, Bierce, it's on your head." Then he and the other agent stomped out of the hospital room.

Bierce laughed again as the men left. "Mrs. Cumpanas, I assume that Dillinger only visits you irregularly, and does not care much where you go when he isn't around?"

"That's Johnnie."

"Very well. Please reach into the bedside table drawer and hand me my wallet."

Cumpanas did so. Bierce extracted a hundred dollar bill and handed it to her.

"I'm afraid that my clothes were ruined by my last encounter with Mr. Dillinger. I will need something presentable for when I leave here. Go to the Brooks

Brothers store and buy me a suit and shirts. Size 36 short, I believe; it will be close enough. Dark blue, pin-striped, double breasted. Come back when it is safe to do so."

Cumpanas looked strangely at Bierce, then rose, tucked the bill in her purse, and left the room without a word, just before the bustling Dr. Stein entered, charts and X-ray plates in his arms.

"Dr. Stein."

"I would like to run a few more tests."

Bierce shrugged. "No need. I should be ready to leave in about two days."

"Oh surely not, Mr. Bierce, surely not. You have miraculously survived being shot through the lung. We cannot afford for you to being released early, only to relapse. Now, let us see the chest wound. We do not want an infection to develop."

Dr. Stein placed his bundle of charts and X-rays on the table, then laid out a small pair of scissors, bandages, and a bottle of iodine. Without asking permission, he drew back the top of Bierce's hospital gown, to expose the chest bandage. Swiftly he loosened it with the scissors and carefully drew it back. Then he shuddered, literally hissed, and drew back. His widened eyes focused on where there should have been a bloody, jagged hole drilled deep into Bierce's chest. Instead, the doctor was looking at an expanse of smooth, healthy skin, with only the slightest impression of a dent in the middle of his torso. Wordlessly, he looked at Bierce, who was smiling in a way that disturbed the doctor.

"I heal rather fast, Dr. Stein."

✦

The following morning one of Chicago's notorious summer heat waves clamped down on the Windy City. By ten o'clock, both temperature and humidity were in the nineties. Ana Cumpanas's orange dress was light, but it was already soaked with sweat. As she entered the hospital, struggling with the clumsy parcels she was carrying, she had hoped to find it was one of the few buildings in the city that had the new-fangled air conditioning. Her hopes were immediately thwarted. If anything, it was hotter and more humid than outside. She passed by sweating, red-faced doctors and nurses in the corridors, too miserable to pay her any attention. As she came up to the door of Bierce's room, she could hear him in quiet conversation with Melvin Purvis. She hesitated, not wanting to go in while the unsympathetic Purvis was there, but Bierce noticed her in the doorway.

Waving cheerfully, he called out, "Come in, Mrs. Cumpanas, come in."

She entered the room, keeping her eyes carefully on the floor. "I don't want to disturb you while you discuss police things."

The haggard-looking Purvis, tie loosened, jacket slung across his shoulder to imperfectly conceal his large Colt automatic, rose wearily to his feet. "Doesn't matter. We've been sweeping every street, nightclub, and whorehouse for your boyfriend—nothing. Coming up with jack."

Cumpanas continued to look at the floor. She would have much preferred to tell her news to Bierce alone. "Mr. Agent Purvis, I think I know how you can capture

Johnnie alive tonight."

Immediately Purvis' exhausted eyes came alive. Cumpanas continued. "He called me. Johnnie wants to leave town, but not for two days. He says the big job must take place in the next two days, so that we have money to live like royalty overseas. He wants us to stay apart until we leave, except for tonight. He says he needs to relax, so he and I should meet at Biograph Theater. It's air conditioned, and he says we will be able to relax most of night there."

Purvis looked inquisitively at Bierce, who said, "This could work much better than trying to intercept Dillinger at Mrs. Cumpanas'. He will be especially careful now, and will just disappear if he so much as smells a Federal agent. It would be almost impossible to hide our presence from him around an apartment building with relatively few people coming and going. Whereas, on a crowded street filled with theater goers, we should have an excellent chance."

Bierce turned his attention to Cumpanas. "Will you do it? Will you lead Johnnie into our trap?"

She hesitated slightly before she nodded. "Yes, if you keep them from sending me to Roumania. I cannot go back there. I cannot."

Purvis shrugged. "Wear that red number tonight. It'll make it easier for my boys to see you."

"It's orange, Mr. Purvis."

"Whatever. Stands out like a drunk at a society ball. Anyway, what film will be playing?"

"Manhattan Melodrama. It's a Clark Gable movie."

"I've seen it, not bad. That Gable guy has a future in front of him in the movies." Purvis narrowed his eyes and gave Cumpanas a cold sneer. "Don't try to rabbit on us tonight. Bierce needs Dillinger alive. You, he doesn't." With a nod to Bierce, Purvis strode purposively out of the room.

After a moment, Cumpanas spoke in a low voice, "I am scared, Mr. Bierce. I think without you there, that man will kill me tonight."

"Then I better be there tonight." With only the slightest of groans, Bierce sat up and twisted his legs so that his feet rested on the floor.

"Mr. Bierce! You cannot get out of bed! It will be weeks, many weeks before your wound heals."

"I heal quickly, Mrs. Cumpanas," Bierce replied as he tentatively stretched his arms. He slowly stood up. "Now, let us try on the clothes you were kind enough to buy for me."

Slowly, with help of a rather intimate nature from Cumpanas, he put on his new clothing. Walking slowly, Bierce approached the small mirror over the sink, looked at himself, and grimaced.

"Not a very good fit. Nothing off the rack seems to be exactly the right size for me. Well, it will have to do."

"Nonsense," replied Cumpanas. "Take off coat and pants. I fix." To Bierce's amazement, Cumpanas took out of one of the shopping bags what appeared to be a complete set of tailoring implements. Amazement turning to amusement, he took off the suit and handed it to Cumpanas. He sat at the foot of the bed, watching Cumpanas work with amazing speed, stopping only occasionally to whip out a tape measure and hold it steadily against some part of Bierce's anatomy. In less than an hour she was done.

"Here. This is much better. Try it on."

Bierce did as he was instructed. Inspecting himself in the mirror, he was astonished. The fit was perfect, as good as any Brooks Brothers he had ever owned.

"Marvelous, Miss Cumpanas. You will make some lucky man a happy husband someday."

Her features clouded. "I had husband once. He drank away all the money then sold me to whorehouse."

Instantly, Bierce stepped forward and took her hands into his. "I apologize deeply, Mrs. Cumpanas. It was wrong for me to jest about your personal life when it is obvious it has not been a happy one. May I ask your forgiveness?"

"It's all right. You meant no harm." Then, acting oddly shy for one in her profession, she asked, "You have wife, Mr. Bierce?"

He gently released her hands. "I did. She died of a cancer of the uterus some years ago. I was with her to the end. Never had I seen such bravery, in man or woman." He paused, then voice lowered almost to a whisper said, "She looked much like you, at least at a distance. For a moment—just a moment—when I first saw you, I thought you were her."

Cumpanas was not used to the relations between man and woman being about anything but animal sex. "I see that you loved her very much."

With a catch in his voice, he replied, "I loved her more than my life." His eyes seemed to glisten. Then shaking his head he said, "You should go and meet up with Dillinger. I promise I will be there tonight to make sure Mr. Purvis behaves himself."

She nodded and left the room. Bierce went to the room's small closet and retrieved his Colt .45 and its holster. Having secured the holster, he removed the magazine—seven in the mag, one in the barrel—enough to deal with anything he was likely to meet. He slammed the magazine into the butt of the weapon and holstered it. He then removed his white Panama hat from the shelf within the closet and placed it levelly on his head. He stepped over to the mirror above the sink. An utterly expressionless face peered back at him.

✦

Despite the heat and mugginess in the corridor that made his bald head glisten with moisture, Dr. Stein bustled along toward Agent Bierce's room in a state of immense happiness. By pure good luck, a fortuitous opportunity had fallen into his hands when Harry Bierce had been brought to his hospital. It was not that his body's defenses were unusual, they were absolutely unprecedented! The man healed at an inconceivable rate from what should have been a fatal injury. There was not the slightest sign of infection that almost always accompanied serious gunshot wounds. There was something unique in the man's immune system, something, that if he could discover what it was, would save millions of lives—and most notably—win him the Nobel Prize. No more struggling endless hours in obscurity with a procession of routine injuries and illnesses. He would be famous, a guest of honor at countless conferences, a tenured professor at an Ivy League university. The whole world would open up to him. All he needed were additional X-rays and blood tests to help unlock the secret hiding within the body of

Agent Harry Bierce!

The doctor paraded into Bierce's room, only to see a young nurse changing the sheets on the bed.

"Where is patient Bierce?" he yelled at the young woman.

Eyes wide with concern, she replied, "Why, he checked himself out not thirty minutes ago, Dr. Stein. I thought you knew."

Without another word, Stein spun on his heels and started running for the elevator. He prayed Bierce was being delayed in settling his bill at the front desk. But as he reached the elevator, he pulled up short, nostrils flaring. Smoke, he thought. Fire? Then the fire alarms began to clang, the sound seeming to come from the corridor leading to his office. Stein ran for all he was worth. As he came within sight of his office, the alarm stopped. Without immediately understanding its significance, Stein noticed that the door to his office was ajar, although he could have sworn he had locked it. One orderly was holding an emergency hose, spraying it into a metal waste can that was spewing black smoke and ash. Another orderly had been engaged in stopping the blaring alarm. He turned and saw Dr. Stein.

"Sorry, sir, seems it was some kind of nasty prank. That trash bin was filled with files, records, X-ray plates. Someone placed it in the middle of the room here and set it alight. At least they seem to have taken care to prevent the fire from spreading, since the can was metal, and where it was placed, the fire was unlikely to spread any further."

The other orderly turned off his hose. Most of the contents in the can were utterly destroyed, all script unreadable—except one plate. Dr. Stein bent over to get a closer look at the Xray. Scrawled along the edge—Bierce, H.

✦

Cumpanas waited uneasily outside the Biograph Theater, all too aware there were armed Federal agents scattered in the crowds of the street. Half of her worried that Dillinger would not show up, the other half feared he would.

Then, from behind her she heard a voice call to her, "Hey, Ana!" With a mixture of emotions she whirled around, only to receive an unexpected shock. It was indeed Johnnie, waiving at her with his right hand, but his left hand firmly encircled the waist of a young, bleached-blonde woman.

A wave of iciness rushed over Cumpanas. "Who is your … friend?"

"Polly Hamilton," replied Dillinger easily. "I'm surprised you two haven't met before, being in the same business. Anyway, it's her place where I've been hiding out since your place seemed too hot. The bulls know I have a connection with you and might be watching your place, but they know nothing of dear Polly and me."

"Pleased ta meetcha," responded Polly, chomping a wad of gum. A woman of indeterminate years, and a few pounds heavier than she should have been, she wrapped her right arm around Dillinger's waist possessively. She smiled, but coldly surveyed Cumpanas.

"Thought I'd give her a treat as well, for taking such good care of me," said Dillinger charmingly. He came up to Cumpanas, pecked her on the cheek, and confidently slid his free arm around her waist. "Let's go in."

Across the street in the entrance to an alley, Melvin Purvis stood, twiddling a cigar in his fingers. He briefly considered lighting it, which would signal his deputy Charles Winstead and the other agents to move in. Instead, Purvis decided to wait. If he gave the signal now, Dillinger would likely retreat into the darkened theater full of innocent bystanders. Best to wait until he emerged. Purvis placed the cigar back in his coat pocket. The movie wouldn't be that long.

✦

"Buck-fifty, mac," said the cigar-chewing cabbie. Harry Bierce, eyes already locked on the garish lights of the Biograph, handed him two dollars and muttered, "Keep the change." He walked slowly toward the theater, the pains in his chest telling him that he needed more time to recuperate. Determined, he locked the pain away into a small compartment in the back of his mind. Something he had learned how to do many years before. Tomorrow, Bierce thought, the President would be arriving by train, and over the next few days Roosevelt would be attending a number of very public events. Dillinger must be apprehended, and he must give the evidence that would bring Huey Long to justice.

Bierce caught sight of a narrow alley just to the left of Biograph's box office and slowly made his way to its entrance. As he settled into position, he noticed a wide-eyed Purvis staring at him from across the street, obviously shocked to see the wounded Bierce present for this dangerous takedown. Bierce smiled, gave Purvis a military salute, and sank back into the shadows.

The wait was less than ninety minutes, but of course seemed much, much longer to the keyed up Federal agents—except for Harry Bierce, who had patiently endured far longer lookouts in his varied career. Then the wait was over, a thickening crowd of happily chatting moviegoers poured out of the cooled recesses of the Biograph into the hot mugginess of a Chicago summer night.

Across the street, Purvis saw a tall man exit, each arm around a woman. Purvis could not quite recognize Dillinger, but he could definitely recognize Cumpanas's dress. Muttering "Don't give a damn what she says, it's red, not orange," he jammed the cigar into his mouth, ignited a wooden match with his thumb, and lit the stogie. His keyed-up agents had been watching, and moved into action.

Dillinger was puzzled by Ana's mood. The movie had been excellent, the air-conditioning a heavenly relief from the sticky hot air of Chicago. Yet in contrast to Polly's happy chattering, Ana was as silent as a stone. He would have to shake her out of her mood because he had plans for the three of them when they got back to Polly's place.

Like the flick of a switch, Dillinger's sixth sense for danger kicked in. He looked around wildly until he saw several men hurrying across the street toward him. Flinging his escorts aside, he rabbited to the alley on the left of the Biograph. Surprised, he skidded to a stop before a small man holding a big Colt .45 automatic. In an instant he recognized him as the G-man he had shot at Wrigley Field. The man who shouldn't be alive, much less holding a gun on him.

"Federal agent. Raise your hands, Mr. Dillinger. You are under arrest."

Instantly Dillinger realized from the sheen of sweat on the man's forehead, the slight shakiness of the gun that he held, and the stiff way that he positioned his body, the man was sick from the wound he'd inflicted upon him, and would unlikely be able to respond quickly. Swift as a mongoose, Dillinger reached under his loose white shirt and produced an automatic. Three shots rang out.

Bierce stepped back, astonished by the speed of the criminal's draw, along with the flecks of blood and bits of brain matter spattered on his gun and hand. Staring at the crater of an exit wound just under Dillinger's left eye, Bierce watched, as if in slow motion, the criminal's nerveless hand dropped the pistol to the ground. A moment later, the gangster's body collapsed on top of the gun, and remained there. Unmoving. Bierce, still motionless, heard rapidly approaching footsteps.

"Agent Bierce, are you all right?" Bierce now focused his attention on Agent Charles Winstead, who rushed toward him, a look of concern on his face. In his hand, the agent held a smoking Smith & Wesson revolver.

Bierce regained his composure. "Yes, I'm quite uninjured," Bierce replied, removing a large handkerchief from his pocket. "This," he said as he wiped the gore from his face, "compliments of the late Mr. Dillinger."

Purvis ran up, followed by several other agents. "You idiot, Winstead! We needed him alive!"

Bierce looked at the gory handkerchief in his hand, and impulsively put a corner in his mouth, tasting

Dillinger's blood, a look of obscene pleasure crossing his face. Before anyone could notice, his expression changed to one of self-loathing and guilt. He looked with disgust at the cloth in his hand, suddenly throwing it on the ground.

"It is not Agent Winstead's fault. In fact, I owe him my life. I had intended to confront Dillinger, and if he resisted, shoot to wound. Unbelievably, he was quicker than I had imagined, and my reflexes were slowed by my injury more than I supposed. If we could not take him, we had to kill him. I am just sorry I played such an inadequate role tonight."

"Inadequate!" exclaimed Purvis. "I didn't expect you at all. And if you hadn't been here, he might have made an escape down this narrow little alley, which was the only one I hadn't blocked. I'm a goddamn idiot! We only got this murdering bastard because of you."

Police sirens wailed in the distance. A crowd had gathered at the entrance to the alley. In some mystic kind of osmosis, they seemed to all know that the body was that of John Dillinger. Several of the more ghoulish were darting forward to dip their handkerchiefs in the growing pool of blood surrounding Dillinger's head. This stopped for the moment when Purvis impulsively kicked one of the souvenir seekers in the head. Bierce glanced at the alley entrance. Polly Hamilton was wailing uncontrollably, tears smearing her thick makeup. Ana Cumpanas stared stonily at Bierce, her eyes completely dry.

CHAPTER FOUR

"And so I followed the mob …"

Harry Bierce peered out the small window of the unused, back-up radio broadcast room onto Wrigley Field. The President was long gone, probably on his train back to Washington already. A surprising number of people milled about the stands and field, still excited by the soaring speech FDR gave after the game, still unwilling to return to the drab misery of their homes. Melvin Purvis walked up beside Bierce, and for a minute the two G-men watched in silence as workmen set out to disassemble the platform on which the President, his entourage, and tons of movie and camera equipment had rested less than an hour ago.

Finally Purvis broke the silence. "Say what you will about that crippled socialist bastard, he can sure stir a crowd. Never saw anything like it in my life."

"He may indeed be a socialist," responded Bierce quietly, "but, he knows, as you and I know, that this country is teetering on the edge of revolution. His policies are designed to give hope to a desperate, suffering people, and turn them away from both the fascists and the true communists. He may very well be the only one at this time who can save our republic, and keep us from the chaos sweeping Europe."

Purvis shrugged. "Be that as it may, America came

goddamn close to losing him, and you deserve the credit for preventing that." Purvis walked over and picked up the rifle that had been discovered in this small room.

"A Springfield 30-06, fitted with a military-standard telescopic scope. From that window, it was less than one hundred yards to where Roosevelt was speaking. For a marksman like Dillinger, it would have been almost impossible to miss. Do you think he could have gotten away?"

Bierce shrugged slightly. "Hard to say with certainty, but he would have stood a good chance. We already know that he was a fanatical follower of the Chicago Cubs. As such, he had over the years learned every nook and cranny of this—let's be blunt—mazelike stadium. You remember how easily he eluded you and slipped away after I was shot? I think he planned to do the same after murdering the President. He would wipe down the rifle to remove his fingerprints, and slip out the door of this disused room into a mass of hysterical people. Bold to the point of arrogance, but it just might have worked. No one could have proved who fired the shot. The President's followers would be frantically looking for the murderer in any group that had ever dared to oppose FDR; law enforcement would be paralyzed, riots in the streets would erupt, and, just perhaps, a revolution would be set in motion."

Both men were silent for nearly a minute, then Bierce said, "That is why I want your word of honor as a gentleman that you and your people never breathe a word about this attempt, or about my involvement in taking down Dillinger."

Purvis carefully leaned the rifle against the wall. He then looked at Bierce, silently bothered by the phrase "word of honor as a gentlemen." Who used such language these days. Bierce was an anachronism, yet Purvis could tell the man was absolutely sincere.

"Harry, you have my word, but only on one condition."

"And that is?"

"That I privately tell that bastard Hoover that this was your show. I won't take credit for this, at least with those who matter. Let the blessed public think what they will."

Bierce thought for a moment, nodded, then turned his gaze out the window again. Purvis joined him, and without looking at Bierce, said, "Dillinger had no politics. Someone paid him to do this. You going after that bastard?"

Bierce continued to stare out the window, saying nothing.

"Just want you to know you can call on me. Anytime. Anyplace." Purvis turned toward Bierce and stuck out his hand. Finally, Bierce looked at him, and after a moment shook Purvis's hand in return.

Thereafter, Bierce made his own request. "You know the Immigration people have seized Mrs. Cumpanas. I promised her that I would not let her be deported to the hellish hole that is Roumania."

Bierce dug into the side pocket of his coat jacket and removed a large amount of cash, neatly secured with a rubber band. He handed it to Purvis. "I do not have time to address the wrong due her immediately. Please, use this money to hire a good lawyer to delay deportation as long as possible. Now, good day." Again, he shook Purvis's hand briskly, and left the astonished agent holding six months' worth of salary.

✦

"God damn you to hell, Earl," roared Senator Huey Long, in a voice that sent his two henchmen easing themselves out of the luxury hotel suite, leaving Huey alone with his red-faced brother. "You drooling retard! I give you a simple assignment and you screw it up. You couldn't pour piss out of a shoe with instructions written on the heel!"

"That ain't fair and you know it," replied Earl Long in a terrified, whiny voice. "You told me to get hold of Dillinger, and I did. Ain't my fault the Feds shot him outside a movie house before he could do the job."

Huey paused and did his best to bring his titanic temper under control. He drew in a deep breath and exhaled slowly. He knew Earl was right, that his brother had done what had been asked. Still, he had needed to take out his anger on someone, and his dimwitted brother was the only one on hand.

"All right, Earl, I know it's not your fault. It's just that the damn man in the White House seems to have the devil's own luck. I know you do your best for me. Always have, always will. Don't take what I say serious, brother. It's the rest of the family who treats you like shit, not me. I'm going places, and you're going with me. All the way to the top."

Huey remembered seeing his folks and his siblings treat little Earl like the village idiot, causing the child to cry himself to sleep night after night. He remembered how he stood up for his little brother at the cost of an occasional beating, and had been rewarded by the unreserved adoration of Earl. Huey swore to himself that someday he would have people kissing Earl's ass. His mind snapped back to the issue at hand. "We can't try the direct route again. We've missed twice now. Too much chance it could be traced back to me if we miss a third time. "

"Huey, maybe we should give up trying to take the easy way. Maybe we should work to take the nomination away from him, in two years' time."

"Do you have any idea how much money that would take? The entire deduct box would be a drop in the bucket!"

"Come on, big brother. The deduct box gives us absolute control of Louisiana, with cash to spare."

"Open your eyes! This here is about the poorest state in the Union. We can control it for pocket change. To take the nomination away from FDR, we need to get the support of states like New York, Pennsylvania, Illinois, Ohio. We just don't have the cash for that." Huey Long rubbed his eyes, then continued. "Well, I have been working on a back-up plan, little brother o' mine. We can squeeze our out-of-state friends for more—much, much more."

"I tell you, they have no more to give," Earl replied

"They will if we point out what another six years of Roosevelt's rule would mean to their interests. And who's to say FDR would stop with two terms. How about three? Four? Besides, I think it's time we try to see what we can get from some friends across the ocean."

"Across the ocean? Goddammit Huey, you've gone plumb loco. Why would some foreigners give a crap about who runs the U S of A?"

"They care, never you mind why. A little bird told me they're going to send a representative to talk turkey. You and me are the only people who know that, at least at this end. I want you to meet this representative and sound him out before bringing him to me, quiet like. Find out how much money he can get us. If it's enough to take on FDR in two years, we're back in business."

"Now, just who is this representative you want me to meet?"

Huey Long told Earl, who responded with an uncharacteristic obscenity.

✦

It was an unusually clear morning in New York harbor. On the deck of the ocean liner *Bremen*, the passenger in the dark, conservative suit stared moodily down at the dock where final preparations were being made before the passengers could disembark. His concentration, however, was not on the bustling workers, but on his mission, his family, and what he must do to keep them alive.

His papers identified him as Albert Schmidt, a representative of a large German winery seeking to establish new markets for the fine red wines of the Rhineland. They gave not the slightest hint that he was in fact Franz von Papen, and until the last month, the Vice-Chancellor of Germany. He had doubted that his disguise would pass muster, as his face was well known to the political world. However, Heydrich's experts had been correct—shaving his moustache, dying his iron-grey hair black, and parting his hair in the middle rather than severely combing it toward the back of his head seemed to make him unrecognizable to the Americans.

Although the summer morning was warm, von Papen shivered. Not from cold, but from fear. He had once thought himself a brave man, believed that his service as an advisor to the Turkish forces during the Great War had proven that. He now realized he was a small man, a weak man whose arrogance and miscalculation had placed his beloved wife and five children in mortal danger. He closed his eyes and reviewed the events that had brought him to New York under a false name, doing the work of a common spy.

The worst mistake of his life was to have ever entered the chaotic, political arena of the Weimar Republic. By birth and nature an aristocratic Prussian conservative, he had wended his way through the ever-shifting alliances and hatreds of Weimar, with each shift of the wind getting ever closer to the Chancellorship. He carefully cultivated the aging, increasingly senile President von Hindenburg, encouraging him to bypass parliament, and govern by Presidential decree, as was permitted by the Weimar Constitution. Then, in 1932, von Papen received his reward. Parliament was hopelessly splintered, no one party having a majority. Normally, the largest party would have headed a coalition government with smaller parties. Yet, the two parties with the most members were the Communists, who von Hindenburg hated with every particle of his conservative Prussian soul, and the Nazis, who he, too, despised for their unseemly anti-Semitism, and especially for the low social origins of their leader. Whispering into the aging war hero's ear, von Papen persuaded him to appoint him Chancellor, despite the fact that von Papen was universally disliked and distrusted in Parliament as a scheming opportunist. Impertinently, von Papen felt he did not need to consider Parliament, as von Hindenburg had promised to implement the Chancellor's laws by Presidential decree. Von Papen had made it to the top.

His victory lasted only six months. During his reign, Parliament grew more agitated by his dictatorial role, and Nazi and Communist thugs ruled the streets of the major cities. Even the army had come to despise him, and refused to help restore order unless he was replaced as Chancellor by an army general. With great reluctance, von Hindenburg gave in and relieved von Papen of his duties, but the public disorder only got worse.

Finally, the leaders of the centrist and conservative parties decided that they would have to choose between the Nazis and the Communists. Given the Communists' great allegiance to Stalinist Russia, most felt they had no choice but to turn to the Nazis, whose brown-shirted Sturmabteilung thugs could at least clear the streets. Surprisingly, they neither liked, nor trusted Hitler and his followers. So, when they offered him the Chancellorship, the only other Nazi allowed in the cabinet was the superficially charming Hermann Goering, a highly decorated war hero barely acceptable to respectable society. All other cabinet members were non-Nazis, who were acceptable to the army. President von Hindeburg did, however, give von Papen the position of Vice-Chancellor. In order to keep an eye on the "Austrian corporal," as the dying von Hindenburg sneeringly called Hitler.

And then a dimwitted Dutch Communist burned

down the Parliament building. The terrified legislature voted an "Enabling Act" that allowed the Chancellor to issue laws for the protection of Germany without consulting Parliament or the cabinet. Von Papen abruptly found himself living in a dictatorship run by a racist clearly intending to plunge Europe into another war. Von Papen had seen the previous war and did not want to see another. And although somewhat anti-Semitic, he was genuinely shocked by the blatant hostility, brutality, and discrimination that was being visited on what he considered "good Jews," and which was getting worse by the month.

Much against his will, he slowly recognized that he had played a major role in handing the German state over to a thuggish monster. It hurt his monumental pride, but he could no longer conceal from himself the knowledge that his own lust for power and aristocratic disdain for the lumpish gangsters who ran the Nazi party, had blinded him to the threat they posed to his beloved Germany. Although it cost him weeks of agonized uncertainty, he finally decided it was his duty to clean up the mess he himself had helped create.

Only the army could now remove Hitler and his crew, but they would not move without the word of President von Hindenburg, who still retained the power to dismiss the Chancellor. With von Hindenburg senile and dying, his crippled brain often confusing Hitler with the Emperor Wilhelm, von Papen decided that harsh action must be taken to warn the people against the Nazis, something so dramatic that it would compel von Hindenburg to order the army to eject Hitler from the Chancery, and to sweep the ruffians from the streets.

And of course, von Papen thought wryly, there would have to be a new, non-Nazi Chancellor. And who better than Vice-Chancellor Franz von Papen?

So, with the help of his able secretary, Herbert von Bose, he drafted a stem-winding speech, one denouncing—in no uncertain terms—the lawlessness of the Nazi regime, calling for the end of Hitler's rule by decree and restoring legislative power to the Parliament. He chose to deliver this speech at the University of Marburg, where the students and professors would guarantee him an enthusiastic audience. And they were enthusiastic. They cheered him for a quarter hour after his savoir faire.

But, nothing more happened. Minister of Propaganda Goebbels forbade any mention of the speech on the radio, or in the newspapers. Except to the relatively few who had actually been there, it was as if von Papen's speech had never happened. So, the public concentrated on other things. There were rumors that the head of the Brownshirts, Ernst Rohm, was planning a coup, whereby he would replace the army with the SA oppressors. There were rumors, also, that Hitler was talking to army leaders, promising to curb the SA, if the army would support him. There were no rumors, however, about any speech at the University of Marburg. Then late one night it happened.

Vice-Chancellor von Papen sat in his office, discussing with the loyal von Bose a plan to contact the leaders of the army directly. It being a hot summer's night, the French doors leading into the garden were open. When he heard a faint, but distinctive sound of a pistol shot, followed by the stutter of submachine guns, Von Papen's head jerked up. Prompted by a scream cut short by another burst of fire, both men rose from their chairs and hurried to the window. At first in the distance, the gunfire burst sporadically, then closing in, the men turned to each other, fear overtaking them. No sooner had the men turned away from the window, that through the closed inner-office door, they heard a commotion, shouting, and then von Papen's wife scream, "Franz, help!" This, followed by the sound of a muffled blow.

"Martha!" he screamed, running full tilt towards the door, skidding to a halt as it was thrown open. Two soldiers, dressed in the black uniforms of the SS, towered in the doorway. Both were carrying Mauser pistols. With more courage than he had ever thought he had, von Papen ran at them, shouting, "Martha, I'm coming!" only to have the soldier on the right bring his gun down on the Vice-Chancellor's head with stunning force. He staggered backward into von Bose's arms, his loyal subordinate keeping him from the indignity of falling to the floor.

"Let us have no more of that, Mr. Vice-Chancellor," said a soft, rather high voice from behind them. Von Papen shook himself free of his secretary, and turned toward the open French doors. Two men more men entered, the sight of whom turned his blood to ice. Both were jackbooted; both wore the SS black. One, a short, rather plump man with thick spectacles and the face of a bemused rabbit: Heinrich Himmler, head of the Hitler's SS bodyguard, rumored to soon become chief policeman of Germany. The other, a tall, fit man, blond and blue eyed, the very image of the perfect Aryan: Reinhardt Heydrich, Himmler's chief henchman, already spoken of in whispers as "The Hangman."

Choking back his terror, von Papen spoke in a harsh voice, "Himmler, what does this mean? What have you done with my wife and children?"

"They are all right—for the time being," replied Himmler in a friendly voice. "I take it that your companion is von Bose, am I not correct? The very man who so willingly drafted your Marburg speech."

"Yes, he is," von Papen defended, "but the speech was mine entirely, he only transcribed what I dictated."

Himmler smiled, and gestured to Heydrich. The blond giant drew a Mauser broom handle pistol and shot von Bose in the head. The man fell, but Heydrich kept shooting until his ten-round magazine was empty. At the sight of his friend destroyed, his head literally obliterated, and the acrid odor of cordite filling the air, von Papen puked his guts out all over his prized carpets. When he finished being sick, the devoted Catholic von Papen stepped over to von Bose's remains and made the sign of the cross over them. He then turned to face his own death, putting on a brave face, as a Prussian officer should.

Unexpectedly, Heydrich finished reloading his gun and holstered it. Himmler walked over and perched himself on the edge of von Papen's desk. "The Leader apologizes that he could not be here in person, but he has commitments in Bavaria. He is directing the arrest of Rohm and his catamites on charges of treason." Himmler rearranged the files on von Papen's desk as he spoke. "They will be dead by sunrise." The SS leader folded his hands across his propped-up knee and fixed his gaze upon von Papen. "So will a number of others—the Brownshirts, the army, even those in the Party itself—those who were attempting to overthrow National Socialism."

In a seething whisper, von Papen replied, "When President von Hindenburg hears of what is happening, he will dismiss Hitler from the Chancellorship, and order the army to clear all you Nazis out of office."

After a short laugh, Heydrich's demeanor changed. "The President is in a coma, and all the doctors agree he will never come out of it. When he dies, he will be given a spectacular funeral, as befits a hero of the Fatherland. And after a decent interval, the Leader will combine the powers of the Chancellor and the President. He has also made a deal with the army's leadership. In return for reducing the Brownshirts to an impotent remnant, he will have the army's total support. Of course, over time our SS will undertake the tasks the Brownshirts previously performed, but the Leader saw no need to raise that issue with the generals."

"And now we come to you," said Himmler as he stood and pointed his finger at von Papen as if he were a child. "You have been a very bad fellow. The Leader is very, very disappointed in you. He was inclined to throw you into the cells with Rohm and his fairy friends and have you shot tomorrow morning, but," Himmler bowed slightly, "Goering and I persuaded him that could be unwise. The generals don't care how many SA thugs the Leader has shot, but they would not accept your death. They dislike and distrust you, but you are, after all, a former Chancellor and a Prussian officer." Himmler waved his hands before gathering them behind his back, standing even more rigid, as if he were about to undergo inspection by a superior officer. "That means a lot to those stiff-necked militarists, perhaps the latter, more than the former. So, we persuaded the Leader to accept your resignation as Vice-Chancellor, and promised him that you would use your remaining prestige to perform an important service for the Reich."

Himmler drew a folded document from an inside pocket of his tunic, and threw it on von Papen's desk. "This is your resignation. Sign it."

Fearful, but determined, von Papen slowly shook his head. "I will not. I don't care if you kill me, I will not bow down before you … you Sträftater … you murderers."

"That is a pity," replied Himmler with a sigh. "Heydrich, take the two men at the door and go to where Frau von Papen and the children are being held. You know what to do."

"NO!" screamed von Papen. "I will do all that you ask! Please," he begged. "Just leave Martha and my children untouched." He staggered over to the desk and signed the document without reading it.

Himmler smiled benevolently. "See. That wasn't so hard, was it?"

"What is this so-called service you wish of me?" asked von Papen in a hollow voice.

"You've heard of the Thule Society?"

"Yes. An association of unbalanced crackpots who have some idiotic ideas about the origins of mankind."

The smile instantly disappeared from Himmler's face, replaced by a scowl. "Be careful what you say. Their ideas are not idiotic, and they exercise great power behind the scenes in the Reich. I am one of their Inner Council, with Heydrich as a candidate member."

Von Papen's jaw nearly dropped. He wondered if it was possible for Germany to become any more insane under the Nazis.

Himmler continued to speak. "The subtle pressure the members of Thule were able to bring to bear eased the Leader's path to the Chancellorship." Himmler stopped. "I see from the look on your face that you do not believe me. Well, no matter, your lack of belief will not affect your ability to conduct your duties."

Madmen are indeed running the asylum, thought von Papen. Even so, his family must be protected. "So what is this service you wish from me?"

"There is a secret society in America, one in accord with many of our goals. It wishes our financial support in funding a politician to replace Roosevelt in the White House, a politician who is in accord with many of the principles of National Socialism. This is tempting. Roosevelt despises us, and may try to thwart our future plans. The Leader wishes to be assured that they are a serious organization with serious resources. You will take a ship for New York under a false name, wearing a disguise. There, you will be met by a representative of the American group. He will take you to see those who control it, where you will examine their financial resources. If you are satisfied that they are a serious group, you will be taken to meet their American politician, and, as they say, 'strike a deal'."

With courage he had not known he possessed, von Papen replied, "Why do you think I would give you an honest evaluation?"

Heydrich answered. "Because, after you finish your job, you will return to Germany to see your family.

And you will all remain under house arrest. If later it should turn out you have betrayed us...." The Hangman gestured toward the body on the floor.

"Very well," said von Papen. "It appears I have no other choice."

"Excellent," Himmler replied as he clapped his hands.

"We will begin immediately." Himmler patted Heydrich on the back. "Heydrick will escort you to SS headquarters and begin fitting you with the papers for your new identity. I," again Himmler bowed, "will escort your beautiful wife and children to your country estate, and ensure that a ... ah ... guard of honor is established for them."

Just then, the distant chatter of a submachine gun followed by a scream caused von Papen to jump.

✦

Schmidt shook off his reverie and left his cabin. After descending the gangway, he went to the customs station, and handed his papers nervously to the official, certain that as someone who had, however briefly, been one of the most important politicians in Europe, he would be recognized. On the contrary, Heydrich had been correct about changing his appearance. The bored official glanced at him casually, stamped the passport, and handed it back to him. A relieved von Papen collected his single suitcase and exited the customs building. All at once he heard, "Welcome to America, Herr Schmidt." Von Papen turned to face the speaker, a large, somewhat overweight man with a friendly smile, who enthusiastically shook his hand.

"I'm Jackson Noyes, Mr. Schmidt," the man said in a distinctive Boston accent. "As you were undoubtedly told back in Germany, I will be your guide and your host during your visit to our fair shores."

"Pleased to meet you," responded von Papen automatically, although he had taken an instant dislike to the man.

"Here, let me take your bag. Follow me to our car." von Papen followed the American for half a block until they entered a parking lot, and reached a flashy new Cadillac convertible, the top already down. Noyes threw the suitcase into the trunk and took the driver seat, gesturing for von Papen to take the passenger seat. Barely seated himself, Noyes ignited the engine, and with the V-12 howling, gunned out of the parking lot, turning left on a northbound street. Above the sound of the engine and the wind, von Papen had to speak loudly to be heard.

"I understand that you are to introduce me to some of your, ah, colleagues, as well as some of your resources. I was not given the details. Now that I am here, I would appreciate more information."

Noyes laughed ruefully. "Our organization is quite old, and seventy years ago was close to doing for this country what your Leader is doing for Germany. Unfortunately, we moved too quickly and encountered unexpected opposition. That opposition thought it had destroyed us. What they did not know is that we had boltholes it never dreamed existed, and we still retained stupendous financial resources. We sent some of our best people to Europe to found a sister organization, but moving slowly, never excited suspicion. The Thule Society is the result.

And although even most Party members don't know it, we have been a major supporter of your Leader—and of Herr Himmler. They are grateful to us, and in return will make the resources of Germany available to us, so that we can put a man in the White House who will support our mutual goals."

"Fringe beliefs such as yours are three a penny since the Depression hit," von Papen said, frowning. "Why should Germany back a pack of chanting cultists?"

Noyes was now smiling broadly. "Oh, we are ever so much more than, as you say, 'a pack of cultists'. We are something you would not believe, unless you saw it with your own eyes. That is why I am taking you to see some very curious facilities and people in rural Vermont, and then to spend a couple of educational days in the Massachusetts seaside village of Innsmouth, with a final visit to meet our Grand Council."

"In Boston?"

"No, in an interesting town northeast of Boston called Arkham."

✦

Harry Bierce brought his rented Hudson convertible to a stop just in front of the imposing brick mansion. Killing the engine, he emitted a long sigh; the day and a half drive from Chicago to Kentucky had involved some bad roads, and the constant jolting had tired him. In addition, he did not look forward to his meeting. Still, she deserved the warning he was here to give. He got out of the car, stretched, and started toward the grand front door. He stopped short when his eye caught the image of a woman riding a horse near a distant barn. He hurried toward the barn. The woman must have noticed him, but continued to put her mount through its paces. As he walked directly up to the horse, Mrs. Belasco brought her animal to a stop and smoothly dismounted, keeping the reins in her hand.

The raven-haired beauty smiled arrogantly at her guest. "I didn't expect to see you so soon. Do you need more money?"

"No, your kind gift has been more than sufficient. I have come rather to give you a warning."

"Indeed. Well, come walk with me and warn away." She whistled, and a groom came scurrying out of the barn. Wordlessly she handed him the reigns, then began walking to a nearby pen. Bierce followed, his sensitive nose wrinkling at the foul odor emanating from it. On closer inspection, he could see that the enclosure held ten or twelve large hogs, grunting and snuffling at the muck that covered the ground. Mrs. Belasco leaned on the top railing, looking affectionately at the animals. Bierce held back, distaste written on his features. Mrs. Belasco noticed this and laughed.

"You never did like pigs, did you?"

"Foul animals," he muttered. "I've seen them in the aftermath of battles, feeding on the dead and the not quite dead, eating until there was literally nothing left of the soldier."

"Ah, yes, perfect little disposal machines. That's why I keep them around. They eat the garbage, and then can be sold to the slaughterhouses. Anyway, where have you been lately?"

"Chicago."

"Took the train to Louisville?"

"No. Rented a car and drove the distance. Took more time, but I wanted to get a view of the towns and countryside on the way. Terrible. The people are suffering and in want. Many of the farms are derelict, most of the factories seem to be closed. Homeless men, women, and children could be spotted wandering the streets in every town through which I passed. It's even worse in the South, but not by much. It reminds me so much of those awful times, long ago."

Mrs. Belasco laughed heartily, heartlessly. "I am always and forever baffled as to why you still care for those peasants."

"Those 'peasants', as you call them, are trying to build a better world under a government which encourages them in their dreams of freedom, but seems unable to help them with their daily wants. When I see what is happening in Europe and Asia, I come to believe America and its 'peasants' are the only hope for decency and freedom."

Mrs. Belasco chuckled. "You and your idealism. No matter what government comes, I will continue my pleasures, indulge my desires. And I know you share those desires, no matter how valiantly you struggle to suppress them." She cast him a sidelong glance. "Do not try to deny it. In any event, you do seem to have had some influence on my brother. He has been enjoying the high life of Berlin recently, and has acquired some interesting information. He has joined this delightfully decadent thing called the Thule Society, and has sent me a short message through ... shall we say, unusual channels ... that he wished me to give to you next time we met. He says that the Thule Society is tight with the Nazis, and they've persuaded the Austrian peasant to contact a society in America to investigate the possibility of an alliance."

"Starry Wisdom," Bierce said softly.

"Yes, your old friends."

"I thought they had been beaten into impotence years ago."

"You, of all people, should have known better than that. Anyway, brother says that if the two societies can come to an agreement, they will funnel their resources to support some Southern governor to kick FDR off the ticket in '36. He thought that you would be interested in this information."

"I am indeed. When you can, thank him for his information, and tell him I would be extremely grateful for more such information in the future."

"You know, I believe he will do so," she said thoughtfully. "It seems like some of your idealism rubbed off on him after all. Now, you said you had some sort of warning to give me."

"It is about your missing husband. The Chicago office tells me that the search for him is being upgraded. There is a lot of pressure to apprehend him. It seems several of the victims in the Maine mansion were very well connected, socially and politically."

Mrs. Belasco leaned her back against the railing of the pigpen, smiling strangely. "So what does this have to do with me?"

"I know you two are estranged, and I am glad of it, but in a desperate last resort he might try to hide out here. I warn you against giving him shelter. If you did, you would be an accessory after-the-fact to multiple murders, and all the money in the world won't be able to keep a jury from sending you to the chair. If he shows his face, turn him in. I beg you."

She turned around and looked lovingly at the hogs. "I don't think he will be showing up anytime in the future. Just look at my beauties here, very efficient. They literally eat anything. And, they do not leave a trace."

Bierce's stomach did a small flip. He gave Mrs. Belasco a short, quick bow, then turned and walked quickly to his convertible. Behind him, Mrs. Belasco's laughter sliced through the clear Kentucky air.

Bierce drove two more days to get to New Orleans. The last time he had driven that route had been in 1928 to interview a retired police detective named LeGrasse about a ritualistic murder. That drive had taken four days. Grudgingly, Bierce admitted to himself that Long had fulfilled at least one of his promises: in the last five years he had paved every road in sight, and replaced the inefficient ferries with bridges over the numerous rivers. As he drove through the countryside and the small county seats, he still saw poverty and despair, but he also saw new schools and hospitals—the former still segregated, but the latter obviously admitting black as well as white patients. Bierce reflected that many people in the North would not think of this as much, certainly not worth surrendering freedom to the increasingly dictatorial and corrupt Long machine. Seeing all this, Bierce now understood why he was constantly seeing pro-Long signs and placards in front of tarpaper shacks in the country and in run-down tenements in the towns. Even before the Depression, the downtrodden souls of Louisiana had nothing. Long had given them good roads and bridges, new schools, free textbooks for their children, hospitals and health facilities for all—white and black alike. Of course, the middle and upper classes despised Long's corruption and increasingly dictatorial rule, but the poor loved him unreservedly, and did not give a damn if he took their political freedoms. It reminded Bierce uncomfortably of what was happening in Germany.

As Bierce parked his Hudson near the entrance to the Roosevelt Hotel, he spotted a large gathering a block away. A voice boomed from several loudspeakers. Despite the distortion, he could tell that the voice was that of Senator Long. Bierce decided to delay checking in and go to hear the great Huey Long in action.

A short walk brought him to the edge of the crowd, which he estimated to consist of about 8,000, a respectable turnout, even for a city the size of New Orleans. Although the crowd seemed friendly, even rapt with attention, Bierce noticed that on either side of the speaker's dais stood a large, ugly man in a crumpled suit, whose appearance screamed hired muscle. More disturbingly, toward the back of the platform were about twelve national guardsmen, each with a pistol, and several with Thompson submachine guns. The sight of them made Bierce frown deeply. He then devoted his entire attention to the speaker, who had apparently been winding up the crowd for some time.

"My friends, you know I have been trying to work

with President Roosevelt up in Washington City. I've been telling him that the people of Louisiana—hell, the whole country—have been hurting. All of you, my hard-working friends, be it on the farm or in the factory, you've been working your hearts out, wearing away your health and years, and yet, it's hardly enough to feed your family. Yet is this country poor? Is it?

"NO!" yelled the crowd in unison.

"It is not, my friends. How could it be? Look at all those rich Easterners—the Mellons, the Carnegies, the Astors, the Morgans—why, Mr. John D. Rockefeller alone, is worth over a billion dollars. Now my friends, I don't begrudge a man money that he's worked for. Some of God's creatures are blessed with more ability and luck than others, and more power to them. But how many meals can a man eat, while others go hungry? How many suits can a man have, while others don't have a pair of pants without a patch? How many houses does a man need, when so many have no shack they can call their own? Does this seem a proper state of affairs, my friends? Does it?"

"NO!" yelled the crowd, louder than before.

"But do not despair, my friends! Today I have exciting news! Since Mr. Roosevelt does not seem to have the backbone to take on the rich and get this country moving again, I am forming a new organization to do just that. It is called the "Share Our Wealth Society," and its slogan is "Every Man a King." I urge you all to join it. I urge you to tell your friends to join. Tell your families to join. There are no dues! All I ask in return is help in spreading the good word. Now what does the society propose to do, you may ask? Well, I'm here to tell you.

"We will get the Congress to enact a tax taking away all family properties above a value of five million dollars. We will get the Congress to enact an income tax that will take away all family income of more than one million dollars a year. Now, what will be done with that money?" Huey Long stepped away from his podium and moved to the edge of his stage. Then he pointed his finger at the crowd, his voice booming. "Every family in America will receive five thousand dollars—enough for a home, a car, and a radio!" The crowd roared.

"Thereafter, every family in America will receive an annual payment of two thousand dollars. Two Thousand Dollars!" Bierce could barely hear the man over the thunder of the crowd.

"And every family with a child of proven ability will have that child sent to college, tuition free! Not only that, but the work week shall be limited to thirty hours a week." Long walked back to his podium and turned back to the crowd, and threw his hands in the air. "Now, my friends, do you think that this would make every man in this country a king?"

The crowd went wild, the cheering, deafening. Many in the audience were crying tears of joy as the grinning Long held his arms out, as if he wished it was possible to embrace every member of the crowd at once. Bierce had seen nothing like it—except in newsreels of the Jew-baiter in Germany. He frowned to himself at that thought.

When the audience finally quieted down, Long began to speak again.

"Friends, this is going to be a campaign, but not a campaign of hatred or misery. No sir! Our campaign will be one of joy. And like all campaigns of joy, it should have a joyful anthem. Now, as you all know, I'm a humble man." Both the crowd and Long chuckled. "But I decided to try my hand at writing such a song. Now, I found the words all right, but here before you I admit I found that the notes themselves were beyond my modest ability. So, the head of our beloved LSU Marching Band assigned his notes to my words. He and some of his boys are here this very day to play you the result. Boys, get on up here!"

The conductor and twenty of his students, wearing bright, garish uniforms, crowded onto the platform. After a downbeat, the band began to play the music, while Long cheerfully bawled out the words:

Why weep or slumber America,
Land of brave and true,
With castles and clothing and food for all,
All belongs to you.
Ev'ry man a King, ev'ry man a King.
Ev'ry man a King

But there's something belonging to others,
Enough for all to share,
Winter or Spring,
Sunny June or December,
Ev'ry man a King, ev'ry man a King.
Ev'ry man a King!

Bierce had not thought it possible that the crowd could whoop any louder than it had already, but he was wrong. Men and women trapped in lives of misery had been shown a road to a wonderful life—by a man who seemed only to have their best interests at heart—a golden future, if only they would follow him. They danced and sang the verse, repeating, "Ev'ry man a King," until Bierce could stand no more. He turned away in disgust, and worked his way out of the crowd, anxious to get back to the Roosevelt and get a decent bath, wash away Long's reverie, and get good night's sleep.

Of course, Bierce knew that it was all nonsense, but the desperate poor didn't realize that, although Long would undoubtedly do more to improve their lives if he were in power in Washington, but Bierce thought, as well he imagined Long knew, that he would never even come close to doing it all. Whatever one thought of the rich, there simply were not enough of them to fund Long's utopian scheme—not nearly enough.

Supposing, Bierce thought, he did become president, would Congress enact his laws? Absolutely not. But supposing it did? In no time, it would be clear that the revenues gained would not support what he had promised. He would then be forced to take even more from the rich, and start taxing the middle classes. Bierce knew that when all of this was done, there would simply not be enough capital to provide for the long term investment and development necessary to drag America out of the Depression. The country would become poorer. And even poorer still. Not only would it lack the money to fulfill all of Long's grand promises, there would be no money to modernize the military to face the potential threats from Japan, and a Nazified Germany, which were already on the horizon.

Bierce decided he would begin an extended series

of interviews of Long's enemies, to see if he could find something—anything—that could remove the threat that Long posed to FDR. He realized bitterly that he was not going to be able to get enough evidence to connect Long to the attempts on FDR's life, or even to the criminal schemes set forth in the dead lawyer Rocha's notebook, but he would settle for proof of some lesser crime that would be sufficient to crush his presidential hopes. After all, he reminded himself, the mad dog criminal Al Capone had been responsible for scores of murders, but was in the end, brought down by a simple tax evasion case.

Yes, he would start on a new course to bring Long to justice, but only after a bath and a good night's sleep.

✦

The Ford Tri-Motor was a steady, reliable airplane, and the weather during the trip from New York had been reasonably good. Still, Franz von Papen's complexion was ashen, and sweat rolled down his cheeks. Only the swift action of a smirking stewardess with some towels had kept him from fouling his elegant suit an hour before.

Across the aisle, Jackson Noyes bestowed a cocky smile on the German. He was amused to find von Papen was not quite the "superior man" of which the current rulers of Germany spoke. Noyes chuckled to himself at how shocked von Papen had been when shown certain things in rural Vermont and the Massachusetts town of Innsmouth. Still, Noyes could tell von Papen had been impressed—awed, in spite of himself. Now, all that was needed was to seal the deal with Huey Long.

Over the roar of the three engines, Noyes heard the pretty stewardess announce they were about to land in New Orleans. The only sign von Papen gave that he had heard was that he tightened his hold on the arms of his seat into a death-grip, and tightly closed his eyes. There was a hard bump followed by two smaller ones, and the aircraft landed firmly on the ground. The pilot taxied over to the small terminal building, and one-by-one, killed the engines. Only then did von Papen unclench his eyes. As the door to the passenger compartment was thrown open, the German bolted from his chair and was first out into the sunshine. The amused Noyes followed at a more sedate pace. He found von Papen leaning against the wall by the luggage claim desk, gulping air, the color slowly returning to his face. Noyes approached the airsick German, trying to suppress his amusement.

"So, Franz, you do not have the stomach of a flier."

"I did not claim to," replied von Papen, now wiping the sweat from his face with a large handkerchief.

"It might be something else," replied Noyes with a smirk. "You haven't seemed quite yourself since you met our Vermont and Massachusetts friends. Don't worry, you probably won't need to see them again. They will remain behind the scenes, for obvious reasons."

Gott im Himmel! thought von Papen as he restored the handkerchief to his coat pocket. He wondered if there was any end to the perversions of the Nazis ... to contemplate an alliance with those ... those....

A voice interrupted von Papen's thoughts. "Good afternoon!" said a tall, overweight man who pumped Noyes' hand up and down as if he was trying to get water from a well. The stranger then turned to von

Papen and took the German's right hand in both of his. "And this must be our friend from overseas. I'm Earl Long, Senator Huey's little brother. Big brother has told me you're here to discuss some arrangements of benefit to all. I'm to take you to the Roosevelt Hotel, where the Senator maintains a private suite. Very private. Perfect for discussing private matters. If you both will follow me, I've got a Packard parked on the street."

Von Papen grabbed his bag and, along with Noyes, followed the strange young man with the crazy eyes whom he had instantly distrusted.

✦

After Earl Long had settled von Papen and Noyes into their rooms at the Roosevelt, he escorted them down to the first floor and led them into The Cave, the Roosevelt's high-end restaurant. As its name implied, it had been decorated to resemble an underground grotto, complete with small waterfalls and ponds. Seated in a nook farthest from the entrance, was Senator Long, eating a juicy steak while chatting with a local judge. To either side of the table stood two large, beefy men with bulges under their left armpits. The hour was early, and there were no other diners. Earl Long ambled nonchalantly up to the table and said, "Brother Huey, here are your two visitors from out of town, just as you asked."

The Senator scowled at his sibling. "How many times I gotta tell you Earl, in front of others it's 'Senator'. Gotta show respect for the office."

"Sorry Hu—Senator. Anyway, here they are."

Long spoke to his dinner guest. "Judge, I hope you'll

forgive me, but my visitors' time is short. If you'll excuse us, you can come back tomorrow morning for breakfast and we can continue our talk."

"Of course, Senator," muttered the small, rather plump man dutifully. He maneuvered his chair backward, stumbling clumsily before scurrying out of the restaurant. Long then gestured to his bodyguards and said, "Move off a-ways. Make sure neither you, nor anyone else is close enough to hear." They acknowledged their orders with grunts and moved off. Senator Long turned his attention to his brother and the two newcomers, gesturing for them to sit.

"Brother Earl, I've not met either of these folks. Care to do the introductions?"

"Surely, Hu—er—Senator. This here is Mr. Jackson Noyes, senior partner in the Boston law firm of Marsh, Pabodie, Pickman, and Noyes. His firm is very influential in the politics of New England. Much less publicly, he is on the Council of Starry Wisdom, which can deploy similar power, but only on a very discreet level." Noyes confidently shook the Senator's hand.

"Heard of your law firm in Washington City," said Senator Long. "People say it's got a lot of influence in both parties. I've also heard rumors about Starry Wisdom—some really crazy stuff. On a previous visit by one of your people, he tried to tell me some of what it could do for me. Now, I've heard a lot of shinola in my political career, but what he told me … well, you'll have to pardon my skepticism. I think your man got himself into some bad moonshine and stretched the truth just a little bit."

"You can believe it, Senator," interrupted von Papen in a hoarse voice. "Whatever he has been telling you,

you can believe it."

"My apologies," said Noyes. "Senator, let me introduce you to Franz von Papen, former Chancellor of Germany, and until two months ago, Vice Chancellor under their new Leader. My friends in Starry Wisdom felt that it would be useful to bring in the resources that the new, reinvigorated Germany can make available to us."

Von Papen did not offer his hand, but nodded his head slightly. "Senator, as you can imagine, interfering in the government of a country with which Germany is currently at peace, is a monumental step. The Leader wishes to assure himself that Germany's resources will be used wisely, that our role in changing the government will not become known, and that the plan is certain of success."

Senator Long frowned. "I expect we are in agreement on your one point—the whole country would go plumb nuts if they thought the Krauts were supporting me. But you said I could trust what Mr. Noyes says about the abilities of Starry Wisdom. Just why is that?"

Noyes answered for the German. "I've taken our guest on a little tour of our facilities, introduced him to some of our ... allies. That convinced him that they could deliver as I said. Isn't that right, Mr. von Papen?"

At this, von Papen glanced at Noyes, and began to sweat. Under other circumstances, it may have been the New Orleans heat and humidity. He turned his attention back to Senator Long, and in a quiet voice said, "Yes, Starry Wisdom can provide you a great deal of help. Just pray to God you will not need it."

Long seemed to chew on his lip. "I don't expect you Krauts are helping me because you believe in my Share the Wealth plan. Just what will you expect in return?"

Thinking back to his last meeting with the blond monster Heydrich, von Papen shivered slightly before answering. "The Leader has certain plans for the future. He would like assurances that—"

"Perhaps we should not be discussing details in a public restaurant," interrupted Noyes smoothly. "Besides, we are hungry and need some rest. Is there some private place, truly private, where we could have some extended discussions tomorrow?"

Before the Senator could answer, his brother eagerly said, "Huey—damn—Senator, we've got a good little suite upstairs. We could all meet up there around 9:00, after our visitors have had a chance for a little rest. Sound agreeable to everyone?"

Senator Long looked around the table. No objections were raised. "Well then, that's settled. Let me order you gentlemen a fine New Orleans dinner, and we'll make an early night of it."

✦

It was getting dark when Harry Bierce pulled his Hudson convertible into the driveway of Judge Benjamin Pavy's colonial revival house. He had only taken a short nap in his room at the Roosevelt before he got up and called his friend in the local Bureau office, asking if he knew anyone hostile to Senator Long who would talk to him. The friend had hesitantly recommended Judge Pavy, a well-respected and honorable jurist who had somehow come afoul of the Long Machine. The Judge's reputation for honesty and integrity was unsullied, despite many attempts by Long to tarnish his character, including widespread whisperings that the judge had some black ancestry. Normally, this would be a devastating charge in the Deep South, but the people of his district either didn't believe it, or they didn't care. In short, Judge Pavy could be a sterling witness on the stand, if Long were ever brought to trial.

Bierce walked up to the front door and rapped three times. The door was opened by a tall, heavy-set man in his fifties, with a full shock of white hair, dressed in a somewhat wrinkled, white linen suit.

"Judge Pavy?" asked Bierce, taking off his hat in a show of respect.

"I am," the man said in a profound, commanding voice that must have been the terror of all lawyers in his district.

"Agent Harry Bierce of the Department of Investigation. Thank you for seeing me on such short notice."

"Well, come in," boomed Pavy. "Let me take your hat." As Bierce entered the hallway, he handed his homburg to the judge, who placed it neatly on a side table, then gestured to the first door on the right.

Bierce entered a vast room, which must have taken up a third of the ground floor. Yet the comfortable, lived-in furnishings scattered about the room made it seem welcoming rather than grand. Seated on a large sofa was a plump woman about the same age as the judge. Beside her was a younger, thinner version of herself, cradling a baby in her arms while holding a bottle. Bierce immediately liked her; women in Judge Pavy's class usually handed off all caring and feeding of infants to servants. Standing behind the couch was a thin, dark, bespectacled man who was gently massaging the young woman's shoulders, but his cold, suspicious eyes glared at Bierce through thick lenses.

"Mr. Bierce, I hope you don't mind these people being present during our discussions, but I get so little time with my family I want to share with them every moment I can. The silver-haired beauty is the love of my life, my wife Ida. Beside her is the only slightly more beautiful Yvonne, our daughter, who is holding her son Carl. And behind the couch is the man who has made my daughter so happy, Dr. Carl Weiss, Sr. Everyone, this is Agent Harry Bierce, from the Bureau of Investigation. He is trying to make a case for trying our beloved Senator Long on Federal charges in Federal Court. Have a seat, Agent Bierce. Care for a drink?"

"Thank you, but no, Judge," replied Bierce as he settled himself into an armchair directly across from the long couch. Judge Pavy shrugged, then poured himself a whiskey from the drink cart before taking a seat between his daughter and wife. Having taken a sip, Pavy told Bierce, "Fire away, Mr Bierce."

"My sources tell me that you are the greatest opponent of the Long machine in the state. Would you say that is true?"

The Judge chuckled ruefully. "Your sources are too kind. Our esteemed Senator has many enemies in Louisiana. The trouble with most of them is that their only problem with the Long machine is that it freezes them out of the spoils. I am certain it comes as no surprise to you that Louisiana is monumentally corrupt, has been since the Civil War. Each parish is run by a local 'courthouse gang', usually centered around whoever is their sheriff. The mayor of New Orleans heads his own machine—not big enough to run the state, but big enough to make even Huey sit up and take notice from time to time."

"What issues divide them?"

"Issues?" The Judge laughed bitterly. "It's all about the spoils. Whose cousin is appointed to which state job, which county gets a new road, what town will have a state hospital built. Aside from unanimous agreement that the Negro should be denied any trace of political power, issues seldom come into it. The only thing that can unite them is that Huey Long doesn't share any of the spoils." The judge took another drink and tipped the glass at Bierce. "That, and the fact he does not respect the rich families that have pretty much run things in this state since the last century."

"Is that the reason you oppose him, frustrated ambition?" asked Bierce quietly.

"An interesting question," replied Pavy, who took another sip of his drink. "I suppose I am ambitious. Most men are. But I'm not ambitious for money, patronage, or even high office. I guess I'm ambitious for Louisiana. You've a bit of a Southern accent, Agent Bierce. Your people from Texas or Kentucky?" When Bierce didn't answer immediately, Pavy continued. "Doesn't matter. You're a Southerner. You know how we feel about home and honor. Louisiana is my home, has been all of my life. I love her almost as much as I love my wife and daughter. But it pains me, Mr. Bierce, to the core, to see what people in other states think of my home. A land of shoeless crackers and shiftless darkies, a land of corrupt officials in white linen suits, a backward place where the KKK hangs innocent Negros and allows white killers to go free. A land where there is one form of justice for rich whites, another for poor blacks. That's not the whole truth, Mr. Bierce, but there is enough truth in it to make me angry and ashamed.

"So, I decided to do what I could to bring Louisiana into the twentieth century. I became a lawyer, and I defended the poor and powerless, no matter what their race. People hereabouts got to know me, got to know I couldn't be bought, got to know I wanted to make Louisiana a better place, and eventually they made me judge. In my sinful pride, that was my ambition—to be known as a good and just man, so I could become a judge. Yet, despite my sin of pride, for which I pray for forgiveness nightly, I have done genuine good in my little part of this state."

Without a trace of sarcasm, Bierce said, "I would have thought that your devotion to reform would have made you a supporter of Senator Long. Many have told me he has done much good in this state."

"What good is reform, even prosperity, if we lose our freedom? Already Louisiana is close to a dictatorship. I am one of only a handful of elected officials who are not creatures of the Long machine. Whatever he wants done is done. Even the current governor is well known to be only a recording of Senator Long's voice, and he cannot tolerate even a smidgen of dissent from his will. There is a bill currently before the legislature to physically move my district to a heavily pro-Long area, denying me reelection. Every educated person sees that Long wants to be dictator of Louisiana, and after that, of the entire

United States. That is the reason why in two days the few members of the legislature who are not in Long's pocket will spring a motion to impeach our governor, sending a message to Long. It has little chance of success, even as a surprise, but we have to try something."

"Judge, you are a fool," interrupted Dr. Weiss in a bitter voice. "Long has discovered the secret of success that will sweep him into the White House: his Share the Wealth plan. He has discovered that a politician who proposes to rob Peter to pay Paul will always win, so long as there are fewer Peters than Pauls."

Pavy frowned at his son-in-law. "Carl, you have to have more faith in the people than that. They can be made to realize that if one part of them can be treated unjustly, all of them will eventually be so treated."

"I wish I could have your faith. I really do, Judge. But remember that two years ago, I was performing my residency in Vienna. The residency itself was fine, and I learned a lot, but that was the time when the Nazis were taking over power in Germany, just across the border. The refugees, mainly Jewish, were bad enough. What was worse was the reaction of the Austrian people. Instead of pity, those fleeing the Fascists were mocked and cursed; sometimes stones and bricks were thrown at them, all the while the mobs chanting the Leader's name with hysterical joy."

Pavy waved his hands to quiet his son-in-law. "Carl, you are taking this too hard. That's because of your Jewish ancestry. Europe is not America. We are more tolerant here."

Weiss's face twisted into an expression of bitterness. "Judge, you are a good man, but you overestimate the number of good people. Try growing up in the South with a name like Weiss. And the joke is that I'm not Jewish! I'm Catholic, as is my father, as was his father. Good people, indeed! Don't tell me you didn't read about the lynching of that black man up in Caddo last week. The Sheriff watched as they castrated the man before hanging him! How many other such lynchings are there in a year throughout the South?"

In an uneasy voice, Pavy replied, "Those were exceptions. I never denied there are bad people in the world, and that they will always be with us, but they are small in number."

"That is where we differ. There are enough to elect Long as president, so long as he keeps promising to give to them what the wealthy have. They are too stupid to realize that Long is forging chains of gold that will make us all slaves, not just the blacks!" Weiss's voice had risen to a loud, shrill screech, and his wife placed a comforting hand on his arm. He looked down at her and made a visible effort to control his breathing. "My apologies, Judge, I did not mean to treat you with disrespect. You have been so good to me, better than I deserve. My nerves sometimes run away with me. I will take a walk around the house to let the night air help cure me." Weiss bowed stiffly to his parents-in-law and to Bierce, then kissed his embarrassed wife, and left the room at a fast, nervous clip.

Pavy turned his attention back to Bierce and laughed nervously. "My apologies, Agent Bierce. My son-in-law is a fine man, a respected doctor who volunteers free services to the poor, white or black. The atrocities he saw in Europe have embittered him. He cannot understand that Europe is different from America. Even if Long were to gain the White House, he would not act like that thug in Berlin." Pavy shook his head as if to clear it. "Anyway, I don't have much more to tell you. I've long suspected that a forger named Rocha had done many illegal things for Long. As you already know, that is a dead end, literally. They fished the low-life's body out of the Mississippi last month. I can give you the names of some other criminals I suspect of working for the Long machine. You may be able to get one or more of them to talk, although I would not bet the farm on it. Then you might be able to get a jury to convict, although I wouldn't risk the farm on that, either. Still, I'm glad someone in Washington is interested in stopping Long. It gives me some hope."

Bierce took a small notebook and pencil from an inner pocket of his coat. "Please give me the names anyway. I can be quite persuasive."

✦

Harry Bierce seldom felt tired, yet this was one of the few times. Having been unable to find a parking spot closer than two blocks from the Roosevelt, his normally brisk stride had slowed almost to a trudge. Judge Pavy had given him some names, it was true, but the Judge had cautioned him that they would be unlikely to have directly witnessed any corruption by Huey Long himself. Bierce's exhaustion was more psychological than physical. He was beginning to believe that Senator Long might be truly untouchable.

Bierce was about thirty yards from the entrance

to the Roosevelt when a taxi skidded to a stop with a screech of brakes right in the triangle of light thrown out of the entrance. The instant the cab stopped, a door was thrown open and a tall, thin man erupted from the vehicle, his face reddened with rage. A large, heavyset man followed close behind, throwing some bills at the driver as he exited.

The second man called after the first in a voice revealing the speaker's Boston origin. "Wait!" the man cried, "I only meant to be hospitable. New Orleans is famous for the many and varied pleasures it can provide the visitor. I had no notion you would take it this way."

The first man whirled. Bierce could see the man was in the grip of a barely suppressed fury. In a lightly German-accented voice he replied, "You pig! I am only here because of the threats your friends in my country have made against my wife and children. My every waking thought is consumed by worry for them, by my love for them, and you took me to a whorehouse!"

The second man laughed, saying, "I am truly sorry. I had no idea our mutual friends have proceeded with such a heavy hand."

Seeing the face of the second man, hearing his accent, Bierce was briefly frozen with shock. He recognized the man. Noyes. Jackson Noyes. Bierce's mind flashed back to 1928 and to one of his very few failures.

Bierce had been working out of the Bureau's Boston office. By pure chance he had been in the reception office when Professor Wilmarth, a folklorist at Miskatonic University in Arkham, had stumbled in, shouting incoherently about the murder of a Vermont farmer named Akeley, and the need for the Federal Government to take action, as the local authorities would not. Most of the staff laughed at Wilmarth and made not-so-subtle comments about how even university professors were violating Prohibition. Wilmarth, however, was not drunk. He was, quite simply, terrified for himself and for others. Bierce had taken the professor into a room, talked soothingly to him, and finally managed to get a story of some wild cult in the hills of Vermont that had somehow made away with a farmer named Akeley, a long-time correspondent of Wilmarth's. Wilmarth said the cult was made up of some men, possibly led by a Bostonian named Jackson Noyes and, unbelievably, some sort of intelligent creatures from outer space.

Bierce believed Wilmarth was telling the truth, insofar as the Arkham professor understood it. Bierce had some experience with extreme cults and knew they occasionally used exotic drugs to make members have seemingly supernatural visions. He believed Wilmarth had been fed some such drug, and so discounted the tale of creatures from outer space. On his own, Bierce did some investigation, and found that the farmer Akeley existed and that he, along with many others, had disappeared from Vermont, never to be found, alive or dead. He also found that there really was an Jackson Noyes, a prominent Boston attorney who was rumored to dabble in fringe occult activities at Harvard and Miskatonic. After one disturbing meeting with a smirking Noyes, Bierce decided that something was most definitely foul, probably murderously foul, had been going on in those Vermont Hills, and that he would do his best to bring Noyes and those who conspired with him to justice.

And for one of the very few times in his varied lifetime,

Bierce failed. Akeley's body was never recovered. The Boston Brahmins gathered around Noyes, although there were some hints that this may have been due more to fear than to any liking for the portly attorney. At the end of the day, all Bierce had was Wilmarth. And despite his solid reputation in the academic community, Wilmarth made a pathetic witness. Whatever had been done to the professor had made him a nervous, neurotic wreck. Noyes, acting as his own defense attorney, had torn Wilmarth to bits on the stand. Bierce had cautioned Wilmarth not to dwell on the so-called creatures that Wilmarth insisted he had seen, but under Noyes' cross-examination he had ended up screaming that Noyes and others were allied with monsters from another world wishing to use the earth for their own benefit. The laughter from the jury box told Bierce what the verdict would be long before it was delivered.

Out of pity, Bierce arranged for Wilmarth to receive extended treatment from a brilliant psychiatrist in New York, who eventually convinced the professor that the monsters he had seen had been figments of drugs slipped to him by Noyes and his fellow cultists. The professor was restored to his duties at Miskatonic University, and as nearly as Bierce could learn, was now living a calm and reasonably well-adjusted life. Immediately after the trial, Bierce had done additional investigation in the isolated green hills of rural Vermont, and had found traces that may have corroborated Wilmarth's story. It seemed that there had been some large mining operations—not listed in any government records—that had been abruptly abandoned. Most of the equipment had been removed, but Bierce had recovered some curious pieces of metal of uncertain purpose or origin. He had taken them to scientists at M.I.T. who claimed they resembled no alloy on Earth and could not even say with certainty what minerals had been used to the forge the metals. In the ensuing years, Bierce had seen to it that the Bureau kept track of Noyes and his activities, but nothing out of the ordinary had been noticed.

Until now.

Bierce could not imagine what the socially connected Boston lawyer was doing in New Orleans. He supposed it could be an innocent vacation, but the words exchanged between the German and Noyes indicated it might be something much more serious.

Noyes continued to try to soothe the German. "My apologies. I had assumed that such, ah, entertainment would be to your taste. Berlin is known world-wide for its free and easy ways."

"You speak of the Nazi street trash, and the criminals who gather in any large capital. I am a Prussian officer, sir! I would not bring such disgrace upon myself or my wife."

"Well, well, accept my apologies. I was completely in the wrong. Now, it is time for us to meet with the senator. We all have interests and goals in common."

"So I am told," muttered the German. "Let us get this matter concluded."

"Very well. The senator is in his suite on the twelfth floor. Let's go up now. It shouldn't take too much time."

Bierce's brain slipped effortlessly into high gear. The darkness had kept the two men from noticing him, which left him free to take action. The conversation between Noyes and his accomplice indicated something disreputable, perhaps illegal, involving Senator Long. It seemed to Bierce that fate had finally dealt him a winning hand. If he could only overhear what was discussed, the knowledge might allow him to bring down Long and finally destroy the slippery Noyes. But how was he to overhear? There was no time to place a wiretap. The hall outside Long's suite would be filled with thugs. The rooms, too, on either side of the suite would undoubtedly be empty, as Long was certain to assure his conversations were not overheard.

Bierce looked upward at the dimly lit façade of the Roosevelt Hotel. Every few stories, a narrow, stone ledge circled the building, probably meant to facilitate window cleaning. A plan formed in his head—a plan that would have terrified most people, but not Harry Bierce.

After allowing Noyes and his companion plenty of time to get to the senators suite, Bierce strolled casually into the lobby, nodding to the night clerk, who recognized him. He entered one of the elevators, asking the operator to take him to the twelfth floor. After exiting the car, a quick look to the right showed the entrance to Long's suite, guarded by the young gunsel with crazy eyes, who Bierce had met on his last visit to the Senator. This was a piece of bad luck. Keeping his head low, hoping that he would not be recognized, Bierce turned left then grabbed the doorknob to room 22, the first room to the left of the elevators. Using his body to shield his actions from the young gunman, he produced his lock pick and in seconds had unlocked the door. Like most hotel locks, opening it was child's play to someone with training. Now, thought Bierce, comes the risky part.

Pocketing his small tool, he slipped into the room, locking the door behind him. The lights were on, and Bierce could hear the sound of splashing from behind the closed bathroom door. He had feared that the room would be occupied and had planned to flash his Bureau badge to gain the co-operation of any such occupant. No need, the emanating sounds were uninterrupted, indicating the bather was unaware of his visitor. With catlike tread, Bierce crossed to the window, which like most windows in the hotel was wide open in deference to the muggy nighttime heat of a New Orleans summer. Bierce took a deep breath, and steadying himself by holding the sides of the window frame, he stepped up and onto the window frame, then out onto the narrow stone ledge.

Bierce estimated the ledge to be about six inches wide. Not as wide as it had appeared from the ground, but not too narrow for the short trip he planned. Keeping his arms and back flat against the brick wall he slowly slid his left foot sideways, next bringing his right foot up alongside. After a quick calculation, he found that three windows lay between him and the nearest of the windows of Long's suite. Bierce knew that the one nearest to the senator's room would be empty, but he could not be certain about the other two. He continued. Slide with left, slide with right. Soon he was at the first window. It was open, but no sound or light came from inside. He navigated the opening without incident. Slide left, slide right. Then he came to the second window between him and his goal.

It was dark within this room as well, but Bierce's sensitive ears picked up the sound of soft snoring. As quietly as he could, Bierce continued his sliding journey. He had just cleared the window when he heard a sharp gasp, and a woman's voice say, "Ronnie, wake up! There's someone outside the window!"

This was followed by a snort, and a man's voice said, "Goddamnit, woman! Why'd you wake me up? Gotta bourbon headache I need to sleep off!"

"Ronnie, I woke up and saw the shadow of a man at the window!"

"Hell, you were matching me drink for drink tonight. Your man must've jumped right otta the neck of a bottle. Or you saw a bird fly by the window. There's no man out there … it's a twelve story drop to the street. Forget about it and go back to sleep. And next time, go easy on the hooch."

Bierce heard the sound of a large body rolling over in the bed and settling in. After a few mutterings in a woman's voice, silence reigned. He breathed a sigh of relief, and continued his journey.

He passed the empty room flanking Long's suite without incident. As he approached Long's window, the voices inside became more distinct. By the time he reached the window's edge, he could hear everything inside perfectly.

"You're mighty optimistic, Mr. von Papen, mighty optimistic," said a voice that was undoubtedly that of Senator Long. "I'm not even president yet and you want to dictate policy to me. Mighty peculiar."

"Not dictate, Senator," replied the voice with a German accent. "We simply wish to see our international interests align. We have no desire to try to influence in any way your domestic agenda."

"I'm glad to hear that." Long's voice had acquired a sarcastic tone. "Let me tell you something. I admire a lot of the stuff your boss is doing—dragging your country out of a depression, building good roads, all that—but I don't like what you're doing with your Jews. Don't like it at all. I won't be doing any of that, and the people wouldn't stand for it if I tried."

"I am sure that the Leader will agree that your Jews are entirely your business," replied von Papen, who was sure of no such thing. "Our two nations will always address their internal issues differently. All the leader wishes in return for our financial support is your assurance that should France and England again try to oppress Germany, the United States will stay neutral."

There was a considerable pause, then Long said, "I think I can agree to that. The folks feel they got nothing out of the last war, and wouldn't get anything out of a new one either."

"I see that we are in accord, Senator. It now remains to see if you will be able to honor your commitments to the friends of Mr. Noyes."

"Mighty strange requests they are. You say they want exclusive fishing rights off the New England and Gulf coasts, and a guarantee of there being no submarine or deep-diving operations in those areas? Mighty strange, indeed, and I don't know how our fishing interests are going to feel about that."

Noyes spoke, "Let me remind you, Senator, that my friends will make available to you, two metric tons of gold in bullion, utterly untraceable. I hardly need calculate what that would be worth in cash money. Nearly half again as much as what the Leader will provide you. No competitor, not even Roosevelt himself, will be able to overcome the advantage such wealth will give you."

There was another lengthy pause, then Long said, "Well, I expect we've got a deal, gentlemen. Everyone is getting a little something from it, and that's how politics goes." Long paused again. "You might as well know it now, even if it will be a total surprise to my enemies. Tomorrow afternoon, up in Baton Rouge, I will be declaring my intention to run for President of the United States in 1936."

"Huey, that's too goddamn early!" exclaimed Earl Long.

"Little brother, we need to start now, seeing as how we are getting the wherewithal from our new friends. Throughout his career, people have underestimated that crippled bastard. I will not be making that mistake. Anyway, you fellers want to be in Baton Rouge to witness a bit of history?"

"I must be catching a train tomorrow," replied von Papen stiffly.

"I would love to be there, Senator, but I've neglected my firm's affairs for too long," added Noyes smoothly.

"Huey—ah, Senator—you know I'll be there," chipped in Earl Long. "Been with you straight from the beginning. Wouldn't miss this for the contents of the deduct box."

"Very good. Now, if you'll excuse me, I need to get some rest. Tomorrow is going to be a big day, a glorious day, and I need to get enough rest to be at my best."

Bierce had heard enough. He began the slow shuffle back to the room through which he had entered. The dangerous walk was uneventful, except at one point where an agitated female voice whispered, "Ronnie! Wake up! I tell you there's a man at the window!"

A muffled male voice replied, "I'm not telling you again, woman! Shut up and go to sleep!

✦

Dr. Carl Weiss stood in front of his bathroom mirror, carefully inspecting his suit and tie, brushing away the few traces of lint. He looked down at his black oxfords, and confirmed that they were polished to a bright shine. Then he looked himself straight in the face. His eyes, always intense, now looked like burning coals in the center of black pits. That saddened him. He knew he would probably be dead within twenty-four hours, but he did not want his remains to look as if they belonged to a slovenly, wild-eyed anarchist. He was the son-in-law of the great Judge Pavy, a man he genuinely admired, and did not wish to embarrass more than necessary. Pavy was a good man, a great man, the greatest he had ever personally known.

Nonetheless, the Judge had not seen with his own eyes the refugees from Nazi Germany, pouring over the border into Austria, only to find the Austrians being infected with the virus of Nazism. After Agent Bierce had left, the Judge mentioned that his friends had heard rumors that Long would be making an announcement the next day from the capital building in Baton Rouge. Pavy groused that it was probably about some new plan to loot the state, or steal from the rich to give to the voters. In a flash of intuition, Weiss knew what the announcement would be, and knew that action must be taken immediately—before it was too late.

"Long might not end up as bad as that jumped-up corporal," Weiss said to his reflection, "but he might be even worse and that chance cannot be taken. The Judge will never be brought to understand that the freedom of the entire nation is hanging by a thread. This is the only way." He reached into an inner pocket of his coat, and withdrew a compact Colt .32 automatic. He looked at it for nearly a minute, marveling at how small the sleek, blue-black weapon looked. He snapped the slide to bring a cartridge up from the magazine to the barrel, then returned the Colt to his coat pocket.

As quietly as possible, Weiss turned out the bathroom light, opened the door, and moved into the bedroom, lit only by a dim nightlight. Walking ever so softly, he went over to the cradle that held his sleeping son and kissed him on the top of his head. He wanted very much to do the same to his wife, but Yvonne was sleeping restlessly, turning from side to side, and he dared not wake her. She knew him inside out. If she woke, she would know what he intended, and would do all she could to stop him. So he walked softly to the door of the bedroom, opened it and involuntarily extended a trembling hand toward his wife, barely stifling a sob. Then he left, trying to think only of the long drive to Baton Rouge, and failing.

✦

Flashing his badge while at the same time laying a ten dollar bill on the counter, Bierce obtained Noyes' room number from the ogle-eyed night clerk. As he was about to turn away, the German marched up to the counter, slapped some currency down to pay for his bill, and imperiously demanded that a cab be summoned immediately. Bierce debated with himself whether to arrest the German, but decided that Noyes was the more important figure. Therefore, he ignored von Papen and walked toward the elevators. Passing them, he entered the stairwell. He did not wish to be noticed and remembered by one of the elevator operators. Besides, he realized that the exhaustion he had felt earlier in the day was completely gone, and now, he felt the need to burn off some energy.

He ran effortlessly up the ten flights to Noyes' floor, scarcely breaking a sweat. Quiet as a mouse, he approached the door to Noyes' room. Placing his ear against the flimsy wood, he heard the sound of running water. Knowing that Noyes would be occupied in the bathroom, Bierce brought out his lock pick, and within moments had gained entry to the room. Softly closing the door to the hall, he drew his .45 Colt and silently waited.

A toilet flushed noisily in the bathroom. Moments later, the sound of water running in a sink replaced it. Bierce waited. Finally, the door to the bathroom opened and out stepped Noyes, drying his hands with a small towel, humming a happy tune. The large, plump man took two clumsy steps back as he caught sight of Bierce and his automatic, but he immediately regained his cynical good humor.

Throwing the towel back into the bathroom, he smiled and said, "Well, well, if it isn't Agent Bierce. It is indeed a small world. We haven't met since that day in court when I showed what a neurotic madman that fool Wilmarth was."

"You and I both know Wilmarth told the truth on the stand. It was the abuse and drugs you inflicted on him that turned an inoffensive scholar into a quivering wreck of a man. You and I both know that you, or your group, murdered a respected farmer, and quite possibly others."

"A judge and jury decided otherwise, Agent Bierce. I am an innocent, respected attorney, with friends in the highest places of government. The matter is settled. So, what brings you to my room?"

"I overheard your discussions with Senator Long, along with his brother and the German, and I am arresting you for treason. Your only hope of avoiding the chair is to testify against Senator Long."

Noyes looked shocked, but not for long. "I utterly deny any such discussions."

"I can testify they took place."

"Really? Tell me, Agent Bierce, did you obtain a warrant for your spying on me? Let me remind you that under the Supreme Court's exclusionary rule, evidence of conversations taken without a warrant is not admissible in a court of law. Do you have any other evidence of these so-called discussions? Do you? I can tell from your silence that you do not."

Behind his gold-rimmed spectacles, Bierce's pale blue eyes had acquired a strange, glowing intensity. "Nonetheless, I am arresting you and taking you to jail."

"Agent Bierce, really. I would be out in as long as it would take to wire certain friends in Massachusetts. There would never be a trial. I will guarantee that your persistent attempts to have me convicted of murder, attempts that were rejected by a jury of my peers, were signs of derangement on your part, of paranoid delusions. I nearly had your badge the last time you tried this. Rest assured I will get it this time. In fact, I believe I will sue for damages. You will be eating out of trash bins before I am finished with you." Noyes took his jacket from the bed, put it on, and straightened his tie. "Shall we go? This will be fun."

In a motion so fast it seemed a blur, Bierce brought the barrel of his heavy automatic crashing down on Noyes' head. The Bostonian fell to his knees, too stunned to even cry out. Quickly holstering his gun, Bierce grabbed the semi-conscious Noyes under the armpits, dragged him to the open window, and stuffed him through it. Noyes came to enough to utter an agonized scream, which ended with a wet crunch as he hit the pavement ten stories below.

Bierce glanced out the window, his face expressionless, and then muttered, "You were right. There will be no trial." He then quietly left the room. No one was in the hall to see him in the stairwell as he went to his own room to pack his few belongings and check out before the Roosevelt was crawling with local police.

Through an open window two stories above Noyes room, a woman's voice exclaimed "Ronnie! I heard a man scream!"

"For the last time, SHUT UP woman, and go to sleep!"

✦

The procession consisted of five vehicles: four police cars, two in front, two in the rear, sirens blaring, filled with heavily armed state police. The fifth car was a large open Packard, with a driver and bodyguard in the front seat. Senator Long, Governor O.K. King, Earl Long, and the Senator's beloved son Russell, current star football player at Louisiana State University, were all crowded in the back. The convoy of vehicles rolled up to the capitol building in Baton Rouge, while the crowds, who had been waiting for hours, went wild. As the men exited the car, uniformed officers cleared a path for them. The Senator bound up the steps, followed by his excited brother and son. Governor King, a willing tool of the Long machine, was excited as well, but his bulk and incipient heart disease dictated a more stately ascension on the capital's steps. At the top stood two separate groups of the National Guard, strictly at attention, Thompson submachine guns ported across their burly chests. The Long party inserted themselves between the two groups.

Russell Long leaned over to Earl Long and virtually shouted in his ear, "Uncle, look at this! Where did they all come from?"

"Our boys have been rounding up the faithful since late last night, nephew."

"But do they know he's going to announce he's running for President? I thought that was a secret."

"It is, although many of them probably have guessed. But for most, all they needed to know is that your dad wanted them to come. They love him. And he loves them. Look at him, and look at the crowd!"

Russell did as he was told. He looked at his father who was holding his arms high above his head, eyes shining with excitement, looking down at the crowd.

The senator's love for his followers was transparently sincere. The crowd yelled and cheered, looking at their savior with adoration and hope: adoration for what he had already done for them, hope for the more he would do in the future.

At the edge of the crowd nearest to the soaring monument that was the Louisiana Capital, stood an expressionless Harry Bierce. As he scanned the crowd, he shook his head ever so slightly. Although his face did not reflect it, his thoughts were melancholy. He understood how the people would be grateful for the services Long had brought, services denied them by a corrupt ruling elite, but he was depressed by the thought that the people were trading away their freedoms—freedoms unique in the history of the world—for bread and fishes.

Senator Long ceremoniously made quieting motions with his hands. Amazingly, the crowd quieted like a switch had been thrown. A soldier scurried up and placed a clumsy-looking microphone before the senator. Long tapped on the microphone, and was answered by multiple taps from loudspeakers on the tops of various trucks placed on the edges of the crowd.

Without preamble, he began to speak, "My friends, today I bring you great news! As you all know, I have gone to Washington City to persuade our President and Congress to enact the "Share the Wealth" program that I announced earlier this year. Well, that has not worked as well as I had hoped. No sir, it has not. Congress has been bought and paid for by Wall Street, my friends, bought and paid for! The bankers! The moneylenders!"

"The Jews!" came scattered yells from the crowd. Long frowned for an instant, but then continued.

"My friends, the religion of these people does not matter. What matters is what is being done to hold down the good, hard-working Christian people of this nation. These Wall Street people, these Rockefellers, Morgans, Carnegies, and Mellons aim to keep you all down my friends, all down! Even our President, Mr. Roosevelt, is afraid of them!

"Now, you may wonder how, with all of that, I can dare say that I bring you good news?

"Well, I can! Today, my dear friends, I announce my campaign for the Democratic nomination for President of the United States in 1936!"

The crowd went insane with joy—yelling, cheering, many shedding tears of happiness. Hope was palpable, like a viscous thing permeating everything. Long allowed this to go on for ten minutes before gesturing for quiet.

"Yes friends, I am going to take the movement we began here in Louisiana to the other forty-seven states. I will show the poor, the downtrodden, those without hope, those from Maine to California, that they can believe in this country again. I will take the nomination from the weakling Roosevelt, who has proven so unable to resist Wall Street. I will sweep into Washington City with a mandate from the people of this country, and I will make Congress obey that mandate, by any means necessary. I will see to it that the 'Share the Wealth' program is immediately implemented."

Bierce listened as Long recited the same 'Every Man a King' speech he'd given previously. Taking away from the rich to give to the poor. Handing annual stipends to each and every family, a reduced workweek, picking the best to go to college on the government's dime.

Ridiculous, thought Bierce. No, he corrected himself, Socialism. But not Roosevelt's socialism. This was something altogether different.

Finally completely his speech, Long asked the crowed, "Now, my friends, do you think that this would make every man in this country a king?"

"YES!" screamed the crowd hysterically. Then seemingly out of nowhere, the LSU marching band and a chorus appeared on the steps, and began performing "Every Man a King." The crowd joined into the lyrics with unmusical, but enthusiastic yells.

Harry Bierce for the first time understood how it must have felt for Cicero, that devout supporter of the Roman Republic, to watch Julius Caesar address the crowds, and have them respond with unthinking adoration, throwing their freedoms down at the feet of the Great Man. As he turned away with disgust, he spotted a lean, well-dressed man walking quickly toward the unguarded side entrance of the Capitol building. Bierce recognized the man instantly as Dr. Weiss, son-in-law to Judge Pavy, intense hater of Huey Long and all of his works. In a burst of intuition, he realized what the intense young man intended. Weaving through the cheering people at the edge of the crowd, Bierce began running faster than an observer would have thought possible.

Senator Long had quieted the crowd once again. "Now my friends, you must excuse me. There are still officials in Louisiana who oppose your will. One of them is the tool of the Wall Street financiers, Judge Pavy. However, my friends I have yet more good news for you. As we speak, our friends in the legislature are voting to abolish the Judge's district. He will no longer be able to hinder your progress and happiness. In fact, after I leave you, I am going to congratulate the legislature on their foresight. But remember, soon—very soon—every last man of you will be a king!" As Long and his party entered the Capitol, the band and chorus again struck up "Every Man a King" and the joyous crowd joined in at the top of their lungs.

The smiling Huey Long entered the rotunda, flanked by his brother and Governor King, his son Russell right behind him. Behind Russell came two hulking bodyguards in plain clothes and two granite-faced state policeman. "Brother Earl," Huey said to his brother, "this is the beginning of a great crusade! There will soon need to be a distribution of the pie."

"Pie?" asked a confused Earl Long.

"Certainly. There is only so much pie. Those who join the crusade early will get big pieces of the pie. Those who join later will get small pieces of the pie. Those not joining at all, those like Judge Pavy, will get … good government!" Laughing at his own cynical joke, he turned to Governor King. "Let's go into the chamber and meet the legislature. I need to determine who will be getting what slice of pie…."

Huey Long's voice trailed off. He stopped dead in his tracks. Before him stood an intense young man with glasses, pointing a small automatic pistol at him. Long did not recognize the young man. Without it really registering, Long heard rapid footfalls echoing down an adjacent marble corridor.

Weiss fired twice. He would have emptied the magazine, but the casing of the second cartridge jammed the ejection port. As Senator Long screamed "Kill him!

Kill him!" his four guards surged forward and cut Weiss down with one shot each. "Father!" screamed young Russell Long as the guards gathered around Weiss's already dead body and emptied their weapons into it, two of them crying as they did so. The explosions of gunfire echoed and re-echoed through the marble corridors; bullets that had missed Weiss or passed through his body ricocheted everywhere. No one noticed Bierce's arrival in the rotunda.

The moment the shooting stopped, Harry Bierce advanced toward the corpse, shaking his head at the damage thirty high-caliber bullets could do to the human body. He then turned his head at the sound of the senator's groaning. There was a small rift in Long's shirtfront; blood was trickling out of it.

As Russell continued shouting hysterically, Earl Long grabbed him by the shoulders. "Calm down!" he said. "It's not that bad. It's not bleeding much, and your dad's still standing." He then turned his attention to the guards. "Boys! Help me get Huey to the hospital!" Supporting the still-erect senator, the guards began walking him toward an emergency exit, followed closely by Earl and Russell. Governor King dithered, looking like a lost child. As policemen, reporters, and common citizens began to rush into the rotunda, Bierce took one last pitying look at Weiss's body, then retreated along the route he had come.

✦

The next day, in a small hospital room Earl Long, Governor King, several top members of the Long organization and a frowning doctor gathered around the dying Huey Long. When he was first examined, the doctors were confident that the senator would recover from his wound; he was fully conscious, and even able to joke with his visitors. During the night, his blood pressure began a relentless fall, and the doctors had determined he had suffered severe, irreparable damage to a kidney. An operation to remove the kidney might have saved him, but by now he was so weakened, that the operation itself would probably do the job. Russell had broken down completely at the news, at which point, Earl kindly but firmly ordered him home. Earl himself had held his brother's hand the entire night, feeling lost, so very lost, unable to imagine a future without his big brother.

Now it was morning. The hospital was surrounded by thousands of citizens, strangely silent, simply waiting. Earl Long gave little thought to the crowds. All he could think of was the big brother who had sometimes slapped him around and mocked his slow mind, but who had protected him from bullies, inside his family and out, and, as an adult, guaranteed him a place at his side as Huey began his meteoric rise to power. Occasionally, he used his free hand to wipe tears from his eyes, which from time to time shone like those of a demented lunatic.

The doctor took Huey's other hand and sought for a pulse. After a few moments, the man sighed, and placed the senator's hand on his motionless chest. "He is gone," he solemnly announced. The men in the room removed their hats. Some sobbed openly. Governor King was the first to speak.

"Earl, you got to tell the folks outside."

"I have no position," replied Earl Long numbly. "It

would come better from you."

The portly King shook his head. "The folks out there don't want to hear from a fat old politician like me. They want to hear from a Long. If not Huey, then the next best thing, his brother."

Earl thought a moment, then nodded. Releasing his brother's hand, he left the room, followed by the governor and the leaders of the Long machine. When they reached the steps to the hospital's entrance, there was no need to gesture for silence. The crowd of thousands was as still as a cemetery at midnight. Forcing himself to speak in as loud a voice as he could manage, Earl Long spoke without preamble.

"My friends, today I have lost a brother…" A collective groan traveled through the crowd. Earl continued, "But so have you. The crusader is dead, but I give you my word, his crusade will continue. Now go back to your homes and join with your family and friends to pray for the soul of Huey Long."

There were scattered calls of "Hang the bastards! Death to Wall Street Jews," and other phrases that rang out through the crowd.

Raising his voice even louder, Earl Long responded "None of that, my friends! There was no conspiracy in bringing about my brother's death. A lunatic doctor did the deed, acting by himself. The state police have already confirmed that. The murderer is dead. Now go to your homes and mourn amongst your own people."

With scattered muttering the crowd slowly broke up. Governor King came up to Earl and patted him on the shoulder. "Well done, Earl. That crowd could have got out of hand. There could have been riots, lynchings, God knows what else. They would have only listened to you. Only the words of a Long could prevent a real disaster. Now boss, what are your orders for the rest of us?"

In amazement, Earl Long responded, "Boss? Governor, you're the boss now that Huey's gone."

"Afraid not," responded King, chuckling ruefully. "I may not be the fastest bunny in the forest, but I know I'll never be anything but a place-holder for the Longs, and I don't mind that. Huey built up a Long machine, and a Long must head it. Russell's too young, so it's gotta be you. So let me repeat: What are your orders, Mr. Long?"

Earl Long was speechless for a nearly a minute as he contemplated a future that he had never imagined would be his. Then he began to give his first orders.

CHAPTER FIVE

"with peace and glory ahead"

Harry Bierce had been standing by the main entrance to the soaring Capitol Building in Baton Rouge for over an hour, watching the line of thousands of grieving people, forming a procession more than half a mile long. The Louisiana sun was blistering, but none of the mourners seemed to mind. Silence pervaded except for the occasional sobbing, as the citizens shuffled slowly up to the building and ascended the steps leading to the rotunda—a just-completed monument that Huey Long had built for himself—all for a few moments to see the corpse of the man who had embodied their hopes and dreams, who had promised them so much.

Earlier that morning, Bierce had flashed his badge to the stony-faced state policemen at the entrance, and had been allowed to go to the head of the line. He entered the enormous, echoing rotunda, and had seen the open coffin, set up on a platform on the spot where Senator Long had been shot and surrounded by elaborate floral displays. He stepped up to the coffin and stared down at the peaceful looking body, clothed in a formal tuxedo that, in life, Long would have disdained. Bierce shook his head, marveling how one man with so much energy, so much ambition, had allowed greed to bring him to such an end. Still wondering at the mysteries of mankind, he'd left the rotunda to enter the blinding Louisiana sunlight.

Across the street and near to the line of mourners, sitting on the grass under a shade tree was a black man with a guitar, blind, perhaps from a gas attack during the Great War. Not quite knowing why, Bierce crossed the street and walked over to him. The man was playing a guitar, and although quite good, the upturned cap on the ground in front of him only contained a scattering of change. Standing quite close, Bierce listened to the mournful song the man was singing. He recognized it as the melancholy song that was sweeping the Depression-stricken nation: "Brother, Can You Spare a Dime?"

They used to tell me I was building a dream,
and so I followed the mob;
When there was earth to plow or guns to bear,
I was always there, right on the job.

As Bierce listened, he scanned the slow-moving line. He saw white families and black families standling close together, the uneasiness normally shown when whites were forced into close proximity to blacks, was absent.

They used to tell me I was building a dream,
with peace and glory ahead.
Why should I be standing in line,
just waiting for bread?

Bierce noticed a farmer in bibbed overalls in the line with three children under the age of ten clinging to him. The children looked bewildered, even frightened, too young to understand exactly what was going on, but not too young to understand something was badly wrong. No woman stood with this family. Bierce made an educated guess that constant pregnancy and grinding poverty had placed her in an early grave. The farmer himself had a lined face with sad eyes, his skin so roughened and burned by the Louisiana sun that Bierce could not decide whether the man was black or white. Bierce supposed that it did not matter.

Once I built a railroad,
I made it run, made it race against time.
Once I built a railroad, now it's done,
Brother, can you spare a dime?

Bierce scanned the newsreel crews and their heavy cameras, the crazed equipment of the radio networks with electrical lines wandering over the ground like snakes, the reporters, the photographers. Normally, he despised the newshounds and their conscienceless pursuit of tragedy and sensation, the way that they would serve up to the public the tragedy and the pain of others in order to entertain the curious. For some reason, today they were subdued, even polite. Bierce decided that they realized that something titanic had happened, something that would affect them, as well as the public forever.

Once I built a tower up to the sun,
brick and rivet and lime.
Once I built a tower, now it's done,
Brother, can you spare a dime?

233

Out of the corner of his eye, Bierce spotted Russell Long in the line, accompanied by his mother and sister. Russell and his sister showed signs of crying, although no tears flowed now. Their faces had the look of bewildered amazement Bierce had seen numerous times on the faces of soldiers who had just been shot, still conscious yet unable to comprehend that their lives were about to end. Mrs. Long walked steadily on, her face stony. Bierce had heard rumors that Huey saw his wife seldom in the last few years, contenting himself with casual affairs with admiring young women. Yet there was brittleness in the way she walked that indicated to Bierce that she did mourn, for the man she had married, if not the man he had become.

Once in khaki suits, gee, we looked swell,
full of that Yankee Doodly Dum;
Half a million boots went slogging thru Hell,
and I was the kid with the drum.

Bierce now focused on the blind performer, tears from his sightless eyes flowing down past the rim of his dark glasses as he sang the last verse in the voice of an angel.

Say, don't you remember? They called me 'Al';
It was 'Al' all the time;
Why don't you remember? I'm your pal,
Say buddy, can you spare a dime?

Bierce reached into his pocket and extracted a ten-dollar bill. He was about to put the bill into the upturned cap when he realized the blind man, unable to see the denomination, could easily be cheated. Placing the currency in the man's hand, Bierce murmured, "Just so you will know, this is ten dollars."

As Bierce straightened, the singer said, "Thanks, sir. It is a sad time, ain't it?"

Bierce considered saying something blandly comforting, but then decided that would not do justice to the blinded veteran who had already given so much. All men need to hear the truth, but this man at this moment, Bierce thought, deserved it unvarnished and real. "It is, of course, sad. But you, of all people, must know that the 'Share the Wealth' plan could not have worked. There's nowhere near enough rich people to have funded it. Yet Long would have tried to make it work, would have tried to seize enough of the nation's wealth to make it work. All that would have done, is take from the country the capital necessary to restart the economy. The Depression would have gotten worse, would have gone on indefinitely, with no end in sight. And he would've have used any means necessary to accomplish his goals. That's not the democracy you fought for."

"Well, sir, you may have the right of it," responded the man, idly picking a few notes off his guitar. "I know Long was a bit of a crook. Know some of the state money stuck to his fingers and those of his kin. I know that some of his ideas weren't thought out, were—what's the word?—utopian. But in spite of his greed for power and money, he cared. He really cared. That made up for a lot, sir. He did give us the roads, the schools, the hospitals, the textbooks. The other high-and-mighty types in Baton Rouge, in New Orleans, they didn't care, sir. Didn't care one damn bit for us common folks. Huey did. Can forgive a man a lot because of that."

Bierce knew there was much truth in what the blind veteran said. "There are others who care, more honest, more capable—President Roosevelt and others. They will make certain that what can be done, will be done. Give them a chance."

"I pray you're right, sir." The man began to strum out a melancholy tune. Bierce turned and, without saying another word, left the man to grieve.

After a short walk, Bierce reached his rented Hudson convertible, got in, and started the powerful engine. Placing it in gear, he roared off, taking the road out of Baton Rouge to the south. He was not headed to New Orleans ... not yet anyway. After a relatively short drive, he turned into the entrance of a rural cemetery. Despite the brightness of the sun, there was a deep sense of loss guarded by ancient, spreading trees dripping moss. He spotted a small party in the distance. Driving toward it, he stopped the noisy car at a respectful distance and walked the rest of the way.

A Catholic priest was standing at the head of a coffin, reading something in a monotone. Behind him, at a discrete distance, stood two men in rough clothes smoking cigarettes; presumably these were the gravediggers. At the foot of the coffin stood the towering Judge Benjamin Pavy, one arm wrapped tightly around the shoulders of his sobbing daughter Yvonne, while his wife stood on the other side of him, dry-eyed, stony-faced. Bierce took a position under the shade of one of the massive trees and watched the remainder of the ceremony, removing his hat in respect.

Finally the mumbling priest finished his reading,

made some gestures over the coffin, and hurried off, not bothering to stop to speak to the family. The two gravediggers simultaneously threw their cigarettes on the ground, and crushed them with the soles of their boots. They then picked up shovels that had been lying there and sauntered over to the coffin and the pile of fresh earth that lay beside a yawning grave. Putting a heavy arm each around his wife and daughter, Judge Pavy gently turned them in the direction of a distant chapel where their automobile was parked. As he walked by the tree that sheltered Bierce, the Judge noticed the federal agent. Murmuring a few words to his wife, he handed off their daughter to her. While they continued on the way to the chapel, he then walked wearily over to Bierce. Judge Pavy did not offer to shake hands, but nodded a greeting to the agent.

"Thank you for coming, Mr. Bierce. As you see, no one else has come, not my other children, not even Carl's father. They treat us like we have the plague." Suddenly the old man's face crumpled like old linen. As a wail of despair came his throat, he buried his face in his hands. He spoke between sobs. "Why, Carl, why? Why'd you leave my baby girl a widow, my grandson fatherless? Why'd you throw away that magnificent mind of yours? Was it because you thought I believed you a Jew, that others too believed the same? That Long was like that thug over in Germany? All that didn't matter; you had a duty … a duty…."

Pavy descended into continuous sobbing for some minutes, then forced himself to stop, wiping his face with a large handkerchief and straightned his shoulders. He then turned his red-rimmed eyes on Bierce and asked him, "Or was it my fault? Was it because I was always venting my hatred of Huey Long and all of his works that he became obsessed with the need to kill Long? Did I persuade my baby girl's husband to throw his life away?"

Harry Bierce normally kept his emotions well in check, but he pitied the old man to the bottom of his strange soul. "Judge Pavy, what Dr. Weiss did was murder, pure and simple. But every man must be responsible for his own actions. I am confident that you never once urged him to commit murder for any reason, good or bad. Having said that, I do not believe him to have been an evil man. He killed, not for personal gain, vengeance, or even hatred. He killed because he thought it would save lives. Take what consolation from that you can. When your grandson is of an age to understand these things, make sure that he knows that his father was a good man who took a wrong path. And don't you give up fighting the corrupt and wicked through the ballot box. You are a good man, too, and America does not have enough like you. You and yours have my condolences. Now, you should go catch up with your family. They will need you more than ever in the coming weeks."

Harry Bierce extended his small hand. Judge Pavy took it in both of his, shook it, then with a slight nod of his head trudged toward the chapel. Bierce watched him until he disappeared inside. Then Bierce strode purposely toward his Hudson. There was so much to do, and so little time in which to do it.

From behind him came the hollow "thunk, thunk" as the gravediggers threw shovels-full of earth on the coffin of Dr. Carl Weiss.

✦

"So, Huey Long has come a cropper, eh? I knew he would, eventually. Tried to tell your bosses in Berlin that, but they wouldn't listen. They were in too much of a hurry. Told them '36 was too soon; told them to wait until '40, when Roosevelt's two terms are up."

Von Papen face held an expression of ill-disguised disgust. He despised traitors—even those who benefited his beloved Germany. The man across from him took a long drag on an unfiltered Camel and blew the noxious smoke in his direction; von Papen did not attempt to hide his coughing response to the cheap American cigarette.

The American smiled, relishing von Papen's discomfort.

"The Leader is not known for his patience," replied von Papen dryly. "Besides, he knows that the limitation of two presidential terms is a custom established by your George Washington, not a requirement of your Constitution. He believes that should he live, Roosevelt will run for a third term in 1940. Perhaps even a fourth in 1944. That is what concerns him. He knows that your President hates Germany in general and the Nazi Party in particular. He has plans for the 1940s in Europe, and does not want American interference, like in the Great War." Von Papen paused to grimace, and then continued. "Having said all that, in my personal opinion I believe you to be correct. Better to be successful in 1940 than fail in 1936."

"I think you're someone I can deal with. You're not like those thick-headed thugs your precious Leader has sent in the past. And don't worry, I don't take much persuading to stay out of European affairs. We got into your Great War, and as near as I can see it all we got out of that was a quarter million boys killed. Still, the terms I've discussed with you people in the past will have to be changed. Without Huey, I'm all you got, and my price has gone up."

Von Papen just barely managed to suppress a sneer. "And just what is your price now?"

"First off, you can tell your buddies in New England to go crawl back in their holes. This is a white man's country, and I'm not sharing it with anyone—least of all those freaks. Second, the money will be twice what I previously said, and all in gold. I'm going to need every ounce of it, especially if Roosevelt tries for a third term."

"I have no power to agree to your new terms, although I will most certainly relay them to Berlin. Personally, I think the Leader will agree. As you say, you are now all he has." Von Papen stood, and bowed slightly. "In any event, I must go. My ship leaves New York for Hamburg in fourteen hours, and I must be on it. That requires I take the very next train north. I will find my own way out." Von Papen clicked his heels, turned, and exited the suite without a backward glance.

Vice President Garner looked thoughtfully at the door, then crushed out his Camel in the ashtray.

✦

Another mercilessly hot day had just ended in Commerce, Oklahoma. In the small bungalow owned by the teacher, she had left all the windows open and kept two electric fans going, but the heat made the air seem almost liquid, made moving about seem like walking through water. The teacher wiped a layer of sweat off her face with a handkerchief, then walked into the dining room

Despite the temperature, she smiled at the sight of her recently adopted daughter, the orphaned child of Constable William Campbell, gunned down by Bonnie Parker last summer. Constable Campbell had no living relations, not even cousins, and there was talk of sending the girl to an orphanage. The teacher had grown up in an orphanage, and had no intention of letting this bright little girl live in a hellish state institution. Instead, she had taken the child in and had not regretted it for one moment since.

The girl did not notice her adoptive mother looking proudly at her. She was writing in a notebook, periodically consulting a high-school level physics textbook, concentrating completely, seemingly impervious to the heat. The teacher was glad that she had formally adopted her, despite the objections raised by her lack of a husband. She had been married in her twenties, but there had been no children before her husband went to the Great War and found a nameless grave in France, and she'd never felt the need to remarry—did not feel the need now. She was certain her late husband would have been proud to be father to the intelligent girl at the dining room table. The smile faded from the teacher's face with thoughts of the future. The girl had a brilliant mind, but she feared it was destined to be wasted. There was barely enough money for the two of them to survive; nothing left over to save for college. Perhaps there would be some sort of scholarship, but, honestly, the best her daughter could hope for would be to find a good man who would appreciate her mind. Most likely it would be some farmer who would keep her fed and pregnant on some hard-scrabble land for the rest of her life.

Unexpectedly, there was a brisk knock at the screen door. The girl looked up from her work with an expression of terror. It broke her mother's heart to see how nervous she was. There was really no need. The people in Commerce were friendly and decent, and aside from some violations of the Prohibition laws, not inclined to crime. In fact, people hardly ever locked their doors. But a year ago, the girl had held her father as his life bled from him on a hot, dusty street. The experience had left its cruel mark on her.

Telling the girl in a bright voice not to worry, that she would see who was there, the teacher went to the screen door and turned on the porch light. Seeing nobody at the door, she opened the screen and peered around. She saw nothing but a paper bag at the door. Frowning, she picked it up and took it inside. She told her daughter that it had been some kind of prank, and the girl resumed her studies. The teacher sat herself in a living room chair to examine the contents of the bag, and was barely able to contain a cry of amazement and wonder. Bundles of currency, mainly fifty- and one-hundred-dollar bills, fell into her lap. A folded note also fell out. Opening it, she read the following:

I have looked into your background and find you a fit guardian for the daughter of Constable William Campbell. Enclosed you will find $20,000 for her support and education. There is no need to report this, if the money concerns you. No one has a better right to it than you, and no one will be pressing a claim for it.

There was no address or signature on the note, which had been neatly printed. Tears began to trickle down the teacher's cheeks. She could not imagine who her benefactor was, but she now knew there was continuing education in her daughter's future.

Four houses down on the opposite side of the street, a figure looked at the teacher's bungalow for a long time, then walked to the next block, got in a Hudson convertible, and roared off into the night.

✦

It all seemed unreal to Earl Long. Here he was sitting in Huey's office behind Huey's desk, seeing a regular stream of Huey's friends and supporters. Even Governor King, who had ignored Earl during Huey's life, was now humbly sitting across from him, asking what he wanted done as to this, that, and the other. It didn't seem right; Huey had always called the shots, and Earl had never imagined it could be any other way. Still, one could get used to such power, thought Earl guiltily.

"So, Mr. Long, we're going to need a lot of money—cash, untraceable—to keep our majority in the legislature next year. And I hate to think what a national campaign would cost us." It was not lost on Earl Long that Governor King was no longer calling him 'Earl,' or the occasional 'Huey's idiot kid brother.'

"I'll see what can be done," replied Earl. "We won't need as much as you think. With Huey gone, there's no presidential campaign. We only need money for the Louisiana elections and to help elect some friends of 'Share the Wealth' in other states. I'll run the trap lines

243

and see how much we can expect."

"Well then, I'll be getting along," replied the Governor as he rose from his chair. "Thank you for your time, Mr. Long." He took his considerable bulk out of the room, closing the door behind him.

Now that he was alone, Earl Long decided to find out just how much was in the deduct box. As he had done on numerous occasions when Huey was alive, he opened up the hiding place and nearly passed out from the shock of seeing it was absolutely empty—no large tin box, no mounds of untraceable cash. Then he noticed it was not entirely empty; there was a small piece of paper in the empty space. With trembling fingers he drew it out. On the paper, in plain block letters, it said:

THE CITIZENS OF THE UNITED STATES
SEND THEIR THANKS.

Dropping the paper from his nerveless fingers, Earl Long collapsed back into the large desk chair and passed out.

✦

Mrs. Belasco was at her desk in the library, rushing to finish some important correspondence. Very special guests were due at any moment, and she had no intention of depriving herself of one minute of the . . . unusual entertainments those guests provided. She frowned at a quiet knock on the closed door, and irritably said, "Come in."

The elderly butler entered, carrying a medium-sized

package wrapped in brown paper. "My apologies, Mrs. Belasco, but this just arrived, brought here by a special courier. I thought it must be important."

"Put it here on my desk and then leave," she said gruffly. The old man did as he was told, softly closing the door behind him. The moment he was gone, she took her gold-plated letter opener and cut away the paper, only to find a neatly stacked block of currency, made up of carefully bound stacks of tens, twenties, and fifties. Although she would have a precise count done later by one of her accountants, she estimated there was about $50,000 cash in this bundle. There was no letter or note.

Bierce. She leaned back in her chair and gave a silvery, chilling laugh. She wondered how he had come into such a sum, and laughed again. Frankly, she had considered the original amount a gift, never expected to see a penny back from the government-salaried investigator. Well, tonight she was going to have a reason to celebrate.

Again, there was a polite knock at the library door.

"Come in," she said.

The elderly butler again entered the library, this time with a badly concealed look of disgust, tinged with fear. Belasco found that amusing, considering the varied things the old man had seen in his many years of service to her.

"Mrs. Belasco, your guests have arrived."

"Show them into the special room in the basement. Tell them I will need several minutes to get prepared."

✦

Ana Cumpanas stared with hollow eyes at the

institutional green walls of the interrogation room that the immigration officer had locked her into, and uttered a vile curse in Roumanian. Despite the promises of Agent Bierce, she had been picked up and processed for deportation back to the barbaric hellhole that General Antonescu had made of her homeland. She knew that today was the day. Any moment, an immigration officer would walk through that door, handcuff her, and take her to the train station for the long trip to New York City, where she would be placed on some rusty steamer for the month-long journey to the land of her birth. She could easily imagine being met at the dock in Varna by men from Antonescu's Iron Guard. She didn't want to imagine what would follow.

The door flew open and, to her utter surprise, Harry Bierce entered the room. Before she could utter a word, he said, "I keep my promises, even if it involves some minor corruption. You are free, Mrs. Cumpanas. Come with me."

She staggered to her feet, and followed Bierce down the corridor and into an elevator. The car opened on the ground floor. Neither of the two guards on duty tried to stop her. They simply gave a nod of recognition to Bierce, then pointedly looked away. Bierce led her out onto the street and down two blocks to where his Hudson convertible was parked. The agent held the passenger door open for her. Still stunned by the change in her circumstances, she gingerly entered the sporty car. Bierce then went around to the driver side and vaulted into the seat without opening the door. He hit the ignition and merged the powerful automobile into downtown Chicago traffic.

Having been silent since Bierce had entered the interrogation room, Cumpanas finally found her voice. "Agent Bierce, I don't get what's going on? Where are we going?"

With his free hand Bierce reached into his inside coat pocket, withdrew three envelopes, and tossed them in her lap. "First things first. You are no longer Ana Cumpanas. You're Helena Klein. You're still Roumanian, but you were born in Brasov, not Bucharest. One of the envelopes contains your naturalization papers. They will withstand any reasonable scrutiny."

Her head spinning, she said, "But … but they have ordered my extradition for today. When I don't show up—"

"That is taken care of," interrupted Bierce. "As it happens, another Roumanian woman was awaiting extradition. She ran a business that, ah, relieved women of unwanted pregnancies. I have paid her a considerable sum to agree to be you. The same venal official who has provided you with your new papers has altered her records to show her as Ana Cumpanas."

In her many years as a prostitute, and then a madam, she had seen and heard of many things, but never anything like this. "I don't know what to say."

"The second envelope contains a thousand dollars cash," interrupted Bierce again. "That should support you until you have established your new life. The third envelope contains a first-class train ticket to Los Angeles, and a letter of recommendation to the head of costuming at a major film studio. I once provided a very great service for her, and she will employ you as a favor to me. The skills you demonstrated repairing my clothes in the hospital proved to me you will do well in such a job, which will not provide wealth but will give you more than enough to live on, and is free of taint of the criminal underworld."

The car roared past a long line of dejected men and women, waiting patiently for their turn at a soup kitchen. Shortly thereafter the train station came into view. Bierce brought the Hudson to a smooth halt before the main entrance.

"What if I just decide to turn in the train ticket for a refund, and start up my business as before?" she said, looking at Bierce speculatively, a slight smile on her lips.

Bierce turned and looked right back at her with an intensity that startled her. "That will be your choice entirely. I believe you have never really had a good choice before you in your life. Now you have one. I hope that you will choose wisely."

The woman who was now Helena Klein frowned. "Why are you doing all of this for me, really?"

Bierce took a deep breath as a look of profound sadness and devotion passed over his features. "Because you remind me of a woman I once loved." He swiftly grabbed her face in both hands and planted a deep kiss on her lips. Just as quickly, he broke off the kiss, reached across her and threw open the passenger door. Wordlessly, she stepped out of the Hudson and closed the door. Bierce roared off, never looking back. She then turned to look at the entrance to the train station and took her first steps toward a new life.

✦

Franz von Papen was terrified as he entered Heinrich Himmler's inner sanctum, but struggled hard to control his fear. When he saw Rheinhard Heydrich was also in the office, standing behind and to the left of the seated secret policeman, it became more of a struggle for him to conceal his terror. Yet somehow, he managed.

Himmler was tapping a file that lay open on his desk with a pen. The expression on his face was bland, as always. He did not invite von Papen to sit. Instead, he launched straight into business.

"The affair with Long has not ended very well, has it? It even appears that Mr. Noyes, our valuable New England contact, committed suicide out of disappointment and chagrin."

"There is more than meets the eye to the death of Noyes," replied von Papen in a carefully neutral voice. "His suicide took place before the murder of Senator Long. In any event, I cannot recommend that Germany rely on what is left of his organization. I met certain of his … key people. My recommendation is that they can in no way be trusted."

Himmler emitted a small, exasperated sigh. "So, we are back to relying on Vice President Garner. I am not sure he can be counted on to support the goals of the Leader."

"Did you meet with Garner on your way home, as I told you?" asked Heydrich in an icy voice.

"Yes, there I am more hopeful. It is true he does not approve of many of the Leader's internal policies, but he is a very dedicated isolationist, and wants no involvement in any future European war. He would never agree to be controlled by us, but his foreign policy positions would align with Germany's long-term interests, should the Leader resort to war. Of course, he is now demanding money, a great deal of money, to support a run for the American Presidency in 1940. He knows we now have no one else to turn to."

Himmler nodded. "Given that you could not have anticipated Long's assassination, you have done well enough. I will report that to the Leader. I will also recommend that he appoint you our ambassador to the Vatican. The Pope looks down his long, Catholic nose at the Party and its leadership and does not have good relations with our current representative. Since you are a well-known Catholic from the old aristocracy, you should do much better."

Von Papen struggled hard to keep his face from showing the relief he felt. "I will be pleased to represent Germany to the Holy Father."

"One final thing," said Himmler, "the Leader would like you to apply for membership in the Party. He feels that our representatives abroad should indicate their solidarity with the current regime."

"I will serve Germany in any honorable way I can, but I will never join the Nazi Party. Never. You may tell the Leader that." To von Papen's horror, the words fell from his mouth without conscious thought.

"No matter the costs to yourself and your family?" asked Heydrich in a voice that sounded amused and enraged at the same time.

Von Papen felt as if a pit yawned before him, but it was too late to take back his words. In truth, he did not wish to take them back. "No matter the cost," he said in a voice near a whisper.

Himmler glanced at Heydrich, then turned his attention back to von Papen, his lips curled in a faint, benign smile. "The Leader thought you would say something like that. He has informed me that it is not mandatory that you join, so long as you continue to serve Germany. Two days from now, you are to meet the Leader to receive your formal commission to Rome. In the meantime, you are dismissed. Go home to your family."

His body trembling ever so slightly, von Papen bowed to the secret policeman, clicked his heels, and left Himmler's office, a slight stagger to his walk. After the door closed, Heydrich turned to his master and said, "The Leader is really going to let that ridiculous old aristocrat get away with such insolence?"

"Do not question the Leader's judgment. He sees that some usefulness can still be garnered from von Papen."

"And should he cease to be useful at some time in the future?"

"Then he will be yours," replied Himmler.

Heydrich smiled broadly, showing his white, sharp teeth.

✦

Harry Bierce sat in a wing chair of his DuPont Circle apartment living room, staring moodily at a framed picture over the fireplace. It was of a woman dressed in the style of the 1880s, flanked by two teenagers, a boy and a girl. The woman was tall and erect, the streaks of grey in her long, dark hair adding, instead of detracting, from her exotic beauty. She stared boldly into the camera, a lovely, enigmatic smile gracing her lips. The resemblance to Ana Cumpanas was slight, but it was there. The teenagers also stared directly into the camera. It was hard to say why, but their expressions indicated cheerfully cruel intelligence.

Bierce sighed, then turned his attention to the large tin box that sat on the floor to the left of the fireplace—the famous "deduct box," the disappearance of which was generating rumors throughout the nation. He felt some shame for having taken it, as he had been raised to regard thievery as strictly dishonorable. Regardless, it would not be possible to return the money to the state employees from whom it had been extorted. And since he would never allow the remnants of the Long political machine to retain it to further their corrupt goals, he had decided to dedicate the money to the benefit of the country.

Now, thoroughly convinced that it was only a matter of time until Germany again was a considerable threat to the United States, Bierce had tried to alert the relevant authorities. Although not long back in Washington, he had already talked to the heads of the Army and Navy Intelligence, who had called him an alarmist. He had talked to Army Chief of Staff Douglas MacArthur, who also dismissed his concerns, although MacArthur's aide, a middle-aged captain named Eisenhower, had listened with a thoughtful, concerned expression on his face.

Bierce had even obtained an interview with President Roosevelt, who'd been informed by Director Hoover of Bierce's role in saving his life and expressed his sincere gratitude. But he condescendingly assured Bierce that America could contain the Nazi menace by providing aid to England, France, and Russia.

Bierce was disappointed, but not despairing. Since official Washington would not take him seriously, he would use the money from the deduct box to set up his own, private intelligence service. He would then deliver up priceless information when those in Washington finally awoke to the threat. According to Mrs. Belasco, her brother was already in contact with the Nazi inner circle and, much to Bierce's surprise, had shown a willingness to inform on their plans. Maybe there was some real humanity there. He would have to find a way to contact him directly without having to go through Mrs. Belasco, though.

There were more immediate things to accomplish. He could hardly leave such huge sums of cash lying about his apartment. He would have to open a number of safe deposit boxes and banking accounts in various names. And before that, he needed to make his final report to Director Hoover. Bierce stood up, placed his fedora neatly on his head, and headed out on the long walk to Bureau headquarters.

✦

Earl Long was at his desk in the office he unofficially occupied in the Capitol, trying to decipher some reports on parish voting patterns, when Governor King burst in, face red with excitement.

"Mr. Long! Mr. Long! I've got to talk to you!"

Long frowned at the genial, nonentity that his brother had placed in the governor's mansion. "Calm down, Governor. What is it?"

"I've got the state coroner's final report on your

brother's death. You got to see it!"

Earl Long rubbed his tired eyes. "I've been at these damn papers for too long. Just tell me what it says."

"Well, in summary it says your brother died when a .32 caliber bullet perforated his kidney and small intestine, causing fatal bleeding."

"So? We know that bastard Weiss shot Huey with a .32."

King paused to take several deep breaths before saying, "Mr. Long, the coroner had a ballistics test done on the bullet, just as a matter of routine. Mr. Long, I don't know how to say this…"

"Spit it out!"

"The bullet … it didn't come from Weiss's gun."

Earl Long stared slack-jawed at the Governor for a moment, then almost shouted, "Of course the goddamned bullet came from that Jew's gun! It was a .32!"

King vigorously shook his head. "But it wasn't the gun that fired the bullet that killed Huey."

"I was there myself. So were you. We saw Weiss fire twice!"

"In this report, they say they did pick up two .32 slugs at the scene. One smashed the watch of a bodyguard next to Huey, breaking his wrist; the other buried itself in the woodwork of a bench."

Earl Long was silent for a full minute before saying, "It must have been a ricochet from one of the shots fired by the guards. They must have shot Weiss thirty, forty times after his gun jammed. One of the slugs must have gone wild, bounced off the marble floor, and hit Huey."

Again King shook his head. "The coroner thought of

that and checked on the guns of every last one of the guards. They were all .38s or .45s."

Long and King stared at each other. Finally, the dead senator's brother asked, "Then who killed Huey?"

"We probably will never know," replied Governor King, taking out a large handkerchief and mopping his brow. "Mr. Long, this is a goddamned mess! What am I going to tell the press? What am I going to tell the people?"

"You tell them nothing!" snarled Earl Long. "You're right, we'll probably never find out who actually fired the bullet. But that doesn't matter. His political enemies were behind it. We're going to pound them with responsibility for Huey's murder, pound them so hard that Huey's people will stay in power in Louisiana for the next generation! But if there is public doubt as to who fired the bullet, they might be able to wiggle free of the responsibility. We need to bury this, bury it so deep it will never see the light of day. Governor, you take this report back to the coroner and tell him it is unacceptable. He needs to change it to show the bullet that killed Huey came from Weiss's gun. The coroner and any of his people having knowledge of this report should be told if they tow the line, they will be taken care of. If they don't, then they will also be taken care of. Just in a different way."

King visibly gulped. He now knew for certain what he had only suspected: Earl Long was just as hard and ruthless as Huey had been. The governor gingerly took back the report and said, "Yes, Mr. Long." as he tiptoed out of the office.

Earl Long swiveled his chair to the window and

stared out of it blankly for some time. Finally, his voice almost breaking with emotion, he murmured, "Who fired that bullet, big brother? Who killed you?"

✦

"That's it, then," said Hoover, tapping a pencil on the final report given to him by Bierce. "Long is dead, the worst of the Midwest bank robbers are dead, the plot against the President's life … dead. Good job, Agent Bierce." The words seemed to come unwillingly from Hoover. His mouth looked as if he had been sucking a lemon.

"There is still the matter of the long term threat from the Nazis to this country," replied Bierce. "I spoke personally to the President on that, but he seems to feel he has it all under control."

The Director pointed a finger at Bierce like a gun. "Now, that's something else I wanted to talk to you about. You went over my head to Roosevelt without clearing it with me. I won't have it! I don't care how good an agent you are, I won't have it. In the future, if you ever feel the need to talk to the President or the Attorney General, come to me first. You know me, if you've got a good reason, I will grant you permission. But I have the final say on such political contacts. Is that understood?"

"Yes, sir," responded Bierce, his face blank.

Having delivered his reprimand, Hoover relaxed the expression on his face. "As for the Nazis, I agree with you that they pose as great a potential threat to this country as the Bolsheviks. But as you saw in your talks with the intelligence people, now is not the time to press it. We need more evidence to open their eyes to the threat. I'm establishing a special counter-intelligence unit, and I would like you to be part of it."

"I would be honored, Director. Would this new unit also be looking into the activities of Noyes organization in New England"

Hoover seemed to mull the notion over for a few moments, then said, "I think that would be a good idea. We've had our eye on the late Mr. Noyes for some time, but he was excellent at covering his tracks. Now that we know he was conspiring with potential enemies of this country, the Bureau can pursue his organization with more vigor. You're going to need to see some highly classified documents on a raid made on a coastal village in Massachusetts in 1928 to understand the ... peculiar threat that could come from that organization, and then you will need to make a trip to see some prisoners being kept in the Naval Penitentiary in New Hampshire."

Hoover looked out his window at the darkening sky. "It's Friday, and it's late. Go home and get some rest over the weekend. I will have the files ready for you Monday morning."

"Thank you, Director." Bierce rose from his chair, bowed slightly, and left the office.

Hoover sat with a thoughtful look on his face for several minutes. Then, he opened the lower right-hand drawer of his massive desk, and removed a large file with "Bierce, Harry" neatly typed on the cover tab. He flipped past several tabs containing routine personnel documents until he came to one that had only a photographic copy of an old glass-plate picture. Hoover had always taken an interest in the American Civil War, and in his extensive readings he had come across this picture. With some difficulty, he had traced down the original at the Smithsonian, and had it enlarged and photographed.

The photograph was one of many taken in the summer of 1865 during the victory parade in Washington of General William Sherman's returning army. On the reviewing stand stood grim-faced President Andrew Johnson, inadequate successor to the martyred Abraham Lincoln. To one side of the president stood Secretary of War, Edwin Stanton and Chief of Staff, General Henry Halleck. On the other side, General Ulysses Grant and Sherman himself stood. Between the shoulders of the dignitaries in the front row could be seen some lesser officers in a second row: General Rawlins, the bearded, pale-faced chief of staff to Grant; Colonel Parker, a full-blooded Indian on Grant's staff, whose Native American features were unmistakable; and a third officer.

The third officer was a small, slight man, dressed in the uniform of a staff lieutenant colonel. His light colored hair was swept back to fall to his shoulders, pale eyes seemed to stare directly into the photographer's camera through wire-rimmed spectacles. Aside from the length of his hair, the officer bore an uncanny resemblance to Harry Bierce, exactly as he appeared today, even though the photograph had been taken seventy years previously. Hoover had made discrete inquiries among a number of Civil War historians, but none could put a name to this blond officer.

Hoover sighed as he considered the photograph. He supposed it was possible that the officer just happened to have an amazing resemblance to Harry Bierce, perhaps his father or an uncle. Some sort of relative. Still, Hoover did not think so. Something in his gut told him different, and he always listened to his gut. He remained still, studying the picture intently as he had the past several nights.

✦

Harry Bierce had not gone directly to his apartment after his late meeting with Director Hoover. He had wandered the streets of Washington for several hours, deep in thought, ignoring the numerous homeless who shuffled aimlessly along the streets, until he found himself on the bridge between Georgetown and Arlington, staring eastward along the course of the Potomac.

He was now alone, except for the occasional passing car. To his left, he took in the brilliantly illuminated Capitol Dome, completed during the Civil War as a symbol of Abraham Lincoln's faith that the country would endure. To his right, on the Virginia side of the Potomac, he saw the former home of Robert E. Lee illuminated by spotlights, and the center of a cemetery holding the remains of tens of thousands of young men who had given their lives for the United States. Bierce shook his head solemnly at the thought. So much sacrifice, so much waste, just that America might survive as one. And he knew there was to be more such sacrifice in the near future, much, much more. Not just of lives and treasure, but of principles and honor. He hoped that such sacrifices would not be in vain, that America would continue to be the last, best hope of the world.

He reached into his coat pocket and removed the small Colt .32 automatic he had taken from the Bureau evidence room, the gun that had killed the Mayor of Chicago and that had nearly killed Franklin Roosevelt. It was exactly the same as when he took it, except that now, one cartridge was missing from the magazine. He looked around to make certain he was unobserved, then he hurled the gun far out into the river, where it disappeared with a small plunk. A barely visible ripple spread out from where the gun had disappeared. He turned north and began walking in the direction of his apartment on DuPont Circle. He knew he should try to get a good night's rest.

There was going to be so much to do. So very much to do.

AFTERWORD

This is a work of fiction. For reasons of the plot, massive liberties have been taken with the historic record. To name a few: Mayor Cermak died in a hospital the day after he was shot, not in the car; the "Night of the Long Knives" took place a full year before the assassination of Huey Long, there is no indication whatsoever that Vice President Garner was anything but a loyal American, and there is no indication whatsoever of a Nazi connection with the Long organization.

On the other hand, some of the seemingly unbelievable events mentioned in the novel really did occur. To name a few: before he died in the hospital, Cermak really did tell Roosevelt that he was glad that it had been him who was shot, not the President-Elect. Bonnie Parker and Clyde Barrow really did accomplish the seemingly impossible feat of freeing two of their gang members from a Texas prison, the dying prison officer really did extract a promise to kill Bonnie and Clyde, rather than capture them alive (a promise that Hamer honored), and although confusion surrounds the issue to this day, it seems possible that Huey Long was not killed by a bullet fired from Dr. Weiss's gun.

Although this story is fiction, it was my intention to give the reader a flavor of the times that were so important to making us the country we are today while sharing an entertaining story. If I have done those two things, my job is done.

The following are brief notes on some of the historic figures who appeared in this story.

Clyde Barrow (1909-1934) and Bonnie Parker (1910-1934) - Brought up in a Dallas, Texas slum, Clyde Barrow was arrested for stealing cars at the age of fifteen. Thrown into prison with adults, he was repeatedly sexually assaulted until he finally beat one of his assailants to death with a pipe. The authorities were not overly concerned and brought no charges. When he was released, he made no effort to go straight, but embarked on a career of increasingly serious crime and violence. Bonnie Parker was married at fourteen. When the marriage, not surprisingly, broke up, she went to work in a diner, where she is reputed to have met Barrow in 1931. Bonnie and Clyde immediately took off in a joint life of crime. They and other members of their gang killed at least nine police officers and five unarmed civilians before Frank Hamer and his men brought their murderous rampage to an end. Starting with the release of a film in 1967, pop culture began to romanticize them and their exploits. One wishes the families of their fourteen victims could be heard on this subject.

Ana Cumpanas (1889-1947) - A Roumanian immigrant, Ana Cumpanas pursued a career as a prostitute and madam in Chicago. In return for a $5,000 reward and a promise not to be extradited, she led John Dillinger into an FBI ambush wearing a bright orange dress (not the red dress of legend and newspaper accounts). The promise not to extradite her was not kept. She was deported to her native land in 1935, where she lived the rest of her life in obscurity.

John Dillinger (1901-1934) - The son of a poor Indiana farmer, John Dillinger got an early start on his life of crime. Released from prison in 1931, after serving nine years for robbing a grocery store of $50, he immediately began a crime spree that would end only with his death. Forming a gang with a fluctuating membership, he would specialize in bank robberies; his crimes ranging across the nation from Florida to Arizona, Indiana to South Dakota. Despite being a stone-cold killer, his good looks and outrageous antics caused newspapers and their readers to look upon him with some indulgence. One time when he was captured, he bluffed his way out of jail with an "automatic" that he had carved out of a bar of soap and darkened with shoe black. He had learned how to walk on his hands while in prison, and amused his gang members (and hostages) with stunts based on that skill. Despite dozens of successful bank robberies, life on the run was expensive. At the time he was killed outside the Biograph Theater in a federal ambush, he was found to have only a few hundred dollars.

John ("Cactus Jack") Garner (1868-1967) - A long-time Texas Congressman who attained the position of Speaker of the House in 1931, Cactus Jack Garner was Franklin Roosevelt's only serious competition for the Democratic Presidential nomination in 1932. As part of a deal to seal his nomination, FDR gave Garner the Vice-Presidential spot. During his time as Vice President,

Garner drifted further and further from Roosevelt, being isolationist, anti-labor, and anti-black. The final straw for the President was when Garner unsuccessfully challenged him for the Presidential nomination in 1940. In retaliation, FDR replaced Garner on the ticket with Henry Wallace. Wallace caused his own problems for Roosevelt, but that is a story for another day.

Frank Hamer (1884-1955) - Hamer was a legendary Texas Ranger. In his career he had survived being shot seventeen times and, in turn, had killed no less than fifty-three armed criminals. His reputation in Texas was such that armed, cornered desperados would often quietly surrender when he simply announced his name. In the 1967 movie about the exploits of Bonnie and Clyde, he is portrayed as stupid, cowardly, and vindictive. Vindictive he might be, but never stupid or cowardly. When the movie was released, Warner brothers was sued by Hamer's widow and son for defaming his character. The studio settled out of court for an undisclosed sum.

Heinrich Himmler (1900-1945) - A physically small man with the face of a timid teacher and the soul of a demon, Himmler rose continuously in the Nazi regime from being the head of Hitler's personal bodyguard until by 1944 he was clearly the second-most powerful man in Germany. Always maneuvering to gain more and more power and authority for himself, he became head of all police forces, including the dreaded Gestapo. He was the architect who created the infrastructure of murder squads, death camps and factories to implement Hitler's genocidal Holocaust. An agnostic with a hatred of all Christianity, especially Catholicism, he directed a massive campaign to implement a kind of pagan

Nazi state religion which even Hitler found to be a bit strange. He believed in all kinds of mystic fads, and in the middle of Nazi Germany's fight for existence, he devoted considerable state resources to "proving" various fringe theories. He took over various advance weapons projects, such as the Me-262 jet fighter and the V-2 ballistic missile. He even found time to dabble, unsuccessfully, in secret attempts to influence American politics. In the last months of the war, he attempted to negotiate a separate peace with the Western Allies, actually believing that they would make him head of a post-war Germany. Captured by a British patrol, he committed suicide by swallowing cyanide, taking fifteen minutes to die in agony. It was a far, far easier death than he deserved.

John Edgar Hoover (1895-1972) - Appointed head of the scandal-ridden Bureau of Investigation in 1924 (it only became the Federal Bureau of Investigation in 1935) and remaining in that post until his death in 1972, J. Edgar Hoover was a controversial figure in his lifetime, and remains so till this day. Using tactics that were questionable, even by the looser standards of his time, he reformed a corrupt and incompetent organization into a model for the world. He was accused of politicizing the agency by threatening elected officials with release of embarrassing information. Without defending what was, in essence, blackmail, I believe this was usually done to prevent these officials from politically interfering with the agency, and to maintain its status as an impartial protector of the public. In the years since his death, the Bureau has been increasingly politicized, to the detriment of its effectiveness.

Although many of the tactics the Bureau used during his stewardship are of unquestioned unconstitutionality, it should be noted that there was little criticism when he used such tactics to break up the Midwestern crime spree of the 1930s, Axis espionage/sabotage efforts of the 1940s, organized crime activities of the 1950s, and Ku Klux Klan violence of the 1960s. It was only when the FBI turned such tactics against groups favored by the intellectual elite that such people swiftly discovered their objections to the tactics. It should be remembered that Hoover was a product of his time, and that he was personally incorruptible, bequeathing to his country a nonpolitical national police.

Earl Long (1895-1960) - Earl Long probably suffered from bipolar disorder, a disease largely untreatable during his lifetime. He would often suffer periods of bizarre, almost manic behavior. Despite this, and because of his relationship to the martyred Huey Long, he was quite a successful politician in Louisiana. He served as Lieutenant Governor from 1936 to 1939, then as Governor from 1939 to 1940, 1948 to 1952 and 1956 to 1960. Late in life, he entered into a relationship with an "exotic dancer" named Blaze Starr, outraging and amusing the people of Louisiana in equal amounts. His angry and embarrassed wife had him committed to the state insane asylum. While there, he did some research and confirmed that under state law the fact that he was committed did not remove his powers as Governor. He promptly fired the head of the asylum and appointed a crony as the new head, who immediately signed an order for Long's release. Perhaps Earl was not as insane as people thought.

Huey Long (1893-1935) - Despite his continual claims in speeches to be of humble origins, Huey Long was in fact the son of a wealthy landowner in northern Louisiana; this claim so humiliated his father that in later life they were completely estranged. A brilliant speaker and a tireless campaigner, Long was Governor before his 35th birthday. As Governor, he built up an efficient, ruthless political machine that stopped at nothing; even kidnapping was used to remove an opponent for a while, if it was deemed necessary. He promised the people of Louisiana many things, and delivered many of them: free textbooks for poor children, roads and bridges to end the isolation of the rural poor, new schools and hospitals, even for the then-disenfranchised blacks. Elected to the United States Senate, it became very obvious that Long was intending to challenge Franklin Roosevelt for the Presidential nomination in 1936, running on his "Share the Wealth" program. Although Long was wildly popular with the poor of Louisiana, and increasingly those of other states, those 'better-off' acquired a growing hatred for the man. Some of the opposition was generated by Long's increasingly dictatorial methods; some by selfish opposition to spending much money on the needs of the poor. At the height of his popularity, Long was apparently shot by Dr. Weiss. To this day, there is some doubt that Weiss fired the bullet that killed Long.

Frank Nitti (1886-1943) - Starting out as a bodyguard to Al Capone, Frank Nitti impressed his boss with his intelligence and business acumen, rare qualities in the criminal underworld of Prohibition Chicago. Nitti was rapidly promoted through Capone's organization until he was the number two man. When Capone went to prison for tax evasion in 1931, he designated Nitti as his successor. In 1943, Nitti was charged with several serious crimes related to his attempts to have his mob infiltrate the film industry. Already suffering from cancer, fear of a long prison sentence caused him to shoot himself.

Franz von Papen (1879-1969) - Von Papen was a Prussian nobleman who served on the German General Staff during World War I. Entering the confused politics of the Weimar Republic, he was Chancellor of Germany for a few months in 1932, but lacked enough support in the parliament to continue in the position. With no one party able to command a majority in parliament, a coalition government was established in January 1933, making Hitler the Chancellor. But with only two other Nazis in the Cabinet, it was arranged for von Papen to be Vice-Chancellor (the non-Nazi members of the government assumed he would act as a check upon Hitler). After the fire in the Reichstag, a panicked legislature voted Hitler wide emergency powers, which were added to upon the subsequent death of the senile President von Hindenburg. As the Nazis established sole control of the government and began to implement increasingly brutal and anti-Semitic legislation, von Papen decided he needed to speak out. At the University of Marburg, he delivered a speech denouncing the excesses of the Nazis. Propaganda Minister Goebbels guaranteed that the speech received no coverage, Himmler had the friend who had helped von Papen draft the speech brutally murdered, and Hitler accepted von Papen's "resignation" as Vice Chancellor. His life was spared—foolishly or bravely— when von Papen refused to join the Nazi Party, despite several "requests" to do so. He lived quietly throughout the war, his political activity being limited to serving as Ambassador to Turkey. After the war, he was tried at Nuremburg as a war criminal, but was acquitted largely on the evidence of the Marburg Speech and his refusal to join the Nazi Party. His attempts to re-enter politics after the war were unsuccessful.

Dr. Carl Weiss (1906-1935) - Dr. Weiss was a rising young physician, married to the daughter of a fierce critic of Huey Long. Perhaps because of that, or because he had done post-doctoral research in Vienna and had witnessed the rising tide of fascism first hand, or for both reasons, he shared his father-in-law's hatred of Long. There is no doubt at all that Weiss fired two shots at Long on that fateful day in 1935, but there is a small but persistent doubt shared by some researchers that either of those shots was the one that killed Long. In any event, Long's bodyguards pumped no less than sixty-two slugs into the young doctor's body.

Guiseppi Zangara (1900-1933) - A five foot tall veteran of the World War I Italian army (which trained him to be a sniper), Zangara immigrated to America, failing to find success due to increasing health problems. On 15 February 1933, during a speech FDR was giving from the back of an open car, Zangara fired five .32 caliber shots; four people were wounded, and Chicago Mayor Anton Cermak was killed. Conspiracy theorists have argued that Cermak, who had sworn to clean up organized crime in Chicago, was the real target. Nevertheless, Cermak was standing next to the President-elect of the United States, and it seems unlikely that the cautious Frank Nitti would have ordered a hit when the bullet might have struck Franklin Roosevelt. There are some strange facts surrounding the case. For instance, the shooting took place on 15 February, while Zangara was tried, convicted, and executed by 20 March. Even in those days, that was an astonishingly fast process. It might almost seem that someone was anxious to see Zangara under the ground before he could do much talking.

ACKNOWLEDGMENTS

My deepest thanks to my agent Jeanie Loiacono whose faith in my writing launched my career, and to Kristina Blank Makansi who made my draft actually readable.

ABOUT THE AUTHOR

After receiving his Juris Doctorate from UCLA, Jack Martin worked for The Department of Defense and the aerospace industry, specializing in contracts and regulatory issues. While tracing his Californian ancestry back to the 1830s, Martin developed a passion for American history and the mystery genre. With encouragement and support from his beloved wife Sonia, he began writing. Sonia passed away on Christmas Eve 2009, following a brave battle against ovarian cancer. He promised her he would finish the books and become a published author. He is dedicated his first novel to Sonia, the love of his life.

Martin has five books published by Fireship Press: *Alphonso Clay Mysteries of the Civil War: John Brown's Body, Battle Cry of Freedom, Marching Through Georgia, The Battle Hymn of the Republic* and *Hail Columbia*. Learn more about them at www.fireshippress.com.

www.jacksmartin.com
www.blankslatepress.com/jackmartin

CPSIA information can be obtained
at www.ICGtesting.com
Printed in the USA
FFOW04n0851180815
15966FF